Wolf Tales III

Wolf Tales III

KATE DOUGLAS

APHRODISIA

KENSINGTON PUBLISHING CORP.
http://www.kensingtonbooks.com

APHRODISIA are published by

Kensington Publishing Corp.
850 Third Avenue
New York, NY 10022

ISBN: 0-7582-1388-3

First Kensington Trade Paperback Printing: January 2007

10 9 8 7 6 5 4 3 2 1

Printed in the United States of America

Dedication

I want to thank my husband, Doug Moore, who loves me in spite of myself. Life with a writer is *not* easy and he has patiently encouraged and supported my dreams for the past thirty-five years. (I've always maintained if I'd been married to me, I would have murdered me years ago and just hidden the body.)

Much love and appreciation to a friend and fellow author Kathyrn North for never giving up on me, and to my dear friend Peggy Bloom who always finds time to listen to my complaints—in fact, she hasn't hung up on me once in over thirty years!

Special thanks to my editor, Audrey LaFehr, for allowing me to tell Wolf Tales my way. She has given me the most amazing gift of literary freedom with this series, and I will always be grateful for her generosity.

PART ONE

Deception

Chapter 1

She really needed to get the ceiling patched. Shannon Murphy stared at the ugly crack running from one corner of her bedroom to the light fixture in the middle, only vaguely paying attention to the man diligently licking between her legs.

His short, coarse hair irritated her inner thighs. He had a death grip on her buttocks that would surely leave bruises, and while he slurped and licked her pussy with enthusiasm, his tongue managed to miss her clitoris completely.

Shannon tilted her hips, hoping Robert would take the hint and lick where it counted.

That doesn't sound right. Robert? Richard?

Shit. She couldn't remember his name.

Whoever, he missed his cue. His tongue stabbed her pussy, then he sucked her labia between his lips. His slurping grew louder and his fingers tightened on her butt.

Bruises. Definitely bruises.

The ceiling caught Shannon's attention again. Maybe she could talk the landlord into new paint? A different color? That would be nice. Change was good, wasn't it?

Not always. She really thought she'd been ready for a change when Tia Mason moved out, but Shannon missed her friend. Badly. She glanced at the clock. Tia would have brought her to climax at least a couple times by now. Yeah, Shannon definitely missed Tia.

What a strange phone call from Tia this afternoon! So unlike her. Tia hadn't made much sense, other than to scare the crap out of her, but Tia seemed to think Shannon might be in some kind of danger. Enough danger that a new acquaintance of Tia's was on his way to Boston to protect her, a man who worked for Tia's father, Ulrich Mason.

Robert, or Richard, or whoever the hell he was, crawled up Shannon's body and slobbered on first one breast, then the other. Shannon's nipples didn't respond, even though he sucked and licked the flat, soft circles. Then he rammed his hard little latex-covered dick between her legs.

Dick! That's it! He calls his cock Big Dick . . . and he's . . . Richard!

Shannon sighed with relief over the remembered name and lifted her hips, searching in vain for more penetration. There certainly wasn't anything remotely big about the little pecker banging around inside her totally unaroused pussy. She wished he'd hurry up and finish.

He grunted like a pig, slamming his pelvis against her mound with each thrust. Shannon thought about faking an O, but she had to draw the line somewhere.

Suddenly Richard's body stiffened. He squealed.

How the hell had she managed to bring home a guy who squealed?

Depression settled over Shannon, along with the full weight of the man who hadn't turned her on enough to leave her wanting more of the same. She shoved his inert body aside and crawled out of bed.

A stray thought flitted through her mind. She wondered about the guy headed to Boston and her apartment at this very moment. Hopefully he was younger than Tia's dad . . . young and sexy and very good looking . . . and really good between the sheets. Shannon glanced at the man in her bed and shuddered.

"I'm going to take a shower. I'd really appreciate it if you'd let yourself out before I'm through."

Richard lifted his head and stared at her, obviously not comprehending.

Shannon shoved her tangled hair back from her face. "This was a mistake, Richard. Take Big Dick and go home. Don't come back. I'm sorry." She turned and walked into the bathroom, still muttering to herself. "Really, really, really sorry."

Jacob Trent glanced at the piece of paper in his hand and shoved it back in his pocket. He'd thought about renting a car at Logan Airport, but the broad's address was in Boston's North End, land of no parking, so he looked for a cab instead.

Let Luc Stone pick up the tab, along with the rest of the expenses, since the trip was obviously Luc's idea. Right about now, Jake figured his buddy Lucien would do anything to keep Jake's sorry ass away from Tia, the pack's only bitch . . . and Luc's intended mate.

Jake wished he could blame Luc for what was, without a doubt, the biggest fuck-up Jake had ever engineered in his life. He'd been stewing about it all the way from San Francisco to Boston, wondering exactly why he'd been chosen for this assignment. He'd rather have gotten the details from Luc, not AJ. If Luc had been the one to call, it might have given Jake a chance to apologize.

Obviously, Luc didn't want any part of him right now. Jake wished he knew, though, if this assignment was punishment or an honest job.

He rubbed at the raw bite wound on his throat. It itched like a son of a bitch, which meant it must be healing, but the raw wound was a reminder of the really shitty thing Jake had done to his best friend.

Make that, his best friend's woman.

Jake sure as hell owed Luc—and Tia—an apology. One did not try to fuck as wolf with the pack alpha's bitch. Jake still couldn't believe he'd been so stupid, but for the first time in his life he'd lost it. His Chanku side had gone totally out of control.

Tia was just so damned hot. So ready, on her hands and knees in front of him, her pussy all wet and soft, her scent rising up and grabbing Jake by the balls until he'd totally lost sight of who and where he was.

Even now, almost three thousand miles away and possibly facing banishment from his pack, Jake still tasted Tia on his tongue, still felt the hot, wet pulsation as her clenching pussy grabbed his fingers. Jake's body tightened with the memory. His nostrils flared.

Then shame won out. His cock quieted. The air whooshed out of his lungs.

Tia'd been damned generous with her body, willing to take each man in the pack without hesitation. Only Jake had fucked things up, shifting from man to wolf in mid-thrust, planning to catch her unaware with his wolven cock.

Figuring in some convoluted corner of his horny brain that if he tied with Tia, if he took her as his mate while in wolven form, she'd be his. She'd bond with him, not Luc, and become Jake's mate for life. Like it was that simple? Like Tia didn't have a brain and feelings and wasn't already head over heels in love with Lucien Stone?

Jake felt like a damned fool. He'd risked everything to tie with the only female Chanku shapeshifter any of them had ever known.

Fortunately, Tia had been faster and Luc's aim was off, or Jake's story would have been all she wrote. When Luc had shifted to wolf and gone for Jake's throat, he'd gotten a mouthful of fur along with his hunk of Jake's flesh.

Otherwise, Jake wouldn't be standing here at Logan Airport, looking for a cab.

Feeling like a total jerk, remembering.

Nope. He would've been dead.

Shannon turned off the shower, rubbed lotion over her arms and legs, then wrapped one fluffy towel around her dripping mass of hair and another around her body. She stepped out of the bathroom in a billowing cloud of steam.

She wasn't alone. "Richard, I meant it when I asked you to leave."

The man sitting with his back to her stood up. It wasn't Richard. No, this man might have his hair cut military short like Richard's, but there the resemblance ended. Tall and muscular, he filled her bedroom with menace. His eyes were hidden behind expensive dark glasses, his hands encased in black leather gloves. He radiated danger without saying a word.

Tia's frantic phone call slammed into Shannon's mind. Was this Tia's friend? No. Nothing about this man felt right. Shannon took a step back, but strong arms caught her around the waist, lifted her off the ground. A leather clad hand clapped over her mouth. Shannon hadn't even seen the second man standing beside the bathroom door.

Frantic, she twisted and bucked against his ironlike grip, kicking at jeans-covered shins with her bare feet. Her right hand came free. Shannon raked her fingernails along a sturdy forearm.

"Son of a bitch."

The man shook her so hard her teeth rattled. Her towel fell off her hair, spilling down over her eyes, blinding her. The towel around her torso slipped and twisted around her body, tangling in the man's gloved hands.

Shannon tried to take advantage of her attacker's compromised grip, but the first man grabbed her ankles and quickly taped them together. Still wriggling and twisting for all she was worth, Shannon was dumped unceremoniously on her belly on the rumpled bed. With two large men holding her down, she could barely move. One bound her hands tightly behind her back, almost dislocating her shoulders.

Then he flipped her over, but before she could get a good look, another strip of tape went over her eyes. The last strip covered Shannon's mouth, leaving barely enough room for her to breathe.

Shannon sucked air through her nose. It wasn't enough! Panic gave her strength. She bucked and twisted her body as meaty, leather-clad hands grabbed for her. Still wet from her shower, skin slick from lotion, she slipped free of first one set of hands then the other.

She was falling. Sliding off the edge of the bed amid curses and kicks, large hands grabbing at her slippery body with bruising strength, throwing her face down on the bed once more.

Shannon couldn't breathe, couldn't see it coming. Had no way to prepare for the knee in the middle of her back and the sharp prick of a needle in her left buttock. Pain blossomed outward from the injection site. She saw stars and flashing lights behind the tape, then felt herself falling, as if from a very high point.

Falling through thick wads of cotton, falling deeper and darker into oblivion.

Jake paid the cabby and got out just down the street from a three story brick apartment building sandwiched in among a row of identical structures. A couple of street lights had burned out, leaving the neighborhood bathed in shadow. He set his leather travel case down and checked the address on the slip of paper barely visible in the low light, then studied his surroundings. Streets in Boston's

North End were notoriously narrow, but this was little more than an alley.

A large black sedan filled the entire lane in front of number twelve. Jake noted its presence, felt a shiver of anticipation along his spine. According to AJ, Ms. Shannon Murphy resided in a two bedroom apartment on the third floor. Jake knew Shannon had been Tia Mason's roommate for almost ten years, but little else about her. If AJ was right, the woman was quite possibly in danger from the same crooked politician who had gone after Jake's boss and Tia's father, Ulrich Mason.

AJ hadn't told Jake precisely why Mason, and now Ms. Murphy, had been targeted, but he'd dropped one tantalizing bit of information. There was a chance, a very slim chance, Shannon Murphy might carry Chanku genes. Unaware, unawakened, yet potentially Chanku, a shapeshifter just like Tia and the rest of the members of Pack Dynamics.

That alone would have brought Jake to Boston. The fact she could be in danger because she might be Chanku made it imperative he come. Jake smiled grimly into the darkness as a huge weight lifted from his chest. He hadn't really thought it through before. If Luc had chosen Jake for this assignment, maybe, just maybe, it meant he'd found it in his heart to forgive his longtime friend.

Thank God Ulrich was safe. Jake didn't know all the details, only that Ulrich had been kidnapped then rescued, all while Jake was racing around the woods of northern California, so fucked up he hadn't known where to turn. While Jake's packmates were busy saving their boss's life, he'd been trying to build up enough courage to go home with his tail tucked between his legs and ask Luc and Tia for forgiveness.

Thank God for AJ's call. Jake had grabbed this job like a lifeline, a chance to do something for the pack. The more he thought about it, the more Jake wanted to believe this wasn't an assignment made in retribution, to get him away from Tia. He hoped like hell Luc had decided to give him a chance to atone for his unforgivable behavior.

She might be Chanku.

Or not.

Hell. What a mess.

If only he had a better feel for what Luc really wanted.

Jake shoved the slip of paper into his pocket and pulled the collar of his leather coat up over his ears. He touched the bandage he'd taped over the wound on his throat. The bloody scab looked a lot worse than it felt and he really didn't want to scare the woman half to death.

He grabbed his bag and started forward, then stopped. Someone was coming down the stairs. Jake slipped back into the shadows and waited.

Two men lugged a large canvas sack between them. It looked like a military duffle bag, filled with something big and obviously heavy. Both men appeared well built, but they grunted with effort as they carried their load to the back of the sedan and set it carefully on the ground.

It didn't take a genius to figure out what they had. Or who. Jake quickly stripped his coat off and slipped out of his shoes. He quietly unzipped his pants just enough to slide them down his legs. Cool air raised the hair across his thighs.

One man opened the trunk, then turned to help the other lift the bag. They rolled it into the back and stared into the dark interior for a moment.

Jake's shirt and boxers landed quietly on the pile beside him.

"You think there's enough air?"

"Better be. We're supposed to deliver the package alive and unharmed."

"The bitch is in better shape than I am. Did you see what she did to my arm?"

The first man laughed. He never saw what hit him. The wolf burst out of the shadows aiming directly for the man's throat. He went down, hard, his head bouncing off the cobblestones.

The wolf spun around, his attack silent and deadly. The second man reached for his gun. The wolf took him down before he could pull the weapon from his shoulder holster.

Like the first, this fellow hit the ground hard with the full weight of the beast bearing him to the rocky street. He landed hard with his arm trapped beneath his body. Panting, the wolf stood over him, glancing from one still body to the other, waiting to see if either man moved.

Blood trickled from a head wound on the first man, but he appeared to be breathing. The second man's arm had twisted at an awkward angle. He was unconscious as well, but still alive. Satisfied he wasn't leaving two potential corpses behind, the wolf trotted back into the shadows.

Within moments, Jake emerged fully dressed. He dragged both bodies behind a large trash bin, then raced back to the car. The keys lay on the ground where the first man had fallen. Jake shoved them in his pocket and carefully opened the duffle bag.

Even in the darkness she was beautiful, though still unconscious. There was no doubt in his mind this was the woman he'd been sent to protect. Jake carefully pulled the tape off her eyes and mouth. It left darker marks against her pale skin.

She was lean and long limbed and completely naked. Her fair skin gleamed in the low light. Already, dark bruises marred her arms and legs and spread across one hip. Her long hair hung in damp tangles. The woman's captors had practically folded her in two to fit her into the bag. Jake pulled a knife out of his boot and sliced through the duct tape holding her arms and legs together, then slowly dragged her out of the bag. Her hair hung down in wet ribbons as he carried the woman around to the back door of the car.

He opened the door and stretched her out as much as possible on the back seat. She was tall and he had to bend her knees to make her fit. Slowly Jake ran his hands over her sleek body in search of injuries. She was warm, living satin beneath his fingers. His Chanku senses brought him the sound of each breath she took, the rush of blood through her veins, the slow but steady beat of her heart.

He felt his awareness shift. She was no longer a victim to be protected. Jake touched warm, breathing woman, inhaled her freshly bathed scent and found her primal essence beneath the perfumed soap and body lotion. His body tightened as awareness blossomed into desire, as desire fed arousal.

Suddenly, Jake's fingers brushed over a hard lump on her left buttock, what felt like an injection site. He blinked, returning immediately to *here* and *now*, aware once again of the danger.

They'd drugged her. *Bastards*.

Anger surged, hot and visceral, beyond any reaction he should have felt. His skin shivered. Jake's mind filled with the image of the wolf, but instead of taking down the two men, he was ripping their throats, leaving their mangled bodies in the open for all to witness.

With effort, Jake brought himself under control. *Logic.* He had to act and think logically. Not thinking was a good way to get himself, even the young woman, killed.

She was alive. Obviously drugs, not injury, kept her unconscious.

He'd heard them say they wanted her safe and alive. Jake brushed her hair back from her forehead and gazed at her perfect features. Her beauty tore at him and he clenched his free hand into a fist. He'd have to assume whatever they'd given her wasn't dangerous.

He had no idea when she might awaken and the night air was cold. After searching for a minute, Jake found a blanket on the floor, tucked under the front seat. He covered her, then tossed his suitcase in the back and quietly shut the trunk. After another quick check to see that the woman was breathing okay, he climbed into the driver's seat.

Jake grabbed the steering wheel in both hands and took long, steadying breaths, forcing both his libido and suddenly jangled nerves under control.

After a moment, he stuck the key in the ignition and started the engine. The original plan, staying here to protect Ms. Murphy, was not an option. Whoever wanted her knew where she lived. Odds of keeping her safe in Boston weren't in Jake's favor, especially since he had no idea who he was dealing with. Slowly, he edged the big sedan down the narrow street, then pulled out onto a wider road.

Jake had no idea why anyone wanted to harm her. No idea, even, why Ulrich had been kidnapped, but according to AJ it was all connected.

It had to be tied to their genetics, the fact each of them carried the genes of the shapeshifting Chanku. The secret, the fact they existed at all, grew harder to contain each year, especially with the number of cases they'd worked since the terrorists hit New York.

If the public at large ever found out they lived side by side with an entire race of beings able to shift from human to wolf and back again—talk about the shit hitting the fan.

Instantaneously, at will. Unlike the werewolves of legend, dependent on the phases of the moon, Chanku never became mindless creatures ruled by bloodlust.

Jake shook his head, almost snarling at the irony within the thought. No, they only became mindless when they were Jacob Trent faced with a wet and ready Chanku bitch. Damn! Would he ever find forgiveness for that one act of stupidity? It never should have happened.

He was a sentient being, a thinking creature. He had

powers beyond anything mere humans might imagine, but he couldn't control his damned dick.

Jake should have known better than to try and mate his alpha's woman. Luc had every right to go for his throat. Had every right to kill Jake. No one would have judged Luc badly.

The bite itched. Absentmindedly, Jake rubbed it.

The woman in the backseat stirred, then quieted once again. Jake glanced back over his shoulder, then turned his attention back to the road. It was almost midnight. There was hardly any traffic this late at night.

Still, the drug must be wearing off. She needed clothing, but he couldn't leave her alone in the car until she awakened. If she came to while he was in a store, she'd be terrified, might even try to escape.

He really didn't want Shannon Murphy to get away. Already Jake felt oddly protective, drawn to her on a gut level, intuitively, instinctually. He'd never reacted quite this way to a woman before.

Except Tia.

Like attracting like? Did he instinctively recognize another of the same species? This one might be Chanku. A woman like Tia. A female who would completely understand the needs and desires of another just like her.

Unawakened. Unaware of her potential, in danger because of her ignorance, entirely dependent, for now, on one Jacob Trent.

Jake glanced into the rearview mirror and grinned. If this was punishment, Jake owed Lucien Stone big time. He rubbed at the healing bite on his throat once again, then pulled around a slow van. Merging into the fast lane, he headed north on the interstate.

Almost an hour passed before Jake noticed any more movement in the back seat. Shannon stirred again. Jake heard her groan, then the sharp intake of breath that told him she must be awake.

"Ms. Murphy? Are you okay?" Jake looked in the rearview mirror, saw that she was wrapping the blanket tightly around her body and trying to sit up.

"I think so. Who are you?" She held up her right arm, stared for a moment at the duct tape still hanging from her wrists, then looked up. Her gaze met Jake's in the rearview mirror. He couldn't tell the color of her eyes. Wondered if they were the same green and amber as Tia's. As his own.

"I'm Jacob Trent. Call me Jake. I'm the one Tia sent to protect you. I'm sorry I didn't get here sooner."

"Ah." Shannon closed her eyes and nodded. Her voice sounded slurred. "Tia's friend."

Tia's friend? Would they ever be friends, after what he'd done? "Yeah. Tia said she called you. Explained I'd be coming out here. Are you okay?"

Shannon reached up and brushed her long hair out of her eyes. "I think so. A little woozy. A lot naked." She readjusted the blanket to wrap it more tightly around her body. "Where are we going?"

"North. I'm taking us up into Maine until we can figure out why those two wanted you. I've got a cabin up there. It's isolated and sort of rough, but it's a good place to keep you out of sight for a few days, at least until we know what's going on."

"About the naked thing . . ." Her eyes, looking directly at his in the rearview mirror, were steady.

Jake had to give her credit. She didn't scare easily. He couldn't imagine what it would be like, waking up out of a drugged sleep in the back of a car, wrapped in nothing but a blanket, traveling through the dark with a complete stranger.

He flashed her a smile. With any luck, it would reassure her, not scare the crap out of her. "Once we get into Maine, I know where there's an all-night shopping center. They've got everything from clothes to groceries. I figured I'd go in and get you something to wear, then once you're dressed, you can come back with me and we can shop for supplies."

Jake glanced up again as she nodded. "Why don't you get some sleep. We've got a long night ahead of us. Whatever drug they shot you with is probably still in your system." He grabbed a water bottle off the front seat and handed it to Shannon. She took it with a grateful smile.

"Thanks. My mouth feels like cotton."

Jake watched in the mirror as she upended the water bottle and drank almost half of it. Her throat glowed like an ivory column in the light from passing cars. Jake glanced briefly at the road but watching Shannon's reflection claimed him once again. She smiled, handed the water bottle back to him and once more stretched out on the back seat. She didn't ask about the men who'd tried to abduct her, or even comment on what had happened. Maybe it all seemed like a bad dream at this point.

Jake took a sip out of the water bottle, imagining the taste of Shannon's lips on the cool plastic. He turned his attention back to the road ahead, relaxing for the first time in days, as he guided the sedan through the dark night.

She really must be one sick puppy, to feel aroused by a stranger hauling her bare butt through the night to Lord knows where. Shannon wrapped the blanket close around her shoulders and lay down in the wide back seat, scrunching her butt in tight against the soft leather. Whatever drug they'd shot her with must really pack a punch, because she felt as woozy and hungover as if she'd combined drugs and booze and bad sex.

Well, she'd definitely had the bad sex.

What the hell happened tonight? She'd booted Richard and his Big Dick out the door, taken her shower and walked into a nightmare. Where were the men who attacked her? Had the stranger in the front seat dealt with both of them?

Were the two who attacked her still alive? Still a threat

to her safety? How had Jake managed to rescue her from two dangerous men?

She had no idea how big a man Jake was, though his shoulders were definitely broad enough to go with a fairly tall frame. It looked as if he'd shoved the driver's seat as far back as it would go, obviously adjusting to long legs. She hadn't been able to see him all that well in the pale reflection from the dashboard lights, but she noticed he wore his hair unfashionably long, so that it curled around his collar. His jaw was shadowed with at least a day's growth of beard and there was something dangerous about him, almost feral, something that appealed to whatever base instincts seemed to rule Shannon's body and mind.

She heard a rustling in the front seat and blinked, surprised she'd almost fallen asleep again. Jake glanced back in her direction, then he shoved his leather coat over the seat. "Here. It's pretty soft. Maybe you can use it for a pillow. Get some sleep. We've got about an hour until we get to Biddeford. That's where the store is."

"Thank you." Shannon grabbed the coat. Her fingers sank into the soft, creamy leather, still warm from Jake's body. She folded it over and tucked it beneath her head. It carried his scent, a tantalizing blend of man and forest that reminded her of something, some place just out of memory's reach.

Inhaling deeply, filling herself with Jake's heat and scent, Shannon felt herself growing drowsy once again. She should have been frightened, or at least uneasy, traveling through the night with a strange man, her naked body wrapped in nothing but an old blanket, with no idea where they were headed.

She wasn't. Maybe it was the drugs, but for the first time in ages, Shannon actually felt calm, even relaxed. Snuggling her cheek close against the soft leather coat, Shannon sighed and let her thoughts drift. After so many years in the city, there was something comforting about a man who reminded her of the forest.

Chapter 2

"Ms. Murphy? Shannon, wake up."

Shannon raised her cheek away from the soft coat, disoriented and confused. She looked up into the dark eyes of
the man she'd been dreaming about and blinked.

It hadn't been a dream. She really was bare-ass naked,
wrapped in a scratchy blanket in the back seat of a car
headed somewhere away from Boston in the middle of the
night. Shannon shoved her hair out of her eyes and focused
on Jake's face. They must be in, or near, a town somewhere,
because pale light from an outside source filled the interior
of the car, casting dark shadows over the harsh line of his
jaw, the high, angular cheekbones, the long nose.

Questions twisted in Shannon's mind . . . how, and why,
and who, all coiled together into a seething mass impossible to untangle. Then Jake smiled. Just the right side of his
full lips quirked up, but he didn't look like a man who
smiled often. The questions melted away, just disappeared
like black mist on a night wind.

Shannon felt like an idiot, reclining on the back seat
awkwardly supported on one elbow, clutching the blanket
to her chest and staring at Jake. The interior of the car sort
of closed in around her until all she noticed was her racing

heart, her weeping pussy, her taut nipples standing at attention beneath the blanket.

Who was this man? Why did her body react so powerfully to his presence?

"Are you all right?"

She took a deep breath, let it out. "I'm okay. I think I'm awake, though all of this still has the feel of a very strange dream."

Jake nodded. "I imagine it does. You're really quite calm, considering what you've been through tonight. I hope those two didn't hurt you."

Shannon realized she was grinning like a fool. She couldn't believe her reaction to the man. Even the rumble of his deep voice turned her on. This close in the confines of the car, his scent filled her head, drew her closer. She took a deep breath and had to bite back a moan of pleasure, before shaking her head. "Only my pride. I've taken a lot of self-defense classes. Not a bit of it helped."

"What happened? How'd they get in?"

Shannon frowned. She'd wondered that herself. *Ah . . . Richard*. "I had a visitor who took off when I went to shower. He must have left the door unlocked. The men were in my room when I came out of the bathroom. I only saw one at first. The other grabbed me from behind."

"You left your mark. I heard him grousing about scratches on his arm."

"Good. How did you. . . ? They're not dead, are they?"

Jake shook his head. "No, but they'll probably have really bad headaches come morning. One of them may have a broken arm." He reached for the door handle and glanced back at Shannon. "I'm going to pick up some clothes for you. What do you want me to get? What size?"

"Sweats would be great. Then I can go in with you and buy what else I need." The reality of her situation suddenly hit Shannon hard. "I don't have any money, no ID. I don't . . ."

Jake held up his hand. "Don't worry about it. I'll take care of everything and we can settle up later. What size?"

"Medium. Tall if they have it. Something dark."

"Okay. I'll lock the doors, but I'm leaving the keys with you. We're just outside the regular parking lot, hopefully away from any surveillance cameras. You should be fine here. We're going to have to think about ditching this car at some point. It's the one your two buddies were driving. I imagine by now they've got some sort of bulletin out on it. It might even have a tracer so be real aware of your surroundings, of anyone acting suspicious."

Shannon was still trying to digest that bit of information when Jake nodded and slipped out of the car. He moved gracefully for such a big man. In fact, he was absolutely beautiful—long, lean, and dangerous looking, he reminded her of an untamed beast, a deadly predator of the night.

Shannon watched him all the way across the parking lot to the brightly lit store. Overhead lights caught him. Shannon realized his hair, which had looked so dark inside the car, was actually light brown, sun-streaked. His jeans hugged the most perfect male ass she'd ever seen, and his stride was long and smooth and surprisingly graceful. Though he didn't seem to hurry, he covered the distance between the car and the store in mere seconds.

When he disappeared behind the doors, Shannon released the breath she didn't know she'd been holding. Leaning back against the soft upholstery, she closed her eyes against this totally unreal new reality. She had no clothing, no credit cards, no identification, not a penny to her name. Without her cell phone she couldn't even call Tia and find out what was going on. All the info she had was what she'd learned from Tia's very brief call and what little Jake could tell her.

Something else Jake said flowed back into Shannon's mind. This car had belonged to her attackers? She rubbed her fingertips over the soft leather upholstery. It was no rental—not something this expensive.

With that thought, Shannon wrapped the blanket tightly around herself and crawled into the front seat. The glove box was locked but she opened it with the keys. No registration, no clue of ownership. Nothing beyond the owner's manual and a couple of maps—one of Boston, another of the Washington DC area. Still, whoever wanted Shannon probably had money and power, especially if her attack was somehow connected to Tia's father's abduction.

What in the hell could she possibly have in common with Ulrich Mason? Shannon hadn't seen him in ages, though he'd always been perfectly friendly to her. She'd long suspected Mr. Mason knew about Shannon's intimate relationship with his daughter. Knew and didn't mind a bit, something that should have surprised Shannon more than it did.

What she'd had with Tia would always hold a special place in Shannon's heart. Of all the friends and lovers she'd known, only Tia seemed to understand how Shannon perceived the world. Of course, the fact they'd both lost their mothers when they were small, had both been raised by distant, difficult fathers, had a lot to do with the special sisterhood they shared.

Shannon's mother had died of cancer, but Tia's mother had been murdered. Had her friend discovered any of the details of her mother's death? Shannon was almost certain that was Tia's main reason for returning to San Francisco.

That, and the fact that both of them had recognized something lacking in their relationship. They still loved one another, still had great sex together, but each of them had begun searching for that elusive something missing in their lives.

Shannon wondered if Tia had found what she'd been looking for. She wondered if there was an end somewhere to her own personal quest, a pot of gold at the end of Shannon Murphy's rainbow?

With that thought, Jacob Trent's image slammed itself into Shannon's mind. His stark, unrelenting features, the feral gleam in his eyes, the strength in his lean yet muscular frame. There was nothing gentle about him, nothing soft. Jake was all hard angles and harsh lines, a man who had faced life as a battle to be fought and won.

Shannon lay her head back against the seat and closed her eyes. What was it about Jacob Trent that attracted her so profoundly? Why, when there was nothing welcoming about him, did she feel as if he beckoned her, as if he needed her as much as she needed him?

A dull, pulsing ache spread from Shannon's womb to her breasts. She wanted to touch herself, to run her fingers through the moisture gathering between her legs, but the thought of Jake catching her masturbating in the front seat kept her fists tightly clenched around the blanket. Her clit throbbed, needy, overly sensitive. Shannon squeezed her legs together and bit back a moan. Hell, she was sitting alone in a car in a shopping center parking lot in the middle of the night. Not the most sensual of settings.

A soft tapping on the window jerked Shannon out of her reverie, yanked her back from the temptation of her fingers settling into the slick heat between her legs.

Startled, she turned and looked directly into Jake's unusual eyes. Glowing amber in the reflected light from the parking lot, their primitive heat and bestial intensity reminded Shannon how precarious her position truly was.

Naked, on the run from some unknown threat, trusting her life to a total stranger with the eyes of a wolf and sex appeal beyond belief. Wondering if any of this would ever make sense, Shannon unlocked the car door.

* * *

How a woman with tangled hair, dressed in cheap, black, men's sweats and leather moccasin slippers could give him a hard-on went beyond Jake's imagination, but his cock had come to attention the minute Shannon Murphy stepped out of the car wearing the clothes he'd bought for her.

Jake hadn't realized how tall she was, but standing beside him she was nearly eye level, which put her at almost six feet tall to his six four. He'd seen her naked and unconscious, wrapped her nude body in that old blanket and thought she was pretty, but standing here, looking him in the eye with that sexy grin and those gorgeous green eyes, Shannon just about put him over the edge.

Green eyes? Not amber, not like Tia's. Maybe she wasn't Chanku after all. Weren't the eyes the giveaway? Jake felt a little of the air whoosh out of his lungs, but when Shannon turned away to walk toward the store, his cock begged him to follow.

Chanku or not, she was gorgeous. There was something untamed about her, something savage and ruthless, and it called to him, made him hunger. Tall, loose-limbed and athletic, she had the build of a swimmer with broad shoulders, a small waist, and a sexy flare to her slim hips. Jake pictured her in leather, her perfect little ass encased in smooth black leather cupped close against her cheeks, defining the line between them.

He practically groaned, imagining her kneeling in front of him, her ass in the air, her long, dark red hair sweeping her shoulders as she peered back at him over one naked shoulder.

Shannon turned just then, glancing back over her shoulder, a twinkle in her eyes. Something slammed Jake in the gut, that knowing look, as if she read his thoughts, as if she knew every fantasy swirling around his horny brain.

Jake smiled back, then followed Shannon into the

brightly lit store. An idea was forming in his mind . . . one that would get Shannon in leather and the two of them far away from whoever threatened her safety.

Of course, his plan didn't take into account the threat Shannon posed to Jake. It had been a long time since a woman left him this unsettled. A very long time.

As in never.

Shannon grabbed a cart and headed toward the back of the store. Jake followed, content to watch the smooth flow of her hips under the clinging knit pants. Shannon reached for a bottle of shampoo and another of conditioner. She held a large size and a small one, as if weighing her purchase.

Jake cleared his throat. It was now or never. "Think minimal, okay? I want to dump the car as soon as we can, get off the beaten track. I'm thinking motorcycle. Are you okay with traveling on a bike? It's not all that far to the cabin. They're not going to be looking for us on a bike. The drawback is, we won't be able to carry as much stuff."

Shannon looked at Jake and set the larger bottle back on the shelf. She had a huge, mind-boggling, gut-wrenching smile on her face. "I love it. I'll need jeans and boots and a coat, though."

"Wait until we get to the dealership. There's one north of Portland and they'll have gear. Leather's safer." *And a hell of a lot sexier.*

What the hell was he thinking? Someone was trying to kidnap her, and all Jake could think of was the sweet curve of her ass in tight, black leather pants. What it would be like to peel those pants down over her muscular thighs, bury himself deep inside her welcoming heat.

As if she'd welcome him in the first place. Damn. There was only one way to find out. He had to get her in leather.

Shannon nodded, agreeing with Jake as he continued, selling himself on the idea as much as Shannon. "Let's just pick up the basics for now, find a place to get some sleep for a couple hours. Tomorrow we ditch the car and buy a bike."

"Just like that? You think we can do it that fast? Just walk in and pick out a motorcycle and go?"

Jake thought of the Pack Dynamics credit card in his wallet. Virtually untraceable, credit unlimited. "When you've got the money, you can do just about anything you want. C'mon. Let's get the stuff we absolutely need for tonight, then find a place to sleep. I don't know about you, but I'm exhausted."

Shannon had assumed Jake meant to sleep in the car. Instead he pulled into a small, neatly landscaped hotel parking lot south of Portland, Maine. While Jake got a room, Shannon gathered up the bags with their purchases. Jake walked back to the car, grabbed the heaviest of the sacks along with a leather overnight bag, and carried them up the outside stairwell to the second floor.

Shannon realized her heart was pounding, and it wasn't from the short climb up a flight of stairs. Jake had gotten one room, but how many beds? She watched him insert the card key in the lock with what should have been a sense of dread, but instead was pure anticipation.

Jake flipped the handle when the lock clicked and opened the door, but he paused and looked back over his shoulder. For the briefest of moments, Shannon saw something flicker in his eyes, some emotion she'd not seen before, a question? A sense of vulnerability, as if he expected her to turn and run away?

Turning away was the last thing on her mind. Shannon smiled and stepped through the doorway ahead of Jake. The room was small and clean, dominated by one huge bed covered in a thick down comforter.

Shannon's pussy clenched. Her suddenly erect nipples tingled against the soft knit fabric of her sweatshirt. She piled her bags on a small table in one corner and took a deep breath. "This was a good idea. I'm exhausted."

That wasn't all, but how do you tell a total stranger how turned on you are? That he makes you so damned hot all you can think of is stripping off your clothes and tackling him? After she peed. Some things couldn't be ignored. Embarrassed now, Shannon experienced a moment's shyness. "I need to use the bathroom, then it's all yours."

Jake nodded. He grabbed the remote for the TV and flipped it on, giving Shannon more privacy. She found a toothbrush and some paste in one of the bags and went into the small bathroom. The moment she closed the door behind her, she leaned back against the solid wood. Why, when she had absolutely no compunction about picking up a relative stranger in a bar did her attraction to Jake leave her feeling so rattled?

It made no sense. He was a man. It was obvious he was interested in her. Hell, for some reason most men were, though Shannon really couldn't understand why. She didn't flirt, didn't go out of her way to hunt for a man. They just seemed to gravitate her way, each of them as desperate as she was.

Some she took home, others she ignored. Lately, she'd taken home a few she should have ignored, but they'd seemed so needy.

Maybe that was Jake's difference. Maybe, for the first time Shannon could recall, she was the one who needed. Jake seemed totally self contained. Other than that brief glimpse she'd had, he came across as a man used to getting what he wanted. Used to being in control. Tia, with all her dreams of wolves, would have called him an alpha male.

"Damn, Tia. What the fuck have you gotten me into now?" Grinning at her own sense of drama, Shannon used the toilet, then checked to see if her legs felt smooth. At least she'd showered and shaved them before her kidnapping. *Good Lord*. She should be giving thanks she was still alive, not worrying about hairy legs and body odor!

Still wearing her warm sweats, Shannon quietly slipped back into the room. Her dreams of hot sex with Jacob Trent slipped away on a smile. Partially propped up against a mound of pillows, Jake lay stretched out on the king-size bed. He slept, one hand clutching the remote control resting on his flat belly, the other flung over his head. He'd taken off his shirt and partially unzipped his jeans. A large white bandage covered the left side of Jake's throat and Shannon wondered briefly what injury it hid. She hadn't noticed it before. His feet were bare. Like his chest, they were dusted with dark hair.

In sleep, the harsh angles of Jake's face had softened, the worried frown between his eyes relaxed. His light brown hair glowed like old gold in the soft light from the bedside lamp.

It was three in the morning. He'd arrived late in the evening from California, which meant he'd probably been awake close to twenty-four hours.

Shannon slipped the remote out of Jake's hand and turned off the TV. She lifted his legs to pull the blankets free of their substantial weight, then covered Jake with the quilt. He mumbled something, then slipped lower into the pile of pillows.

Shannon turned off the light and crawled carefully into bed beside him. Jake's soft breathing soothed her, the warmth of his strong body next to hers gave Shannon a sense of comfort she'd not felt before. She lay there in the darkness, sadly aware she couldn't remember the last time she'd actually slept with a man. Uncountable numbers had come to her bed for sex, but she'd always asked them to leave when they were done.

This entire day had been one strange episode following another. First Tia's frantic call, then the kidnapping, then rescue, then flight . . . now this, whatever *this* was. Jake's arm snaked around Shannon's body and he pulled her close, fitting her ass into the cradle of his thighs. He grunted, buried his nose in her hair and settled back into sleep.

Not the wild and steaming sex she'd imagined just a few minutes ago, but definitely satisfying. Smiling in the darkness, Shannon gave in to her overwhelming need for rest.

Strange dreams followed her into sleep. Amber eyes glowed out of the darkness and a wolf howled close by. At some point she felt too warm and stripped off the heavy sweats. Later, Shannon might have heard a shower running, or was it the rush of a woodland stream flowing over worn rock? She dreamed of dark paths in damp woods, of racing naked through wet grass and tangled willows, leaping streams with a sense of freedom, a strength she'd never experienced. Her heart swelled with joy so pure, so all-consuming, it affected her sensually, filled her soul with passion, made Shannon, for the first time in her life, feel whole.

As if that final, unknown part which had forever been missing had somehow slipped itself into place and completed the puzzle that was Shannon Murphy.

A sound woke her, or maybe it was the quiet. Shannon blinked sleepily and gradually came more awake. Stretching, her body tingling and aroused as if she'd just reached climax, Shannon slowly opened her eyes. Jake stood at the end of the bed, his wet hair combed back from his forehead, lean hips barely covered by a white towel, and his eyes . . . his eyes glowed amber like the wolf in her dreams. Glowed with desire matched only by Shannon's.

She'd only known him a few hours. She'd known him all her life. Without hesitation, Shannon lifted the blankets aside and made a space for Jake in the bed next to her. His long fingers loosened the knotted towel and let it slowly fall from his lean hips.

He was only partially erect, his tumescent cock swelling out of a dark nest of hair even as she watched. Shannon licked her lips, imagining that perfect, uncut cock slipping into her mouth. Imagined the taste and texture of Jake's balls, the feel of his swollen penis moving slowly down her throat. Stretching her lips, teasing her senses with the taste of man. She swallowed and the sound seemed loud in the silence stretching between them.

Jake moved as if he were caught in the same web of fantasy holding Shannon. Slowly stretching out over the end of the bed, he rested one knee on the mattress. His left hand hovered for an endless moment over her leg.

The tension between them built, stretched thinner, tighter. When he finally touched her, Shannon gasped. Her head jerked up. Jake stared directly into her eyes for a mere second, then he looked back down at her leg, at the point where his hand rested just below her knee.

Did Jake feel it? Did his palm tingle with the sense of power racing between them? He had to know what she felt, had to realize something magical was happening. He leaned over and placed a soft kiss on the inside of her leg, next to his palm.

A shiver raced up Shannon's inner thigh, directly to her clit. She felt a moan catch in her throat, a needy whimper yearning to break free.

Raising his head, maintaining eye contact, Jake crept closer, crawling the length of Shannon's body, his hand sliding oh, so slowly along her thigh to the swell of her hip. He carefully slipped into the warm indentation of the mattress where Shannon's body had been, gliding against her until Shannon felt his heat surround her, from the spot where his toes touched the bottoms of her feet to the warm pressure of his chest against her breasts . . . to her lips.

His breath carried the minted scent of toothpaste, an

ordinary, pleasing aroma. *Familiar.* His body's essence, though, was something more, something ancient and long forgotten, a primal scent that stirred Shannon in a manner she'd never experienced. Once again she thought of the forest, wondered at the memories that couldn't be, memories drifting from beyond her understanding.

Questions she'd not known to ask somehow gave her the courage to bridge the small distance between her mouth and Jake's. Trembling, aware of him as she'd never been aware of any other partner, male or female, Shannon pressed her lips against Jake's mouth.

She felt his warm sigh, the hardening of his body as his arms wrapped her in a tight embrace. Jake devoured her mouth, slowly but surely finding every sensitive spot with his tongue, his teeth, his lips.

She'd never had anyone make love to her mouth before. Not like this, with such thorough, single-minded attention. Jake's tongue explored the full interior of Shannon's mouth, his teeth nipped at her lips and he suckled her tongue in an open invitation to do the same to his.

Moaning, Shannon pressed her hips close to Jake's, felt his cock swell against her belly. Breathing slowly and surely, he kissed the corner of her mouth, then carefully worked his way along her jaw, paying close attention to the length of her throat, the sharp line of her collarbone. Moving lower, Jake licked just the tip of her left nipple, teasing Shannon with the briefest of strokes.

She arched her hips and whimpered. His hands swept the length of her torso, tangled in her small thatch of pubic hair and tugged. Jake's lips tightened on her nipple, sucking hard and pressing the swollen tip against the roof of his mouth. He moved across her chest with tiny, sucking kisses and repeated the process, slowly suckling and licking Shannon's other breast, then moving lower, kissing the sensitive flesh over her ribcage, dipping his tongue into her navel.

His long fingers slipped carefully into her sex, spreading her fluids up and over her sensitive clit, gently torturing that tiny bundle of nerves. Shannon bit the inside of her lip, fighting the sensations as she reveled in Jake's skillful touch.

Her skin burned but her body shivered. Her womb ached and the muscles in her vagina clenched with each beat of her heart, each thrust of his fingers. She clutched at Jake's shoulders, tilted her hips high to force his fingers deeper. Instead, he slowly dragged his fingers out of her warm and wanting pussy and knelt between her legs. He lifted her buttocks, holding her cheeks in his big hands, lifting her higher, closer to his mouth.

She felt the rough glide of Jake's fingers over the bruises Richard's clutching fingers had left, felt the warm breeze of Jake's breath between her legs. Twining her fingers in the wrinkled sheets, Shannon closed her eyes. She whimpered again, a strangled cry deep in her throat.

Jake sat back on his heels and raised Shannon's legs over his shoulders. She opened her eyes, shocked he would hold her so high, hold her up to his mouth like some carnal feast so that only her shoulders rested on the bed. Jake stared back at her for a moment. His eyes gleamed in the darkness and he licked his lips, as if savoring her taste.

There was a look of wonder on his face, an expression that confused Shannon. What did he feel when he looked at her like this? Why did he affect her so deeply, make her want him so much? What was it about Jacob Trent that seemed to know what was missing in Shannon's life? Could Jake fill the emptiness she'd known for so long?

Then his big hands lightly massaged her bruised and sore buttocks. He lifted her even higher. Jake dipped his head, his tongue lightly caressed her clit, one thick finger rubbed back and forth across her sensitive anus, and Shannon bit her lips to keep from crying out in ecstasy.

* * *

Tasting Shannon Murphy's intimate flavors was the equivalent of taking communion with whatever gods had suddenly blessed his life. Jake's tongue dipped into her creamy nectar and he actually felt the sting of tears behind his eyes.

Damn, but he'd gone down on hundreds of women, enjoyed their myriad flavors and tastes, yet never, not once, had he felt this powerful connection, this rush of sensual need, of almost painful arousal. Breathing deeply he drew her scent into his lungs and felt his cock stretch beyond its already hard length.

Shannon moaned when he tongued her clit. The needy sound turned him on even more, so he gently suckled the erect bud between his lips, licking tenderly at the sleek bit of flesh. She lifted her pelvis, pressed her sex tighter against his mouth and he licked deep inside, swirling his tongue over the slick, clenching tissues. His nose pressed close against her folds and he breathed deeply, inhaling her scent.

How he wished he could shift! If only he could use his Chanku tongue to taste her, his wolven body to love her. The more sensitive Chanku taste buds and ability to smell even the lightest scent would make an almost perfect experience even better.

Shit. Any better and it might be fatal.

He lifted his head for a moment, breathing deeply, fighting for control. Heart pounding in his chest, Jake was almost certain he heard the rush of his blood, the throbbing veins in his cock. Shannon's scent drew him back. Once more he dipped his head to feed between her legs.

While his tongue learned the secrets of Shannon's sweet sex, Jake's fingers stroked her taut buttocks, found the cleft between her cheeks, pressed lightly at first, then with more force against her anus. He felt her push against his finger and knew she was no stranger to this kind of touch. Groaning against her pussy, his hips beginning to sway in longing, Jake dragged his fingers through her dripping fluids for more lubricating moisture, then slowly but surely gained entrance through her anus, pressing his finger deep into Shannon's hot, tight passage.

She whimpered, not a sound of pain but of longing. Her muscles grabbed his finger. Held him.

Lost in a haze of pure lust, Jake licked and nipped and sucked, matching the rhythm between his mouth and probing finger, taking Shannon with him. His thoughts floated free, his need, his physical and emotional arousal, his wonder, all coiling and melding, bringing him to the edge of climax.

Jake hovered on the precipice, held fast by sheer will alone, but his mouth and hands took Shannon over. Her body tensed, her knees locked against the sides of his head. He felt her scream before he heard it, sensed her orgasm seconds before her body went rigid. Her back arched, her pussy gushed, filling his mouth with her unique tangy taste.

Jake's cock felt ready to explode, his balls ached, and suddenly, inexplicably, his mind caught her mental touch. Shannon's orgasm, her need, her surprise, her unbelievable response to Jake's lovemaking.

He held her there, right at the peak, far longer than he'd ever held another woman . . . kept her in the throes of her orgasm, her muscles clenching, heart pounding, while their minds fed, one from the other.

Finally, Jake brought Shannon slowly down, still caught in the wonder of that brief communication, licking her gently between her legs, sliding his finger out of her backside, then stretching her legs limply along either side of his body. Jake leaned over and found his jeans on the floor beside the bed, fumbled for a condom and tore the wrapper with his teeth. He took his cock in his hand, almost afraid to touch himself, he was so close to coming.

His hands shook so that he could barely sheathe himself,

but he finally managed to get the condom over the head of his weeping cock. He'd never regretted more the use of protection. Disease was not a factor—his Chanku genetics made him impervious to human bacteria and viruses—but until he knew whether or not Shannon was Chanku, Jake couldn't risk impregnating her.

He'd heard the guys say they didn't think they could get a human woman pregnant once they became Chanku, but no one really knew for sure. None of them had been willing to take that chance.

Smoothing the condom down the length of his cock gave him a moment to regain control. When he was safely covered, he wrapped his fist around the base and pressed the broad head of his cock against Shannon's sex. She was so damned hot and wet, slick with her juices, with his saliva. Slick and ready and waiting. Her body jerked when he touched her, so sensitive and ready for him. Jake thrust his hips forward, slipped into her fast and deep, and buried his full length to the root.

Adjusting himself between her legs, filling her even more, Jake raised his head and met Shannon's bemused gaze. She looked at him with wonder in her eyes. Wonder and a look of confusion. Then she raised her hand and touched the side of his face, a simple gesture that left him feeling almost giddy.

Jake thrust hard, going as deep as he could, pressing his cock against the hard mouth of her womb, then slowly withdrawing. Again he filled her, and once again withdrew. He kept his gaze locked on Shannon's, watched her face, the expression in her eyes as once again he brought her to the edge, teased her with each thrust, then reached between their sweaty bodies and found her clit.

Shannon's eyes widened in shock, her mouth formed a perfect "O" and she clutched his hips with surprisingly strong hands. Stroked his thighs, cupped his buttocks much as Jake had held hers. He rocked within her slowly, riding out her climax, still holding on to his.

Moments later, her breathing once again almost steady, Shannon smiled at him, a secretive, almost teasing smile. She rubbed her hands over his ass, stroking the skin in ever tightening swirls, finally discovering his balls.

Holy shit! Jake clenched his butt muscles in reaction and ground his teeth. She almost had him, almost forced him to come. Those perfect fingers cupped his sac and gently squeezed, then one slim finger traced the line to his ass, swirled around the taut muscle long enough to take him right to the limits of control. Swirled and then dipped inside, deep, hard and fast.

Jake shuddered, thrust hard and froze with his cock pressed up tight against her cervix. His balls tightened in their sac, his lungs quit working, his heart most likely stopped. He felt the hot rush of orgasm, the sense of everything coiling into one tight spurt of seed blasting from his balls, down the length of his cock, filling the end of the condom.

Damn. He ached. The need to plant his seed at the mouth of Shannon's womb left a visceral pain, overshadowing what was, in every other way, the most perfect fuck he'd ever experienced.

Chest heaving, hips still thrusting of their own volition as his seed spilled into the damned condom's reservoir, Jake felt Shannon's mental shout of triumph, heard her joyous exclamation in his mind as she reached yet another climax of her own. Saw the wonder in her eyes when she finally realized they had done more than just have mind-blowing sex.

They had joined both mentally and physically, had found the ultimate pleasure, a pleasure shared equally only when both were Chanku.

They had linked. For the first time in his life, Jake had

linked mentally with a woman during sex. Shaken, he could only stare into her forest-green eyes and wonder if she understood what had just occurred between them.

Arms trembling, heart thudding in his chest, Jake leaned forward and kissed Shannon gently on the lips. When he carefully separated from her body and moved to lie beside her, Jake realized this was only the beginning. If he didn't screw things up, he could share the same feeling with this amazing woman every day for the rest of his life.

Could share it without barriers, with only their flesh meeting, their bodies merging, their minds one. It scared the holy shit out of him. He'd never brought anyone over before, never taken the responsibility of teaching another Chanku about his or her unique heritage.

That had been Luc's job. Luc and Ulrich Mason's. Jake hadn't wanted the responsibility, hadn't needed the emotional involvement that occurred when you showed someone an entirely new world, a world they'd been entitled to, yet barred from—until another Chanku led the way.

Jake wanted it now. Wanted the challenge, the commitment. He wanted Shannon Murphy.

He raised himself up on one elbow and stared into the bright green eyes filled with trust, glowing with wonder, and knew he faced his greatest challenge.

Keep Shannon safe. Protect her at all costs, teach her the joys and the secrets of Chanku.

How would he teach her when he couldn't tell her? Shit. Until he knew for sure that she was Chanku, he couldn't say a word.

Somehow, he'd figure out a way. He had to. But most of all, he had to make Shannon love him. After this one night, Jake knew he would rather give his life than ever give her up.

Chapter 3

Tia Mason shoved both huge wolves out of her bed and swung her legs over the side. "C'mon, boys. It's almost six. We need to head back to the city."

The beasts sprawled limply on the plush carpet, tongues lolling. "Lucien? Tinker? Get your butts in gear. I think I hear Dad and the rest of the guys moving around out there."

The home belonging to the Montana Chanku pack was huge, the San Francisco pack's rooms in a wing away from the main part of the residence. Still, Tia's Chanku senses seemed to be in high gear this morning and the low rumble of voices at the far end of the sprawling home was almost audible.

Maybe a night of sex with two absolutely gorgeous men had something to do with it. Tia stretched her arms over her head, lifting her breasts with the arch of her back. She ached everywhere, but damn, it was worth every single one of those sore muscles.

Especially the ones between her legs. She felt her pussy clench in response, realized both wolves had turned suddenly wide-awake eyes in her direction.

"No. Down boys. Behave."

The darker of the two wolves licked his muzzle, wrapping

his long tongue over the top. At the same time, he let Tia *see* exactly what he was thinking of doing with his long, amazingly mobile tongue.

The image of what he'd done with it the night before caught Tia in midstretch. She felt the thick wash of moisture flooding her pussy, the sharp spike of arousal in her sex.

With great difficulty, Tia brought her suddenly raging libido under control and glared at her mate, Luc, the wolf with all the ideas. He opened his mouth in a full lupine grin, his laughter and love spilled into her thoughts, totally disarming her . . . for the moment.

The larger of the two wolves, his black coat glistening with golden highlights, yawned and shifted. The change from beast to six-and-a-half-foot tall, gloriously naked African-American male was almost instantaneous, the mouth filled with sharp teeth slipping easily into a wide, perfectly human smile. He leaned over and kissed Tia, his mobile lips bringing her right back to a level of arousal she really didn't need so early this morning. There was too much they needed to do.

But damn, Tinker had certainly used those lips in all the right places last night. Her nipples puckered, begging for a repeat performance. Tia bit back a groan.

Tinker slowly, thoroughly, ended the kiss. "Always in a hurry, missy. You need to learn to relax. It's still early."

The second wolf, his thick coat an unrelenting black, yawned and stretched. His black claws raked the plush carpet and left furrows in the thick nap. He turned his head, and in a most un-wolflike manner, winked at Tia.

Then he shifted. Not quite as tall as Tinker, his skin a fair counterpoint to the other man's dark chocolate, Luc had the same rock-hard muscles, the broad shoulders and narrow hips characteristic of all the other Chanku males Tia had met.

The Chanku she loved. It boggled the mind, made Tia want to laugh out loud, to think that a mere couple of weeks ago she'd never even heard of Chanku outside her mother's fairy tales—and as the old joke went, *now she were one.*

Unfortunately, she'd learned quickly that being Chanku carried with it risks unlike anything she could have imagined. Thank goodness her father was safe, for now. The presidential cabinet member intent on creating a breeding farm for shapeshifters needed to be stopped, but now that they knew his identity and plans, they'd won a large part of the battle.

Tia felt a gentle presence in her mind. She glanced at Luc and realized he was *listening* to everything she was thinking.

"Tinker said it's bad manners to snoop in someone's thoughts without permission."

Luc grinned. "Yeah, Tinker would know, wouldn't he?"

Tinker sat on the bed next to Tia. "You know how sorry I am, Luc."

Tia sighed. She'd learned of Luc's role in her mother's death by stealing into Tinker's thoughts. She knew Tinker felt terribly guilty, even though it was something Luc should have told her on his own. She covered as much of Tinker's big hand as she could with her smaller one. "It's not your fault, Tink, and it all worked out for the best." She gazed steadily into Luc's brilliant amber eyes. "I thought Luc had learned his lesson—that you don't hide important things from the ones you love."

Luc shook his head. "I didn't realize you knew about the breeding farm. I thought you were asleep when Cheval was talking about it. I would have told you, you know."

Tia shook her head. "When, Luc? You have to learn to share things like that with me. It's important. Not knowing stuff could get us killed."

"It's hard to change old habits." Luc leaned close and kissed Tia, his lips soft and warm against hers. "I want to be there to protect you."

She refused to be dissuaded, though it was really hard not to kiss him back. Pulling away with a sigh, Tia managed a halfhearted glare in Luc's direction. "The point is, what are we going to do about it? Is Shannon safe?"

"I need to call Jake. He didn't check in last night, as far as I know. Someone would have told us."

A soft tap sounded at the door. AJ Temple opened it just a crack, saw they were all awake and stepped into the room. He still looked rumpled, as if he'd just crawled out of bed. Tia wondered if AJ and his lover Mik had enjoyed each other as much as Tia and her two men.

"G'morning. Tia, your dad wants you to call your friend and see if Jake got there. He hasn't reported in. Ulrich tried Jake's cell phone but it's turned off and he's not answering his messages. Do you mind?"

"Not at all." Tia grabbed a robe and tied it around her waist. She turned to glare at Luc. "You and I need to talk. I'll be right back."

Luc blew her a kiss as she left the room. Tia was glad he couldn't see the grin on her face.

The long table in the dining room was almost filled. Anton Cheval, leader of the Montana pack, his mate, Tia's cousin Keisha Rialto, and Stefan Aragat, another Montana Chanku, already had plates of food in front of them. Alexandria Olanet, Stefan's mate, was pouring coffee at the sideboard.

Tia said a general "good morning" as she and AJ entered the dining room, then she greeted her father. Ulrich Mason looked none the worse for wear, considering they'd only rescued him from his kidnappers a few hours earlier. She smiled at Miguel Fuentes, or Mik, as everyone called him, who was loading two plates with food. Mik handed a plate piled high with bacon, eggs and fried potatoes to AJ, and the two men sat down at the table.

Tia leaned over and gave her father a kiss on the cheek. "Where's a phone, Dad? I'll call Shannon now. It's late enough in the morning in Boston, she should be up."

Anton Cheval handed a cordless phone to Tia. "Good morning. I hope you slept well."

Tia felt her skin flush. She'd hardly slept at all, not with both Luc and Tinker finding such inventive ways to keep her awake.

Anton's knowing grin made Tia blush even harder. Stefan laughed out loud. "Don't let him embarrass you, Tia. It's not like the four of us weren't doing the same things as you guys." He leaned close to Anton and whispered loud enough for everyone to hear, "Next time, I want to be the bottom."

Anton choked on his coffee.

Tia dialed Shannon's number, laughing along with everyone else. When the answering machine picked up, she left a quick message with the phone number in Montana. "No answer. I wonder where they are, so early in the morning?"

Luc and Tinker entered the room. Both men looked freshly showered and, as far as Tia could tell, good enough to eat.

"No word from Jake?" Luc grabbed a plate and handed one to Tinker.

"No." Tia poured herself a cup of coffee and slathered a blueberry muffin with cream cheese. "Should we be worried? Should we fly back there and check on them?"

"Not yet." Luc leaned over and kissed Tia on his way to the table, clearly staking his claim in front of every other male in the group. "Let's give them a couple more hours, then we need to think about heading back to San Francisco. We can make our plans from home base."

Anton Cheval cleared his throat after his coughing spell, wiped his streaming eyes, and glared at Stefan. "The jet is ready whenever you feel you need to leave. Just let Oliver know so he can bring the car around."

"Thank you." Ulrich toasted Anton with his cup of coffee. "I would like to ask Oliver for a lift to the airport whenever the rest of you are ready to go. I feel a trip to Washington DC is in order about now. I have a strong desire to visit with Secretary Milt Bosworth."

"Dad, do you think it's safe?"

"We'll go with you." Luc grabbed Tia's hand.

Ulrich shook his head. "No. This is something I need to do on my own. Less risk of anyone finding out about us. Besides, I want the rest of you available in case Jake needs help." He turned his attention to the leader of the Montana pack. "Cheval, you and yours have been more generous than I ever imagined or expected. Thank you."

Cheval dipped his head in acknowledgment. "We have much to learn from one another. We are, in essence, recreating an ancient culture, an entire species in fact, with very little history on which to base our knowledge. It's imperative we work together, help one another, share what we know whenever possible."

"Agreed." Tia's father took another sip of his coffee and smiled sadly. He grabbed Tia's hand in his. "I wish your mother had lived to see this." He gestured with his other hand, encompassing the entire room, the ten of them together. "For years we wondered if there were others like us. We knew of Keisha and her mother, but no one else. Then you were born, but we didn't know for sure if you were Chanku. A few years later I found Luc, then he found Jake. Mik and AJ joined us. There's no reason to wonder if we'll find others. Not any more. Now we know they're out there."

His cell phone rang. Ulrich stood up as he reached in

his pocket to take the call. He left the room, talking quietly. When he returned a few minutes later, Ulrich was smiling. "That was Jake. Bosworth's men grabbed Shannon, but Jake got to her in time. They're in a motel on the south side of Portland, Maine." He laughed and pointed a finger at Luc. "We're buying Jake a motorcycle. You know that Beemer he's been drooling over? Seems he really needs it to get Shannon away from the bad guys."

"He what?" Luc slammed his coffee cup down on the table. Then a slow grin spread across his face. "Where's he taking her?"

"Remember that cabin he bought a while back, somewhere near the Canadian border? I'm not really certain where it is and I wasn't about to ask when he called, in case someone's monitoring our calls. Anyway, seems as if that's the perfect place to keep Shannon safe." Ulrich was grinning broadly when he sat back down at the table.

Tia frowned, not quite sure what was going on.

"It is perfect." Luc nodded in agreement. "Deep forest, very few people. Does he have enough of the supplement?"

"He has enough."

Tia's glance shifted from Luc to her father. "What the hell are you two talking about?"

Luc patted her on the knee. Her father shook his head, still grinning. "You know I suspected Shannon might be Chanku. Jake's reached the same conclusion. He's not a hundred percent sure, but enough that he's going to get her to a safe place and see if the nutrient has any effect. They'll be safely out of the way, in any case, which gives me time to have my talk with dear old Milton."

Tia was still trying to process her father's comment when Ulrich wiped the napkin across his mouth, folded it carefully at his place and stood up. "Cheval, Aragat . . . Alexandria and Keisha, though the words are hardly sufficient for what you've done, thank you all." He turned to Tia and the men of his pack. "Finish your meal. I have a feeling things are just beginning to get interesting."

Ulrich left the room. Tia was barely aware he'd gone. Her mind spun with Ulrich's casual announcement. Now even Jake thought Shannon might be Chanku. This went way beyond Ulrich's casual suspicion, and it would explain so much. Tia's lover, her friend, her closest confidant until Luc, a member of the same magical race. And, like Tia had been for so long, completely unaware of her own heritage.

Jake sat on the edge of the bed and stared at the cell phone resting in the palm of his hand. Whatever made him dial Ulrich Mason's number? Jake had only meant to check for messages. He really hadn't intended to call his boss, to say anything to the rest of the pack about where he was going with Shannon, his very strong suspicions about her heritage, but now he'd talked to Ulrich, Jake actually felt more comfortable about his plans.

Ulrich hadn't said a word when Jake announced he planned to buy a motorcycle and put it on the Pack Dynamic account. Instead, the old man had mentioned his own quick trip to the nation's capital. Jake shook his head, wondering what Ulrich was up to.

At least now Jake had some idea of why he'd been sent to protect Shannon Murphy, though it was hard to believe a cabinet member was behind Ulrich's kidnapping, that a trusted government servant might be the one who had ordered not only Ulrich's kidnapping, but also Shannon's attack.

Pipes rattled when Shannon shut the water off in the shower. Jake turned off the cell phone and stuck it in his pack just as Shannon walked through the door, emerging out of the billowing steam like a red-haired wraith.

Jake held his arms wide and Shannon walked into his

embrace as if they'd been lovers for years. She leaned over and kissed him, her mouth moving over his in a light, teasing manner that had his cock standing at attention in a heartbeat.

"What's that for?" Jake kissed her back, sweeping his tongue along the seam between her lips. She didn't open for him as he'd expected. Nothing Shannon had done since they first made love had gone as he expected.

She leaned back and smiled at him. "For saving me from those men. For making absolutely exquisite love to me all night long. For letting me have the shower first. Take your pick."

"Exquisite, eh?" Jake leaned forward to nip at her smooth belly. Shannon turned quickly, slipping out of his arms and out of reach.

"Maybe I overstated. It was okay." She propped her hands on her hips, which effectively forced her perfect breasts up and forward.

"Just okay? What happened to exquisite?"

"I was being polite. C'mon. I'm hungry."

Jake wiggled his eyebrows. "So am I."

"For food, Bozo. I think I missed a meal or two somewhere."

Jake wrapped his fist around his erect cock and stroked slowly along the length, rolling his foreskin back from the broad head, exposing the blood-filled crown, then slipping his palm forward, covering it once again. Slowly, methodically, he taunted her with each careful stroke, until he was almost certain her eyes took on the glazed look of arousal he'd aimed for—and achieved—over and over again last night.

"I've got something here you can eat."

Shannon blinked, then took a moment to study what he offered. She wrapped her hand over his, pushing the protective skin back and exposing his sensitive glans. Her fingers slipped over his hand and she swept one finger across the head of his cock, lifting a small pearl of pre-cum from the narrow slit at the end. Making complete eye contact, she lifted her finger to her mouth.

Jake thought his heart might beat right out of his chest.

Shannon slowly sucked on her finger, closed her eyes and swallowed with a look of pure ecstasy on her face. The tip of her tongue slipped out, followed by a glimpse of her teeth as she carefully licked her lips. When she opened her eyes again, instead of the sexy invite he expected, Shannon flashed Jake a saucy grin. "Tastes great, but I was thinking more along the lines of a cup of coffee and a bagel. Now hurry up. It's getting late."

Grumbling, Jake headed for the bathroom. Damn. Would he ever understand women? They'd linked, damn it. They'd shared their souls during sex last night, melded, one into the other in a way he'd never imagined, and she hadn't said a fucking word about it!

Just thinking of what they'd done, the wild, uninhibited sex they'd shared, turned Jake on. He'd lost track of how many times he made her come, lost track of his own mind-blowing climaxes, but he hadn't forgotten the feeling. The frightening intimacy of linking with a woman at the height of orgasm.

Sharing thoughts, sharing sensations, sharing passion.

And all she could talk about was coffee and a damned bagel. *Shit*.

Jake closed the bathroom door behind him, fighting a really childish urge to slam it hard enough to rattle the windows. It wouldn't be the first time he'd beaten off under the warm spray of a shower, though after last night, he'd really hoped that lonely activity was a thing of the past.

He stared at his cock. The damned thing practically stood at attention. How he could be horny after the work-out last night was beyond Jake, but there was no denying the familiar ache in his balls or the insistent glare of his own one-eyed monster. Stepping beneath the warm spray, Jake imagined Shannon, naked in this very spot. Picturing her soft hands wrapped around his cock, Jake reluctantly took the situation in hand.

Shannon managed to keep the smarmy grin plastered on her face until the bathroom door closed behind Jake's perfect ass. Then she slowly sank to the edge of the bed and rested her head in both hands. Dear God, what had she gotten herself into?

Who was this man? Her body still thrummed with desire, her nipples hadn't lost their taut pucker, her pussy clenched with rhythmic spasms and wept with need, just because he'd wanted her again.

Men always wanted her. Women, too. She'd never really known why. Sure, she was attractive enough, though not so much more than any other woman—but that need of theirs, that desire, had never affected her before. Not like this.

For as long as she could remember, Shannon had loved sex. Loved the power it gave her, the sense of control over the hundreds of men and women she'd slept with since she'd first reached puberty over fifteen years ago. Even Tia, for all her strength, had deferred to Shannon.

Not Jake. Never Jake. No, this man had somehow slipped beneath her defenses, found the chink in Shannon's armor and the code to unlock her heart.

Not only that, he'd gotten inside her head. She wasn't going to think of that now. Couldn't allow herself to try and understand what really happened last night. It was too much, too soon. Shannon glanced at the closed bathroom door, listened to the steady tattoo of water against the shower stall and imagined Jake beneath the hot spray.

He'd be stroking that massive cock of his right now. She'd bet good money on it. She'd watched, mesmerized, as he'd slowly slipped the foreskin back and forth over the head of his cock with a natural ease that said he'd done this often and enjoyed it immensely. She'd felt him even then, his thoughts somehow hovering in her mind—Jake's need, Jake's passion.

All wound up with her own mindless arousal, her body's cry for more. A cry she'd ruthlessly silenced. She didn't know him. Didn't understand this connection with him. Until she figured out exactly what was going on, who the hell Jacob Trent really was—*what* he was—and how he managed to wield such sensual power over her, Shannon swore to keep her guard up.

She'd never believed in things like mental telepathy or any of that psychic babble, but she couldn't deny what Jake had done. She'd felt him, understood his thoughts inside her head.

Damn. Except for that one small aberration . . .

Shannon pressed her fist against her mouth, afraid she might laugh out loud. Well, other than *that*, whatever that was . . . Jake was gorgeous to look at, sexier than any man she'd ever seen and, as far as she could tell, intelligent, caring and so damned perfect he made her heart ache. More than enough reasons to move slowly. To watch him carefully and listen closely to everything he said.

Even when he wasn't saying it out loud.

Shannon shoved her wet hair out of her eyes. She was going to have to be damned careful she didn't do something stupid like fall in love. Love got you hurt. It ruined everything. Took away your control. Eventually, it left you alone and wanting.

Shannon thought of her mother, the nights she'd spent crying alone in her room when Shannon's father hadn't come home. Thought of the long months of cancer slowly killing the woman who had already died a little every night Shannon remembered.

No. She'd never allow herself to be so needy, to love so

deeply. No man would have that power to wound her, to leave her an empty shell waiting for a merciful death.

She found her sweats and quickly dressed in the warm outfit Jake had bought her last night, then shoved the extra things they'd gotten into a plastic bag. Wandering slowly across the room to open the heavy blinds, Shannon slowly ran a comb through her tangled hair.

She glanced through the narrow crack in the shades as she reached for the cord to raise them, and stopped. The black sedan they'd driven last night was parked in full view a few spots down from the space beneath their room. Three men wearing dark suits and equally dark glasses appeared to be inspecting the vehicle.

One spoke into what looked more like a radio than a cell phone, another stood to one side, his arm resting in a cloth sling and a white bandage covering one side of his head. Another man had a bandage wrapped all the way around his head, but Shannon knew she'd recognize him anywhere.

He was the one who'd been waiting last night, sitting on the edge of her bed with his back to her. A fourth man moved into view and gestured toward the registration office at the far end of the complex, then took off in that direction at a brisk walk.

Shannon moved quickly away from the window and knocked on the bathroom door. Jake opened it immediately, caught in the act of rubbing himself dry with a fluffy white towel. If Shannon hadn't been so terrified she would have enjoyed helping him.

"Four men, all suits, checking out the car. Two of them were my visitors last night. One just headed for the hotel office."

Jake didn't hesitate. He nodded, slipped past Shannon and took a quick look through the slit beside the blinds. While he dressed, Shannon gathered up Jake's belongings and stuffed them into his leather carry-on bag. She put her plastic bags together into the larger laundry sack the hotel had provided. Neither of them said a word. Shannon had the oddest feeling they had no need for speech. Each knew what the other expected.

Moving swiftly and economically, they had their belongings gathered and were moving down the stairs at the far end of the complex in less than a minute. The stairwell was hidden from the parking lot until the bottom level, which opened directly to the lot.

Jake slipped over the railing on the second level and dropped quietly to the ground behind a large holly bush. Shannon tossed his leather bag to him, followed by her plastic sack, then made the leap herself. It was at least an eight-foot jump, but with Jake waiting to help her, she didn't hesitate.

Jake caught Shannon just as her feet hit the ground, steadying her, breaking the jolt of her landing. With a quick nod of thanks, she grabbed the bag Jake handed her and followed him. Moving soundlessly, he found a narrow trail through the riparian zone bordering a small creek behind the hotel. The trail skirted the parking lot through a tangle of thick brush, then turned at an oblique angle, away from the three men still standing by the car.

Heart pounding, senses on high, Shannon felt a strange exhilaration, an excitement that somehow reminded her of that amazingly sensual dream she'd had just last night.

They broke into a quick jog as soon as they were out of hearing of the men in suits. Racing along the overgrown trail, following in Jake's footsteps, leaping over rocks and fallen tree limbs, Shannon felt as if she could run forever. Her heart and lungs seemed to have found a perfect rhythm. Her legs stretched out in long, powerful strides and she followed Jake's quick pace without any effort at all.

Jake leapt over the creek, aiming for a break in the

brush on the far side of the water. He turned to help Shannon but she was landing lightly beside him even as he stretched out his arm.

He gave her a quick thumbs up and a wolfish grin, then turned and raced up the narrow pathway through ferns and twisted willows. It almost seemed as if Jake were enjoying himself!

Shannon stayed right on his heels until they both broke out of the small forest into a perfectly normal looking neighborhood of older homes and small shops.

They paused on the narrow sidewalk, lungs heaving, eyes sparkling with excitement. Jake leaned close. His amber eyes glinted now with a dark intensity, his lips parted slightly. Shannon stood perfectly still, waiting for his kiss, but he merely reached up and brushed twigs out of her tangled hair, then smoothed it back over her shoulders.

The air rushed out of her lungs on a long, disappointed sigh as Jake turned away, slung his leather bag over his shoulder and took Shannon's hand in his. His palm was warm against hers. She found herself thinking of those long, sensuous fingers, of the things Jake had done with them last night. Of the responses he'd dragged from her, over and over again.

Shannon's pussy contracted in remembered heat. Jake appeared oblivious to her growing arousal. Just like the aftermath of her dream, she felt energized by the run. Euphoric. As if her body had been awakened in some unusual way. So many emotions and sensations raced through her mind, titillated her body. Shannon found it almost laughable, the way the two of them walked along the street as if they were merely browsing through the shops, not dwelling on the amazing sex shared the night before, not catching their breath after running for their lives. She should be frightened, to know those men were following her, that they wanted her for some mysterious reason.

Instead, Shannon felt as if she'd been dropped into a most amazing adventure, complete with her own super-hero. She turned and looked steadily at Jake walking beside her. "What now?"

He gazed down at her with that same grin, the one she remembered when he'd knelt last night between her legs, his face shimmering with her fluids. He'd grinned just that way, then dipped his head between her thighs once more and given her a climax that had left her senseless.

"What now? Why, a cup of coffee and a bagel. Isn't that what you wanted?"

Laughing out loud, Shannon followed Jake across the street.

Chapter 4

Shannon sipped her coffee and nibbled on her bagel while she watched Jake methodically work his way through a huge plate of fried potatoes, scrambled eggs and ham. He ate his meal with the same enthusiasm he showed when making love.

Shannon's sex clenched and her nipples pebbled against the soft sweatshirt the moment the image entered her mind. She hid her grin behind another sip of lukewarm coffee. Every time she thought about Jake, she thought of sex, of his amazing skills and the effect he'd had on her body . . . the effect he continued to have.

She hadn't exaggerated a bit. Last night had been exquisite.

She glanced out the window then back at Jake, only moderately terrified the men would find the two of them sitting here enjoying a late breakfast in such a public place. Jake didn't seem the least bit concerned, but she'd deduced early on that it took quite a bit to rattle this man.

He looked up and noticed her watching him. She saw him frown, then he took a swallow of coffee and pulled a small plastic pill bottle out of his coat pocket.

"What's that?"

Jake grinned at her. Damn but she loved his smile. It felt like a gift rarely given, yet he'd been generous with her.

"Vitamins . . . an herbal supplement. Something Ulrich cooked up. We all take them and they seem to work. I haven't had a cold in at least fifteen years."

No way would any stupid virus invade this man. It wouldn't dare. Shannon stuck her hand out. "What's in them?"

Jake dropped a capsule into her palm and took one for himself. "Mostly herbs and natural stuff. Nutrients our bodies need, according to Ulrich Mason and his cadre of top-notch scientists. I've got plenty and there's nothing in them that can hurt you, but Ulrich says we need to take one every day."

Shannon looked at the capsule in her palm and took a sniff. It smelled like fresh-cut hay. She shrugged and popped it into her mouth. Washing it down with another swallow of tepid coffee, Shannon raised her eyes and glanced up at Jake.

He watched her, his enigmatic expression telling Shannon absolutely nothing of the thoughts behind his mysterious amber eyes. He swallowed his own capsule, returned the pill bottle to his pocket, left money on the table to cover the bill and led Shannon back out into the early fall morning.

The fist that tightened around Jake's chest when Shannon took her first dose of the supplement refused to relax its grasp. If she didn't show signs of becoming Chanku within the next two weeks, Jake wasn't sure he'd be able to handle the disappointment. If she was Chanku, everything her body needed was in those pills. If she didn't show signs of change, somehow he would have to finish this assignment and let her go.

Losing Shannon was too painful even to consider. He forced his concerns to the back of his mind and concentrated instead on getting them both to safety.

Jake checked the bus schedule and decided on a cab. By midmorning they reached a small town north of Portland where they wandered through a motorcycle dealership just long enough to find the bike Jake wanted and the surprisingly comfortable leather clothing he insisted both he and Shannon wear.

Shortly after a quick lunch, Shannon found herself sitting behind Jake on the back of a gorgeous silvery gray motorcycle, dressed all in black leather with a matching helmet protecting her head and sleek black boots on her feet.

Jake wore full leathers as well. It was all Shannon could do not to touch him, to stroke the warm leather and imagine the man inside. Jake's leather pants fit his perfect ass like a glove and the jacket showed off his broad shoulders and narrow waist to perfection.

The young woman who waited on them seemed absolutely mesmerized by Jake. Shannon couldn't blame her, even though she had the strangest desire to knock the clerk silly. It all felt absolutely surreal.

Twenty-four hours ago, Shannon had never even heard of Jacob Trent. Now she owed him her life. Craved his touch. Needed him.

Wanted to possess him.

Not good. Not good at all.

Though Jake appeared relaxed and at ease, Shannon sensed his anxiety, his need to move quickly. He never stopped checking their surroundings, closely watching the highway in front of the shop and paying attention to every little detail.

The only time Shannon even saw him smile was the moment the dealer handed him the keys to his new set of wheels.

They stowed their gear in panniers on the sides of the bike and headed northwest out of Falmouth, putting as much distance between themselves and the men in suits as possible.

By late afternoon Jake figured the novelty of riding a motorcycle had lost its allure for Shannon. Her arms still held tightly to his waist and her soft breasts pressed into his backbone, but she lay heavily against him in total exhaustion.

The attraction of Shannon in leather had only grown stronger for Jake. When he thought of the huge amount of money he'd just charged to the Pack Dynamics account for the simple pleasure of getting Shannon Murphy into black leather, he couldn't help but grin. Luc was going to have a fit.

Knowing he had enough ready cash to pay his buddy back was Jake's only saving grace, but for now he intended to enjoy all the hoped-for repercussions.

They stopped briefly for supplies in a small town, buying just what they needed for the night. A few miles farther down the road, Jake turned off the main route and followed a narrow track through the dense forest before finally turning down the country lane that led to his cabin. He still wasn't certain what had made him buy the place, but the fact it sat dead center in the middle of almost four hundred acres of dense forest certainly made the property attractive to a shapeshifter.

Jake pulled the bike to a stop in front of the broad front porch. The home nestled comfortably among the tall pines, fashioned much like a larger version of log cabins from two centuries past. Jake wondered if he'd ever grow tired of the quiet beauty of this isolated place. He'd only been here a few times since buying the property, the last trip with AJ and Mik.

An image of the three of them together, Jake and both his packmates making love to Shannon at the same time, hit with such intensity his breath caught in his lungs.

"I thought you said it was little and sort of rough. This is absolutely gorgeous." Obviously unaware of the direction Jake's thoughts were leading, Shannon crawled stiffly from the back of the bike and pulled off her helmet. The long mass of deep red hair she'd kept tucked inside tumbled over her shoulders when she raised her arms and stretched.

Jake's gut tightened into one large knot. His cock swelled against the leather pants. AJ and Mik? What had he been thinking?

No way in hell are those two sex fiends getting near my mate. Not until she's mine. Not until we've bonded.

Every move Shannon made turned him on. With her sleek body encased in the form-fitting leather she could've starred in the hottest wet dream ever. Jake wasn't quite ready to include two of his most intimate friends in those dreams, much less reality, no matter how much he enjoyed sex with AJ and Mik.

"What made you buy something so far from your home in San Francisco?"

Jake blinked out of his fantasy and focused on the real thing. "My family was originally from Maine. I came home for my father's funeral a few years ago . . . ended up borrowing a friend's bike and taking a road trip. Somehow I took the roads that brought me up here and the place was . . . right."

Jake shrugged, not really sure exactly why he'd felt the need to own this particular piece of property in such an isolated corner of the world. It had been an almost visceral desire to possess, a need to race through these dark woods with the knowledge the land was his, that the beautiful log cabin belonged only to him. "Working for Ulrich and Pack Dynamics pays well. I guess I just felt it was time to invest my money."

"Good investment. It's beautiful here." Shannon unzipped her leather jacket, opening it just a bit against the late afternoon warmth. Jake caught a glimpse of black lace holding the full swell of her breasts and practically groaned aloud.

He forced himself to turn away, to open the panniers and saddle bag so they could carry their supplies into the cabin. Shannon grabbed a couple of bags while Jake brought the rest.

The door was unlocked. Shannon glanced back in surprise after turning the handle and watching the door swing open.

"I rarely lock it. As remote as this place is, I've never really worried about theft. If someone's lost in a storm, I'd want them to be able to get in without doing any damage." Still, they were here because someone wanted Shannon. Once inside, Jake lowered a heavy metal bar across the door and used an iron spike to lock it in place. Whoever built the house had felt a need for a simple but secure locking system, one he would use to protect Shannon whether they needed it or not.

"Thank you."

Jake looked up and caught Shannon staring at him with a small quirk to her lips. Not quite a smile, more a look of bemused acceptance that her life had taken a sudden, unexpected twist. "You're welcome. No one's going to get through that. I promised I'd keep you safe."

Jake led Shannon through the large main room, past an attractive grouping of an oversized dark brown leather sofa and four matching chairs arranged around a huge fireplace, then into the kitchen which was separated from the great room by a broad bar with stools along one side. He found a kerosene lantern, trimmed the wick and lit it. "We've got solar for power but I like to save that for emergencies. Besides, I like the way the firelight looks."

When Jake turned around, Shannon stood close. Her hair gleamed like burnished copper in the flickering light from the lantern and she stared at him with a look that set

Jake on fire. There was no question of wanting or needing or even whether or not this was a good idea. He leaned close and gently kissed her mouth, tracing her full lips with the tip of his tongue.

She opened for him on a gentle sigh. Jake's arms seemed to move of their own volition, wrapping tightly around her waist, cupping the perfect globes of her leather-clad ass.

He kissed her thoroughly, his tongue tangling with hers, tracing the outline of her teeth, finding the sensitive roof of her mouth, thrusting in and out with a slow rhythm, one Jake realized he'd matched with the gentle thrust of his hips.

Shannon slowly ended the kiss and rested her forehead against his chest. "I promised myself I wasn't going to let this happen again."

Hiding his shock as best he could, Jake pulled away so he could see her face. "Why?"

"Last night. When we made love, you made me come every time. That's not normal, at least for me. And . . ." She shook her head, obviously confused, unsure of what she was trying to explain. "Something else happened. Something really weird."

"I know. We shared some amazing climaxes. I want to do that again . . . and again."

"It wasn't just the sex, Jake. It was something else. Something I can't understand and it scared me." Shannon turned away and wrapped her arms around her waist. "I felt like you were in my head, like I was in yours. I saw *me* through your eyes. Felt what you felt. Experienced the sensation of your cock inside me, the way my muscles grabbed you. Can you explain that?"

Jake cupped her shoulders in his palms. He much preferred the gentle swell of her bottom, but the rigid set of Shannon's shoulders told him exactly how upset she was. She deserved answers he couldn't give. Jake couldn't tell her, not until he knew for certain she shared the same genes. It was an unwritten law of the pack never to divulge its existence.

A law none of them dare break.

"Did you ever stop and think we might be so well matched, the sex so intense, we formed some kind of psychic link?" Jake turned Shannon so that she faced him, his fingers lightly massaging her shoulders. Her green eyes gazed into his with the same intensity he'd felt in her kiss.

"I felt you the same way, Shannon. That's never happened to me with another woman. Never. I made love to you at least a dozen times." He laughed. Shannon smiled in return and her body seemed to relax just a bit. "That hasn't happened before, either. I mean, I can usually get it up when I want, but there's a limit. Last night erased limits. It was pretty intense, but it was also absolutely amazing. I think of our connection as a very special gift. I'd like to see where this takes us. Are you willing?"

Shannon turned away again, moving out of his grasp, obviously avoiding his gaze. She clasped her hands over her belly in what could only be a protective gesture. Jake dropped his hands helplessly to his sides. He wished he could see into her mind as clearly now as he had at the height of orgasm.

"Someone's trying to kidnap me. I don't know why, but they hurt me and scared me half to death. I just met you yesterday, and while I know Tia sent you, I don't know anything about you . . . except that somehow you're able to read my mind, to let me see into yours. Still, you don't know anything about me, either." She bowed her head, her shoulders rose and fell with her sigh. "I might not be at all what you think."

"And what might that be?" He ached to touch her. Jake realized he'd tightened both hands into clenched fists, pressed tightly against his thighs. It was either that or drag Shannon into his arms.

"Do you know Tia very well?" She turned around and tilted her head to one side.

He certainly couldn't tell Shannon how intimately he knew her friend. That he would recognize Tia's taste anywhere, that his hands had stroked her swollen pussy, his fingers found their way deep inside her ass.

Jake shook his head, accepting Shannon's abrupt change of subject. "Not really. She's with Luc. Lucien Stone, her father's right-hand man. Tia and Luc hit it off from the beginning. I wouldn't be surprised to see them end up married."

The color left Shannon's face. "Married? She didn't say anything. Not a word."

Jake shrugged. "I'm just guessing. I wasn't with them when they rescued Tia's dad, but I imagine it's really been intense. I know they've been in Montana and also in Washington DC, though they're probably back in San Francisco, now. The last time I saw them, they were pretty tight."

The half-truths rolled off his tongue as if he hadn't almost gotten himself killed trying to take Tia away from Luc. Jake still didn't know how he would be accepted when he finally returned to the pack. What if they kicked him out, made him find his own way? He wished he could see Luc, fact to face, talk to his best friend in person and then apologize to Tia. Wished he could undo the stupid moves he'd made just a few days ago.

Shannon worried Jake didn't know what she was really like? Jake almost laughed at the irony.

Shannon didn't have a clue what kind of bastard she was with.

It must have been the shock of the past twenty-four hours finally hitting her, but Shannon felt as if she might fly apart, right here in the front room of this gorgeous mountain home, standing mere inches from the one man she had never expected to find.

Too much, too soon, too impossible to accept. She'd experienced heart-stopping fear, unimaginable sexual ecstasy and a terrifying link with the only man in the entire world who had the power to break her heart.

Shannon stared into Jake's amazing eyes and wanted to weep. He had no idea what or who she was. Never in her life, not once since hitting puberty, had Shannon regretted her actions. Now, looking at this beautiful man she felt nothing but self-disgust. She'd screwed anyone she wanted, had sex with total strangers. If he knew she was nothing more than used baggage, would he still look at her as if he wanted to hold her forever?

What would he think if she told him she'd been fucked by more men than she could remember—and just as many women? What would he think of her then, learning he was one in a long line of sexual partners she'd known since she was nothing more than a kid, just one more warm body capable of giving her an orgasm?

Except Jacob Trent was more. So damned much more. Therein lay the problem.

Shannon wanted to scream! She'd never cared before. Never, except for Tia. She and Tia had been lovers for almost fifteen years, sharing men as easily as most women shared outfits. But damn it all, she would not put Tia in the same class as those nameless, faceless partners. She'd loved Tia, still loved her, in fact, but at least Tia had understood. Tia'd been looking, too. Just like Shannon.

Searching. Always searching for something missing, some nebulous piece of herself. Like Tia, Shannon had tried to fill that need with sex. Why hadn't she wondered what it would be like to finally find the missing piece?

Because I never expected to find it. Never expected anyone like Jake.

Shannon's eyes filled with tears. She blinked them back

and held her chin high. Tia had lived the same life, yet Jake said she'd found someone to love, someone who loved her. Did Lucien Stone know about Tia's past? Did he know she'd done everything sexually possible?

Did he care?

"What's wrong, Shannon? Are you upset Tia's found someone? I know you were lovers for a long time. I . . ."

"What?" Jake knew? "But how did you . . . ?"

"I don't know. Tia might have told me. Maybe it was her dad."

Shannon slowly shook her head from side to side. "I often wondered if Mr. Mason knew we were lovers. Are you sure?"

"I imagine so. Not much gets by him." Smiling, Jake reached for her, cupped his strong hands over her shoulders and dragged Shannon up against his chest. "Are you afraid that's going to put me off? That you and Tia had sex?"

She felt his soft laughter rumble in his chest. "Aw, sweetie. I don't care about your past, not how many lovers you've had or what sex they were. We're a lot more alike than you realize. I've been with as many men as I have women. If that's an issue with you, let's get past it now. It's not important. You're important. What we've discovered is important."

Jake's words, spoken so naturally, so comfortably, rolled through Shannon's heart and caught her totally by surprise. She raised her head to see what his eyes might tell her. His calm, earth-shattering words reverberated in her mind. It was hard to imagine Jake with another man, not when he was so damned good at making love to a woman.

He leaned close and literally captured her mouth, kissing the confusion away. Once more his tongue invaded, once again she felt the steady thrust of his hips against her belly.

This time, though, Shannon allowed his kiss to take her.

She let her body find its own natural rhythm, which amazingly matched perfectly to Jake's.

He kissed her throat, his hands moving to the zipper on her leather coat. Slowly he lowered the tab, one metal tooth at a time. He followed with his mouth, kissing the tops of her breasts, sucking at her skin and making wet little sounds that turned her on even more.

Jake peeled the jacket away from her shoulders until it fell to the floor behind her and Shannon wore only the black lacy bra and tight leather pants.

Jake stepped back and stared at her. His smoldering eyes, the catch in his breath, the harsh line of his jaw—all signs of a totally aroused male.

"My God. You're beautiful. Absolutely beautiful." Like a celebrant approaching an altar, Jake knelt in front of her and carefully unfastened the zipper on her pants. Shannon felt the cool rush of air as he tugged the tight leather down over her hips. He left the waistband resting on her thighs as he leaned down and slipped her boots off her feet. Tugged her socks with them, slowly worked her pants down over each foot.

Standing in the middle of the large room dressed only in tiny scraps of black lace panties and bra, Shannon had never felt so exposed in her life. Or as aroused. Jake sat back on his heels and studied her body as if he could watch her forever. Still fully dressed, he slipped his leather jacket off his shoulders.

His blue chambray shirt strained across his broad chest. The leather pants bulged between his legs. Shannon's gaze darted to his crotch, then back to his dark amber eyes. Jake slid his hands along her thighs, raising gooseflesh wherever he touched.

Shannon's nipples puckered against the lacy bra. Her panties barely contained the fluids seeping from her swollen sex. Jake leaned forward, went down on his knees and inhaled. Shannon watched his chest expand as he breathed in her scent and something deep inside her flowered into life.

Slowly, firmly, Jake pressed his mouth against the triangle of fabric barely covering her damp curls. His breath flowed hot and moist over sensitive tissues. Shannon whimpered, the sound forming deep in her throat.

Jake's hands cupped her ass and he tugged her closer, nibbling now, his teeth scraping the wet satin panties, nipping at her clit through the fabric. Shannon's knees almost buckled. She spread her legs to give Jake better access, then reached forward blindly, grabbing his shoulders and hanging on for balance.

Jake's tongue stroked over the wet fabric, licking Shannon between her legs. Slow, steady strokes, the sensation blunted by wet satin, teasing strokes that brought her hips forward, made her fingers tighten on his shoulders. Made her tremble.

He nipped at the fabric, pulled it aside with his teeth, catching the elastic in the crease between Shannon's leg and her labia. The narrow band pressed against the side of her clit, forcing that tiny bundle of nerves forward.

Jake gently ran his tongue over her, then blew cool air over the damp trail. Shannon closed her eyes against the waves of ecstasy, shivered and locked her knees to keep from falling.

He tugged at the scrap of wet fabric with his hands, then pulled her panties off. Shannon lifted one foot, then the other. Though she'd been wearing little more than a thong, she suddenly felt even more exposed, more naked than she'd been.

A stream of liquid trickled down her leg, hot where it left her sex, cooler as it moved slowly along the sensitive flesh of her inner thigh. Jake tilted his head to one side and licked the cooling trail from knee to groin, then lapped her fluids at their source. His tongue was a hot, fiery brand, marking her.

He licked as if her juices fed him, stabbed deep inside her swollen cunt then suckled her throbbing clit. Shannon's climax built, the tension in her muscles strained her entire body. Her fingers clutched Jake's shoulders, she thrust her hips forward. Jake's big hands stretched across her buttocks, holding her to his mouth. Biting and sucking, licking and nipping he lifted her against his mouth until she balanced on her toes while Jake sucked her clit between his lips.

His hands squeezed her buttocks, rode the sweaty cleft back and forth. Shannon felt the blunt end of one finger probing against her ass, pressing slowly, inexorably moving forward, finding entrance and thrusting deep.

Reason fled and Shannon screamed. Her legs buckled, her fingers dug into Jake's shoulders and she collapsed against him. Held upright by his ravaging mouth and two fingers buried deep in her rectum, she felt boneless, nothing more than a clenching, spasming mass of sensation.

Jake's fingers slipped free of her ass, his arms lifted her, and Shannon felt herself being draped belly down over the back of the large leather couch. Somehow, the fact she still wore the lacy bra, still felt the tight clasp between her breasts made her feel even more naked, more exposed. The lace rubbed against her nipples. Her breasts felt too constrained, trapped within the fabric. Lying this way, belly down over the chair, the lace confining her breasts emphasized the fact she was bare everywhere else.

Vaguely, Shannon heard the familiar sound of foil tearing, then a rustling whisper when Jake's pants and boots hit the floor. Moisture seeped between her nether lips. She felt the cool trickle of fluid along the inside of her thigh.

Jake's hands stroked the smooth skin of her buttocks. Shannon's heart rate sped up and her pussy clenched in anticipation. Not many men were interested in taking her this way. None with Jake's sensuality, his gentle yet passionate touch.

His hand slid along her backbone, found the edge of her bra and traced it around to the front. He released the clasp, freeing her breasts, then pulled the cups aside until her nipples pressed into the soft leather couch. He left the straps on her shoulders, the narrow band across her back emphasizing her nudity even more.

Then Jake rubbed something cool and slick between her cheeks. Shannon shivered when he stroked her there with the broad head of his latex-covered cock. Her nipples puckered, her fingers tightened on the smooth leather.

She felt the head of his cock pressing solidly against her anus, the rough texture of his hair-covered legs rubbing the backs of her thighs. Forcing herself to relax, spreading her legs wide, Shannon waited for the burning, stretching pain that would quickly give way to pleasure. Waited impatiently for Jake to breach one more of her defenses.

Jake wrapped his fist around his cock and counted to ten. He'd grown past counting to gain control years ago, but something about this woman kept him right on the edge. Her taste? Maybe that was it. Shannon's flavor was ambrosia, her fluids the milk of the gods. Damn, he felt like an absolute fool around her, but she drew him, her body calling to his as if there were no other man on earth who could satisfy her insatiable needs.

In spite of the fading bruises from her ordeal, Shannon's ass was perfect. Like two halves of a peach, the pale flesh was firm and smooth and all his. He didn't have any regular lube but the hand lotion he'd found by the sink would work. Shannon didn't seem to mind. Damn, she was as ready as he was.

She was always ready. He'd never found a female anywhere who came even close to satisfying his needs, but Jake had the feeling this amazing woman was just warming up.

He rubbed the lotion along the narrow cleft between

her cheeks, pressing against her perfect little asshole with each pass. She pressed back, inviting penetration, but he teased her, circling the muscle, slipping down to massage her perineum, then once more pressing against her tight sphincter.

They hadn't said a word, not a single thing since he'd kissed her. Jake wondered if Shannon was searching for the link they'd shared last night. He hadn't felt her in his mind yet, though he'd kept his thoughts open, accepting.

She moaned and moved her butt as if she were begging for his penetration. Jake grabbed his cock and slipped it back and forth along the hot valley between her cheeks, finally halting at the rosy ring of muscle, pressing. Retreating. Pressing again, harder this time.

Shannon whimpered, a sound of need, not pain. The muscles in her back flexed, her legs straightened as she raised herself to meet him. Jake held his cock in his fist, squeezing himself to the point of pain for an ounce more of control. He pushed the broad crown against her tightly puckered opening. Felt the muscle relax just a fraction and increased the pressure. This time he gained entrance.

The feeling of that taut little muscle grabbing his cock, surrounding it, almost took Jake over the edge. He realized he was counting again, this time the number of deep breaths he took to hold on to what little control remained.

Shannon pushed back against him as he surged forward. Hot flesh grasped his cock, squeezed him, pulled him deeper. He wanted to shout out some kind of cheer when he finally slipped all the way inside her hot channel, when his balls touched the wet folds of her pussy.

Shuddering, his breath rushing in and out of his straining lungs like a bellows, Jake held perfectly still and fought off his need to come.

Shannon wouldn't have it. She thrust back even harder against him, then pulled slowly away. Not to be outdone,

Jake took a deep breath and matched her rhythm, driving into her heat, slipping out almost to the very end of his cock, then thrusting hard and deep again.

He knew he couldn't last, not with sensation this powerful, but he rode her as hard as he could, realizing almost at once this woman could take him. All of him. Could easily take whatever he offered, would welcome anything he did to help her find release.

He reached forward and caught her breasts, one in each hand. Pinching and tugging at her taut, puckered nipples, Jake added his groans to Shannon's cries. The room filled with the hard slap of flesh meeting flesh, of harsh breaths and loud groans, the creak of wood and leather as Jake forced Shannon against the back of the couch with each penetrating thrust.

Suddenly Shannon arched her back and screamed. Her muscles tightened around Jake's cock like a vise. His control slipped another notch. He knew he had only seconds before his climax boiled up and out of his balls, knew there was no time left to even appreciate the process.

It happened then, the link he'd searched for. He felt the pressure, the fullness of a huge cock filling his ass, only it was Shannon's experience and he was in her mind and she was in his. He knew she felt the clenching pleasure that was almost pain, would feel the hot coil of seed exploding from the end of his cock, the frustration of feeling it caught in the latex reservoir of the condom.

What if she questioned his frustration?

He had no choice but to use protection, no choice but to maintain the deception he was fully human. Until he could tell Shannon the truth, Jake had to continue using condoms as she would expect any lover to do.

Would her mind catch the reason *why* he protected her each time they made love? Would she understand the depths of his deception? The fact he still couldn't be sure, couldn't know until she'd had at least a week of the supplement, enough time to make the change from human to Chanku?

Jake shut those thoughts down the moment they entered his mind. He couldn't risk her wondering, couldn't chance her questioning him.

Shannon arched her back and cried out as Jake pounded into her receptive body. Her long, low cry took Jake even higher, caught his final thrust as he filled her. Shouting incoherently, his voice harsh and inhuman in his own ears, Jake gave in to his climax. Gave in to the rush of semen from testicles to release, the taut pressure in his balls, the overwhelming pleasure of this woman's body.

Jake's spasms went on for what seemed forever. He lay across Shannon's back, lungs heaving, heart pounding, his balls aching from the power of his orgasm. It had never been like this.

Never. No other woman had affected him so powerfully, crawled so far inside his mind that he'd actually *been* her. Jake had felt his cock plowing into her ass as if it was his own butt getting reamed, still felt the softening pressure as if his own ass muscles squeezed and surrounded a man's cock.

It was unsettling, to say the least. Unsettling and exciting as hell. Jake sighed and wrapped his arms around Shannon's waist, buried his face in her tangled hair and planted a soft kiss on the back of her neck.

She must be Chanku. She had to be, but until he knew for sure, Jake would wait. Already he felt the need to claim her. To take her as wolf, to tie with her in the way of Chanku and make her his mate forever.

Not yet. He couldn't. Not until she'd had the supplement long enough for the changes to happen. Until Shannon could become wolf. It would happen. It had to. No normal human could affect him like this.

He let out a deep breath, still covering Shannon's body

with his own. His cock throbbed deep within her swollen tissues, her muscles clenched and pulsed around him. The sense of being Shannon faded slowly away. Jake tightened his arms around Shannon's waist and nuzzled the back of her neck. She turned her head, her eyes drowsy and sated, her lips swollen, and stared solemnly at him.

"Jake? What's *Chanku*? Why do I hear that word in your mind? It sounds familiar, something I remember from a long time ago."

He shook his head, let her think he was too exhausted to answer. There were no words. Nothing he could say until he knew for sure. Only one thing was certain.

He would run tonight. Once Shannon slept, Jake would find solace in the forest, in the primeval depths of the thick woods where the wolf held mastery of all around him. He would run and he would pray to whatever gods watched over the beasts of the forest, whatever gods protected the man he was. He would pray that soon he could take this woman to mate.

PART TWO

Discovery

Chapter 5

They showered together, made long, slow love once more beneath the stinging spray, then shared a steak and salad for dinner. Shannon rarely ate red meat but for some reason the rare beef tasted like ambrosia. She stared at the bloody piece of meat on her fork and shook her head, caught between amusement and dismay.

It must be all the sex. Damn, she'd never felt so sated . . . or quite so sore. Of all the men she'd been with over the years, none was quite as insatiable as this one.

Or so well endowed. She looked up from her meal and grinned at Jake. He smiled back. The flickering lantern light turned his hair to molten gold and his eyes to liquid amber. Shannon noticed a brilliant glow about them, a sparkle that hadn't been there before. She might be exhausted, but Jake looked ready for anything.

He reached for the bottle of wine to refill their glasses. His shirt gaped open and Shannon noticed he hadn't replaced the bandage on his throat. Whatever injury he had was almost healed, but a jagged red scar ran from the side of his throat to just above his collarbone.

"I keep meaning to ask what happened to your throat." She thought of his rescue of her, the way he'd avoided the men searching for them with such ease. "Did you get shot?"

Jake shook his head as he poured wine into Shannon's glass, then his own. "No. Attacked by a large, justifiably pissed-off canine. Luckily, he missed." He concentrated on the wine so she couldn't see his eyes. The thought of an animal going for this man's throat terrified her. "He didn't miss by much. What were you doing?"

Jake looked up at her, finally, but his expression appeared guarded. After the intimate evening they'd shared, Shannon felt as if he'd suddenly erected a wall between them.

"I tried to take something he was protecting. I guess he wanted to teach me a lesson. Are you familiar with Pack Dynamics . . . Ulrich's company?"

Talk about your non sequitur. "Tia said it's a detective agency."

Jake nodded. "Yeah. Something like that. We do a lot of different jobs. Last week, I stuck my nose where it wasn't wanted and I paid for it. End of story." He wiped his mouth with his napkin and took a swallow of wine, but Shannon had the feeling there was a lot more to the tale than he told.

It was just as obvious she wasn't going to hear it tonight.

Suddenly she yawned. It felt so good, she did it again, stretching her arms over her head. "C'mon. Let's get the dishes done. I really need to get some sleep."

"I'll do them. It's been a long day for you. Go on to bed. I'll be in later."

Shannon nodded. She carried her plate to the sink and kissed Jake as if they'd known each other for years, but sexual intimacy such as they'd experienced tended to do that to people. Grinning, she headed for the big bedroom with the king-size bed. As tired as she was, Shannon was thankful she'd taken the time earlier to make it up with

fresh linens. Even though the cabin had two other bed-
rooms, there'd been no discussion of sleeping arrange-
ments. They didn't need to talk about the obvious.

Jake took his time cleaning up the kitchen, grabbed a
big pillow off the couch and walked quietly on bare feet
back to the bedroom to check on Shannon. She slept
soundly, her hair glistening like burnished copper across
the pillow in the low, flickering light from the one candle
burning in the room.

He leaned over her and felt an almost painful pressure
in his heart, as if that damned organ wasn't quite sure how
to deal with the rush of feelings that swamped him when
he looked at Shannon Murphy. More than just beautiful,
she had the spirit he needed in a mate, the intelligence and
humor and sense of self Jake had never experienced with
another woman.

Not even Tia Mason.

He stood up straighter, aware that the guilt he'd carried
over wanting Tia was gone. Replaced by need, by an emotion he feared to name.

Replaced by love. Jake closed his eyes against the sharp
sting of tears. Damn. That was so *not* what he needed
now, not until he knew for sure.

Quietly tucking the bolster pillow in beside Shannon,
Jake bunched the down comforter over the lumpy form.
With a last look at Shannon sleeping peacefully in his bed,
Jake turned away, and went outside.

Brilliant stars blanketed the autumn sky, a pale sliver of
moon hung in the south and there was a hint of frost in the
air. Jake stood on the porch for a moment, listening to the
sounds of the night, breathing in the utter stillness and
fresh scents of the forest. Then he stripped off his clothes,
folded them neatly and set them in a corner of the porch.
For a brief moment, he glanced back at the house, shivering in the chill air.

No sign of Shannon. Thankfully, she still slept.

Jake shifted quickly, leaning over as he made the change. His hands hit the porch as wolven paws, ebony nails digging into the wood. With a last glance toward the house, the wolf leapt off the porch and raced toward the dark forest. He paused, very briefly, to take a quick glance at the silver motorcycle parked in front. Then, tail held high, the beast blended into the shadows.

Shannon awakened to total darkness, at first disoriented, then merely groggy from sleeping so soundly. She knew she'd been dreaming, but of what, she wasn't certain. Someone or something had called to her, awakened her. The candle had burned itself out and the only light came from the silvery moon hanging low on the horizon, shining through the parted window curtains.

Quietly, so as not to disturb Jake, she grabbed her sweatshirt off the end of the bed and pulled it on, then walked out into the main part of the house. Padding quietly on bare feet across the icy cold, wooden floors, she shivered in the darkness.

Moonlight glinted through the front window, calling to her. Still half asleep, Shannon grabbed an afghan off the couch and wrapped it around herself, then opened the front door. The night air felt icy against her bare legs. Moonlight glowed on the small clearing in front of the house and the forest hovered, dark and mysterious, on the far side.

The ethereal beauty stopped Shannon in her tracks. She listened for a moment, wondering once more what had awakened her, then walked slowly and soundlessly across the porch and leaned against the wooden railing. She almost went back for Jake, so strong was the need to share this moment, but she knew he was exhausted. Tonight, she'd let him sleep.

As cold as it was, she didn't expect to be out there much longer, but it was just so damned beautiful.

A flash of something caught her eye, a slight movement on the far side of the clearing. Straightening up, Shannon squinted, as if that would help her see in the almost total darkness. Again. Something big. What the hell was that? She leaned over the railing, staring until she thought her eyes might cross.

Suddenly, an animal moved out of the shadows, gliding into a sliver of silver moonlight. A big dog? No, the ears were wrong, the body too large, too powerful.

Her mouth went dry. It was a wolf. Wild and free, right here in the front yard of Jake's home. Damn. She wanted to get Jake, to share this with him, but Shannon knew the minute she made a move the creature would disappear as silently, as mysteriously, as he'd arrived.

She watched as the wolf walked slowly toward her, hardly breathing for fear of frightening it away. Finally it stopped, a mere six or seven feet from where she stood. The night was dark, but there appeared to be just enough silver in the animal's coat to catch the reflection of moonlight. It stared right at her, the amber eyes strangely familiar, unbelievably intelligent. Shannon thought of the dream she'd had, of running through the forest and the sound of a wolf's howl. Her skin suddenly erupted in goose bumps.

The wolf was obviously aware of her, had to have seen her, yet it didn't run. It watched her as closely as she watched it. Shannon felt no fear, only a marvelous sense of wonder along with a vague regret that Jake still slept. He should be here, sharing this amazing moment.

What was the animal thinking? It cocked its broad head to one side, its long tongue lolled out of its mouth and Shannon had the distinct impression the animal was laughing at her. She wondered if it might be tame, if it had been raised as someone's pet, but the beast, for all its composure, looked fiercely wild.

She noticed blood on its chest and around its muzzle, as if it had recently fed. No pet would hunt alone at night. No, this was a wild animal. Free, a true denizen of the forest.

Suddenly, the wolf turned around and glided back into the forest. The meadow stood empty in the moonlight, as if the creature had never been. Shannon stared for a long, long time at the spot where the animal had stood.

Wondering. Thinking about the events that had brought her here, about the man sleeping in the room on the other side of the wall.

As if he'd heard her thoughts, Jake wandered out of the cabin. He was naked, his hair mussed, and he rubbed the sleep from his eyes. "What are you doing out here? It's freezing."

He wrapped his arms around Shannon and she realized his skin was cold. He must have come uncovered because the heavy down comforter was more than adequate.

"I saw the most marvelous thing, Jake." She pulled the afghan off her shoulders and wrapped Jake inside its heavy folds with her, felt the press of his muscular body against her back. "There was a wolf, a beautiful silvery wolf right here in the front yard."

He yawned, nuzzled the top of Shannon's head with his chin. "Yeah. I've heard there are wolves in the area. Surprised one would come so close to the house, though."

Shannon shrugged her shoulders. "It's been empty for a long time. The wolf probably wondered who was hanging out in his forest. It was beautiful. I wish you could have seen it." She turned inside the warm afghan and kissed Jake on the chin, familiarly, as if they'd been together for years, not hours. "Come to bed. It's the middle of the night."

Jake kissed her. "Go ahead. I'm gonna take a leak. I'll be inside in a minute."

Shannon laughed. "Men are so disgusting. Don't pee near the house."

His teeth glistened white in the moonlight when he smiled. "I would think you'd be more concerned about the wolf eating me than whether or not I peed near the house."

Shannon shook her head. "He didn't seem at all dangerous. More like he was curious."

Jake's arms wrapped tightly around her body. He turned her so that she faced away from him, and nuzzled his chin in her hair. "Oh, I wouldn't underestimate the wolf. He's dangerous all right. Very, very dangerous."

Shannon twisted in Jake's arms so she could see his face. "Do you think so? He didn't seem at all threatening and he was right there, really close."

"Definitely dangerous. Now get inside. It's cold out here."

Jake put her away from him with a quick kiss. She grabbed the afghan off his perfect body and headed into the house, almost preternaturally aware of Jake's heated stare as she walked away.

Jake waited a few minutes, listening. He heard the toilet flush, the sound of running water, then silence. Once all was quiet, he grabbed his neatly folded clothes from the corner of the porch where he'd left them and quietly carried the bundle back into the house.

Jake left the clothing on the end of the couch, next to the recently replaced pillow, then went into the bedroom where Shannon waited. *Damn.* Tonight had been way too close. Cocky after chasing down and killing that rabbit, he'd had a full belly and an empty mind.

He hadn't even seen Shannon standing there in full sight on the porch. Had almost bounded up the steps and shifted right in front of her. Luckily he'd managed to get around the house, in through the back window, remove the pillow, and meet her outside before she could catch him.

He needed to run. Had needed tonight. Shifting was like breathing, but he couldn't risk getting caught. Gut clenching at the near miss he'd had this night, Jake quietly crawled into bed beside Shannon. She rolled over and snuggled close against him, warming his body, heating his blood.

He tucked her head under his chin, wrapped his arms around her soft body. How long before he'd know? According to Tinker, Tia had begun to show signs of her bloodline within days of starting the supplement. What about Shannon? Would she change as quickly?

Would she change at all?

She had to. Jake took a deep breath and felt her sigh in reply. He loved her. Crazy as it sounded, after just one day with this woman, he knew he couldn't live without her.

She was the lock to his key, the air his body needed to breathe. The missing piece to the puzzle that had always been his life.

Shannon's body settled into sleep, her lips pressed against Jake's throat. He tried to imagine life without her. Impossible. It was already growing difficult to remember life before her.

Sharp nails scrabbled across the rocky promontory. Nose to the ground, she followed the trail, searching for her mate. He must be close. She sensed him, a presence in her heart as well as her mind, and knew he couldn't be far from here. She glanced out across the dark abyss, awash in moonlight, and felt the stirrings of wild things in the tangled forest below, felt the soft autumn breeze ruffling the thick fur at her neck, felt the silence. Quiet so absolute it was a tangible thing.

Turning her nose to the sky, she howled. A long, low cry of mourning and regret, a cry that carried with it the heart of the she-wolf, the sense that nothing would ever be the same. Then she turned and trotted away from the rocky ledge, blending in among the trees, her nose leading her toward the one who loved her most.

Shannon awoke to the scent of bacon frying and steaming coffee, the remnants of her dream a shadowy part of her conscious mind. By the time she'd thrown on her sweats and made it out to the kitchen, the details had faded into the morning and Jake was stirring scrambled eggs in a pan on the stove. He held out a cup of coffee as she entered the room.

"Goodness. I had no idea you were so domestic." She inhaled the fresh scent of coffee and took a sip. *Perfect. Was there anything at all wrong with this man?*

Leaning against the tile counter, she watched him through the steam rising from her cup.

"Comes from living with a bunch of guys. Someone's got to learn to cook or we'd all starve to death."

"Who do you live with?"

Jake glanced her way, then looked down as he scraped the eggs away from the edges of the iron skillet. "The rest of the pack. That's what we call ourselves—the pack. Ulrich Mason, Tia's dad is the boss, but he lives on his own over in the Marina District. We're based in San Francisco. Mason's backed off a bit in the past few years and turned more of the operation over to Lucien Stone. Luc, AJ, Mik, Tinker and I all live in a converted row house in the Sunset. It's like apartments with a central kitchen . . . more of a rooming house, I guess."

Jake set the skillet back on the burner and pulled a tray out of the oven. He glanced over his shoulder at Shannon. "Have a seat. Looks like everything is ready."

He placed the tray, piled high with fried potatoes, strips of crisp bacon and biscuits, in the center of the table next to a large pitcher of orange juice. Then he scooped eggs on to two plates, set one in front of Shannon and the other across the table from her, grabbed his coffee off the counter and sat down.

"Okay. I'm definitely impressed. I have to admit this is better than a cup of coffee and a bagel." She grabbed her napkin and looked up, in time to catch Jake watching her. That's when she noticed the large brown capsule by her place setting and another one in front of Jake's.

"Ah, Ulrich's special blend, right?"

Jake nodded, then downed his with a swallow of orange juice. Shannon took hers as well. If nothing else, the number of times Jake had made love to her in one day was nothing short of unbelievable . . . if one little pill a day gave him that kind of stamina, it had to be good.

Jake called the Pack Dynamics office on his cell phone while Shannon did the dishes. She watched through the kitchen window while he made the call out on the front porch where the signal was clearest. Tall and broad shouldered, Jake commanded whatever space he took. She wished she could hear what he was talking about. It concerned her, obviously, or Shannon wouldn't be up here in the wilds of Maine with a man she'd never met before.

She put the last dish in the drying rack and wiped out the sink. When she glanced up, Jake appeared agitated, as if he were upset about something. Hanging the towel over the edge of the sink, Shannon wandered outside.

Jake ended the call as she stepped onto the porch. "Trouble?"

He shook his head. "No. I hope not." He flashed her a quick smile. "Ulrich's in Washington DC, taking care of business, according to Luc. The rest of the pack's back in San Francisco. Luc said he's thinking of sending AJ and Mik out here later in the week."

"They're two of the guys you mentioned, right?"

Shannon hitched one hip up on the porch railing. "Do you think we're in that much danger?"

Jake shrugged. "I wish I knew. We really don't know much of anything, to be honest. Only that someone kidnapped Mason and a couple of someones almost got you. Until we know for sure what's going on, we need to take every precaution. That means keeping you hidden."

Sighing softly in response, Shannon swept her gaze across the dark forest and deep green meadow, aware of the sense of isolation she felt, the distance from any other human being. So unlike Boston, especially the North End where she'd lived for so long, where everyone knew everybody's business.

She wondered, did any of her neighbors miss her? Had anyone noticed she was gone? She would be on her way to work right now, walking through the Haymarket on her way to catch her ride on the Green Line, Boston's subway.

She really needed to call the office and let someone know she wouldn't be in until . . . when? Shannon looked back at Jake. All thoughts of the mundane, of work or her life before now, fled. Jake watched her with an intensity that was unnerving, to say the least. She wished she could read his mind as easily now as she seemed able to during climax.

Now *that* was unnerving. She still wasn't certain what happened, but the mental link they'd shared, numerous times, now, was amazing. Frightening.

Sexy as hell.

Shannon let the sensations wash over her, the unbelievable awareness of sex from Jake's point of view. Her tight muscles squeezing his cock, the heat and slick fluids easing his passage, the pressure against the hard knot of her cervix when his penis connected tightly with the mouth of her womb.

God, she was getting turned on just thinking about it!

She'd always wondered if she was oversexed, but this was verging on obsession. Pressing her thighs tightly together, Shannon clenched her vaginal muscles, holding back the rush of hot moisture already soaking her panties, flowing between her legs.

Suddenly Jake was beside her, his nostrils flared, eyes narrowed. Shannon had the strangest sensation he actually smelled her arousal, scented the slick flow of moisture. For some reason she thought of the wolf she'd seen the night before, but the image melted beneath the mounting pressure of Jake's mouth on hers, the swift intrusion of his tongue between her lips, the warmth of his breath on her face.

His callused fingers lifted the hem of her sweatshirt and traced the soft underside of her left breast. For all the strength in his hands, he was amazingly gentle, but when he flicked her taut nipple with his thumb, Shannon felt it all the way to her pussy. She moaned into his mouth, thrusting her hips forward, at the same time wondering how she could possibly be so damned horny, her body ready for sex so quickly.

Jake slipped his hand inside the stretchy waistband on Shannon's sweatpants and past the line of her panties. She was wet and ready, her vaginal lips swollen and bathed in fluids. Jake's fingers slipped easily between the sensitive folds. With a groan, he abandoned her breast and dropped to his knees in front of her, yanking her pants down with him.

She raised up on her toes when Jake slipped both her sweats and her panties over her feet. Then he grabbed her buttocks in his hands and held her to his mouth, lifting her toes completely off the ground. His tongue swept between her labia, found the soft sheath surrounding her clit and proceeded to lick and suckle until she thought she might explode.

Hanging on the edge of orgasm, Shannon was suddenly wrenched back to reality when Jake stood up, grabbed her by the waist and deposited her bare butt on the broad porch railing with her back up against the corner post. The wood beneath her rear was ice cold, covered in morning dew and the remnants of a light frost. Shannon shrieked, giggling and clutching at his broad shoulders.

Panting, laughing, his face shining with her fluids, Jake fumbled with his zipper and freed his cock. Shannon reached for him, but he wrapped his fist around the thick length and aimed his cock between her legs, filling Shannon in one powerful thrust.

She shrieked again, caught by surprise when she climaxed on his first long stroke. Jake's hands wrapped around her thighs and he drove into her, filling Shannon on each driving thrust, the wild thatch of dark hair surrounding his cock melding with the neatly trimmed, bright copper between Shannon's legs.

He leaned close and took her mouth with his, kissing her with lips and teeth and tongue, devouring her. She'd never been taken like this, never dominated by any man so completely as she was by Jacob Trent.

His tongue thrust deep, in sync with each stroke of his cock, and she screamed into his mouth, her body convulsing with yet another powerful orgasm.

She felt him then, in her mind, in her heart, his thoughts a jumble of sex and rage and confusion, all caught up in the amazing sensation of his cock riding off her cervix, sliding out to the very edge of her pussy, and thrusting deep once more. She felt the straining muscles in his thighs, the tightness in his groin as he hung on to his own control by mere threads.

Shannon opened her thoughts, gave free rein to her fantasies, acknowledged the powerful sweep of emotion tied into the amazing physical sense of Jake deep inside her body, Jake taking her to heights she'd never imagined.

Jake coming, the tension darkening his face, drawing the tendons and veins out in his arms, the hard muscles of his chest, the taut lines of his throat.

He was wild, untamed, a beast raging beneath a thin veneer of civilized male. Shannon sensed his feral nature, sensed the savage cruelty inherent to the wild side of man. Sensed it, welcomed it, opened her heart and soul and allowed him inside.

She felt the hot spill of his seed against the mouth of her womb. Unprotected. His flesh against hers. Without barriers, without thought of anything other than need, unbearable need no longer denied.

His hips thrust once more, then again. He groaned, a sound filled as much with despair as fulfillment. Finally Jake collapsed forward, his chin resting on her shoulder, his chest rising and falling with each ragged breath he took. She felt him shudder, felt his cock deep inside still spasming, his semen filling her vagina, her muscles gripping him like a fist, squeezing every last drop from his body.

"Oh, shit. I'm sorry, Shannon. I'm so sorry." His words poured out between gasps of stolen breath. "I've never done that, never forgotten protection. I'm sorry . . . I . . ."

She bit her lips to keep the tears at bay. Ran her fingers through the damp tangle of hair curling over his collar. "It's okay. Unless you've got some ungodly disease I need to worry about . . . I won't get pregnant. I can't." She bit back the tears threatening to choke her. For so long she'd considered it a blessing not to worry about babies. Not anymore.

For the first time in her life, Shannon wanted a child. Wanted this man's baby growing beneath her heart. Of course, whatever she wanted didn't matter. Nothing really mattered. It was merely one more count against her, one more negative in a long line of bad karma that defined Shannon Murphy.

* * *

Jake felt the pain behind Shannon's words even as he tried to accept what she was telling him. Now he could admit what he'd been dreaming, the image he'd held in some secret part of his mind since first meeting Shannon—beautiful Shannon—his Chanku mate heavy with his child.

He'd never lost control like this. Never found himself giving in to the beast, taking a woman without protection, without any conscious thought other than the fact he had to fuck now or . . . what? He didn't have a clue.

Except with Tia. Dear God . . . what was happening to him? He'd always been so much in control, so sure of his nature. Not now. Now with Shannon.

He did know he'd almost shifted. Had come so close to changing that he'd felt his muscles strain against the need, had felt the wolf rising strong and dominant inside him.

Shannon's fingers continued stroking his hair, comforting him when he should be apologizing to her. What the hell had gotten in to him?

They'd been standing together on the porch, she'd had a faraway, dreamy look in her eyes, and suddenly he was on her, overwhelmed with need, more aroused than he'd ever been.

It made no sense. No sense at all. He should have been totally sated after last night and the night before. He hadn't had this much sex, this often, for years.

Of course, Jake knew he'd never experienced sex with anyone like he had with Shannon. What happened between them was amazing. Unbelievable.

Absolutely perfect.

He lifted his face from Shannon's shoulder and kissed her lightly on the mouth. There were tears in her eyes. Jake knew he'd put them there, either with his thoughtless words or actions—or both. But how the hell did he apologize when he wasn't sure which thing he'd said or done had hurt her?

The down and dirty sex, or the fact he'd forced her to admit she couldn't have children? Hell, he'd never been good with women, never could figure out how their minds worked.

He sure as hell didn't know why he'd lost control, but he needed to find out. Had to make sure it wouldn't happen again . . . though, if she couldn't conceive, was there really any risk?

Damned right there's risk. Every time he made love to Shannon, he fell a little bit deeper, tied himself to her a little bit tighter. If she wasn't Chanku . . . no, he couldn't think of that.

Jake pulled away from her warm body, felt his shrinking penis slip out of her slick folds as he bent down to retrieve her sweatpants. She took them from him without words.

Feeling less than human, Jake pulled his jeans on, turned away and went into the house to wash up. It wasn't until he got into the brightly lit bathroom that he realized his cock was covered in streaks of blood.

Suddenly it all came clear. Shannon was bleeding, essentially in heat like any wolven bitch. Had her scent brought out the beast in him?

Her Chanku scent?

Jake grabbed the edge of the sink with both hands. Held on so tight his knuckles turned white.

You goddamned sonofabitch.

Could he actually be that lucky? Could Shannon's body be changing so quickly? *Damn*. He stared at himself in the mirror, not knowing whether to give thanks or weep. *Helpless*. He felt so pathetically stupid and helpless. There were so few Chanku, they knew so little about their own kind—and almost nothing about the females.

He grabbed a washcloth, rinsed it out and cleaned himself. Pulled his jeans back up over his hips, but left them unzipped. Slowly, methodically, Jake rinsed out the cloth and threw it in the hamper.

He looked down at his hands. They shook like he had some sort of palsy. He balled up his fists. His arms trembled with the urge to punch something. Anything.

Something important had just happened out there on the porch, something primitive and elemental, and totally unexpected.

The beast had taken over the man, if only for a brief moment in time. Without permission, without warning, he'd almost lost control, almost taken a woman in Chanku form who was under his protection.

Talk about walking on the edge. Wanting Shannon, needing her, feeling her pulling him closer, yet not having that definitive sign she was Chanku was driving him nuts.

Until she actually changed . . . not until then could he be sure. Jake had five more days before Mik and AJ showed up. No matter how much he'd argued for more time, Luc had insisted. Was Luc trying to force the issue? Was this how he intended to pay Jake back for his attack on Tia? Let him get this close to his own Chanku bitch, then turn her over to Mik and AJ?

Damn . . . he hadn't even thought of that. Could Luc be that cruel? No matter. Jake had five more days of supplementing Shannon without interference, no matter what Luc intended.

Getting paranoid, are we?

No shit, Sherlock. He wasn't sure his heart could take it. Shannon was still human, but she was coming in to heat, or at least her pheromones were. Mason had warned them, there was no controlling a Chanku male around a bitch in heat. It was hard enough when the women weren't bleeding, but for all Jake knew, he'd react like that to any woman on her period.

It wasn't like you could tell until you fucked . . .

Mik and AJ, for all their love for each other, would be sniffing around an unmated Chanku bitch, unless the pills worked really fast and Shannon changed before they got here.

Even then, he still had to convince her she wanted him for her mate . . . for the rest of her life.

Shit. Jake whirled around and leaned back against the counter, scrubbing his face with his hands. How the hell was he going to work this? He couldn't warn Shannon what was coming, couldn't tell her about Chanku until he was sure she was definitely one of them.

Once she changed, he had to convince her, had to make her want him enough to be willing to commit. Enough to mate with Jake in wolven form, to bond completely and essentially tie herself to him, both figuratively and in reality.

It wasn't like there were all that many unmated Chanku females around. So far Tia was the only one Jake had ever met, but Tia loved Luc, so if he wanted a mate, it had to be Shannon.

Was that so bad? Hell, no.

Sex between Chanku in wolven form—the ultimate prenuptial agreement. Once tied, the relationship was forever. Unbreakable. If anything went wrong, if either AJ or Mik took her first, Jake could lose the only woman he'd ever loved.

Love? He couldn't even be certain about that. He wanted her. Desired her. Couldn't imagine life without Shannon. Okay, for the sake of argument, he'd call it love.

Five more days. Mik and AJ would be here Saturday. He had five more days not only to change Shannon's entire sense of who she was, but to convince her to link her life forever with a man she hardly knew. One who was currently holding back important, life-altering information from her to suit his own needs.

Yeah, like that would really endear her to him. Jake shook his head in dismay. "Only you, Trent. Something like this could only happen to you." Zipping up his pants, Jake went back outside to Shannon.

Chapter 6

Feeling absolutely numb, Shannon washed herself in the bathroom, cleaning away Jake's semen and her fluids even as her body still trembled. She'd never admitted to anyone the fact she was sterile. Never even told Tia, but she'd just blurted it out to the only man she'd ever considered as a mate. If that didn't turn him off, nothing would. Men like Jake wanted sons. Strong, powerful sons to carry on their name.

He'd not get them from Shannon. She wondered what he was thinking, how he felt about her now? Jake had gone into the smaller bath off the master bedroom. He'd been there for a long time, but Shannon was in no rush to see him right away. Not only was she obsessing over his reaction when she'd said she couldn't get pregnant, she was still trying to figure out what happened out there on the porch.

She'd never experienced sex like that. Never. Good lord, talk about your wild, untamed-animal sex! There'd been a feral glint in Jake's eyes, a sense of otherworldliness about him that might have been frightening if she hadn't been so turned on. She'd felt Jake in her head, felt as much anger as lust when he'd taken her.

Just thinking about the deep, hard penetration, the

need she'd felt in him, made her hot. Made her feel again. Took away the numbness, the pain. Picturing Jake driving deep inside her, Shannon finished cleaning herself off, then glanced down to make sure she'd gotten everything.

Pale streaks of blood covered the white washcloth. Shannon stared at it a moment, confused. She hadn't bled for years, not since the severe infection that damaged her reproductive organs . . . the same infection that rendered her infertile and stamped the importance of condoms into her then-teenaged brain.

Why now? The sex had been hot and rough . . . maybe a small tear? No. She'd feel something like that. Shannon rinsed the cloth and wiped herself again. No blood. Just those first small streaks.

To be on the safe side, she folded up a tissue and stuck it in her panties, then pulled on her sweats. A chill raced across her flesh. Shannon rubbed her hands over her arms, surprised by the sensitivity of her skin. Something about her felt different, but whatever it was remained so subtle she couldn't figure out what had caught her attention.

Shaking her head, she headed back out to the front porch. This whole situation was beyond weird. She really wanted to talk to Tia, needed to find out what the hell was going on, how long she'd be stuck here with a man she hardly knew.

Yeah. Right. A broad grin blossomed across her face. A couple more days like today and she'd know everything there was to know about Jacob Trent. It wasn't easy to hide secrets from a woman who read your mind.

And to think she'd never believed in all that "psycho-babble" stuff! There was no denying what she'd experienced with her own mind.

Shannon was sitting on the front step when Jake finally came out on the porch. She glanced up, smiled at him, then went back to staring at the forest. "Hi. I wondered where you were."

"Cleaning up. Shannon, I . . ."

"Don't apologize. Please?" She lifted her head and glanced at him, then went back to staring at the woods. "I don't know for sure what's going on between us, Jake, but please don't apologize for something we both enjoyed."

"I was afraid I hurt you." Jake sat down beside her, not touching, but close enough to feel her heat. "I don't usually lose control like that, but there's something about you that really gets to me."

She laughed. "You certainly don't need to apologize for that. I can't think of a single woman who wouldn't consider the fact she can make a man lose control something to apologize for. That's a compliment."

Shannon leaned against his knee, her supple body warm and inviting. *Damn.* She was so beautiful. Jake sniffed, wondering if he might actually be able to identify what had aroused him so thoroughly. She smelled fresh and clean, of warm woman and some kind of sweet shampoo. No, there was nothing out of the ordinary his nose could pick up, but his cock was already straining against the tight confines of his jeans.

Shannon shifted, putting more pressure, more of her warmth against his leg. Jake felt the need rising in him, stronger now, felt the fine edge of his control slipping. She must be right at the pinnacle of her heat. He had to get out of here. Had to run but it was daylight and too dangerous for the wolf. Besides, he'd never get away from Shannon without raising her suspicions.

"How long are we going to stay here?"

Her question caught Jake by surprise. "I really don't know. This all happened so fast, we didn't have a plan, or at least there's not one I know about. Mik and AJ should be here Saturday. I think they're planning on staying for at least a couple more days, but it depends on Ulrich's success in Washington and whether or not they can call off the guys hunting for you."

"Why do they want me?" She looked up at him. Jake realized he was staring at her mouth, wanting to taste her again.

He caught himself. "Probably because of your link to Tia and Ulrich Mason. I don't know all the details yet, why they kidnapped Mason in the first place."

But he did know. AJ and told him enough about the breeding farm, the sick plans Secretary Bosworth had for Chanku females.

Shannon took a deep breath and let it out. Jake watched her breasts rise and fall, fascinated by their gentle, unbound swell beneath the sweatshirt. "Is there a store nearby? If we're going to be here that long, we'll need supplies. Plus, I think I might have started my period and I don't have anything with me . . . obviously." She grinned at him. "Talk about traveling light."

"There's a little town just a few miles up the road. Get your leathers on and we'll take a ride."

Take a ride. Is that all this was? The bike practically hummed, slipping along the narrow lane between the tall trees. Jake felt the deep throb of the engine, smooth as silk and just as sensual, the warm grasp of Shannon's hands around his waist, the heat of her upper body pressed against his back.

He'd been in a constant state of arousal since this morning . . . hell, since he'd first laid eyes on her, unconscious in the back end of the damned car. It was more, now. Deeper, More intense. Something had changed over the past few hours. His body's response had reached a whole new level of awareness, and while he wanted to believe it was the proximity of a Chanku bitch in heat, it might just be the vision of Shannon in tight leather pants and jacket. The combination of leather and her perfect body just about tipped his fantasy world on its ear.

They crossed a bridge over a small river filled with cattails and small willows, then entered the old town on a main street shaded beneath brilliant red maple trees. Shannon hung on as Jake coasted slowly past storefronts and empty lots, leaving a trail of swirling fall colors behind them.

Shannon washed her hands and wiped down the counter. The groceries were all put away and they'd eaten a light dinner. She felt oddly restless, yet unusually exhausted from their trip to town. Still, it was too early for bed and, without any television, there wasn't much to do other than read. Taking her glass of wine into the main room, she grabbed the mystery she'd bought in the little general store in town and found a comfortable spot near a gas-burning lamp.

Jake walked into the room, dressed in shorts and expensive looking running shoes. His chest was bare, the muscles rippling beneath the dark hair that arrowed down from his pecs to run beneath the elastic band of his shorts.

Shannon caught herself staring at the dark trail, wishing she could follow it with her mouth. When she glanced up, Jake was grinning at her.

"Should I try and guess what's on your mind?"

She shook her head, laughing. "Nah. I'm much too easy to read."

Jake laughed with her. "You look beat, but I really need some exercise. I'm going out for a run. I'll probably be gone a couple of hours. Will you be all right alone?"

Shannon nodded. "I'll be fine." She gestured at her wineglass and the book. "I've got my survival gear handy. Be careful. It's almost completely dark out. Remember, there's a wolf out there."

Jake leaned over and kissed her gently on the mouth. "I'll be careful and I know the trail well enough. Don't let anyone inside. If you hear anything unusual, lock the door and throw the bar. It'll keep you safe. The cell phone's on the kitchen table."

He slipped out the door, loped across the clearing and disappeared into the dark woods. Shannon watched the space where he'd been, then glanced toward the kitchen table. Just like Jake said, the cell phone sat there, fully charged.

Shannon set her book down, got up and walked into the kitchen. She'd been going along with everything Jake wanted since he rescued her. It wasn't in her nature to accept someone else's control so easily. Rubbing at the weird tingling in her arms, Shannon punched in a familiar number. It was time to look for answers from another source.

She stepped out on the front deck, phone in hand, and found a clear signal. Tia answered Shannon's call to her cell phone on the first ring.

"Ohmygawd! Shannon! I've been worried sick about you. Are you okay? Jake said they'd kidnapped you and gave you some kind of drug. How are you?" Tia took a quick breath, then blurted out, "What do you think of Jake?"

Damn, it felt so good to hear Tia's voice! "Jake is amazing. If your guy Luc is anything like Jake, you're probably having trouble walking."

Tia laughed. "Just about. You wouldn't believe what's been going on since I got back to San Francisco. There's a lot I can't talk about yet, but Shannon, it's so amazing being here with Luc, with my dad, with the other guys. I just heard that AJ and Mik are coming out to stay with you and Jake at the end of the week. Wait until you meet *them*!"

"Don't tell me. They're just as sexy as Jake, right?" Shannon tried to imagine adding two more guys with

Jake's sex appeal. Shivers ran down her arms at the mere thought of all that testosterone in one room.

"Oh yeah. These guys are so hot. I can't wait 'til you meet these two."

"What's the deal, anyway? Why are they coming?" Jake hadn't offered any explanation. In fact, he'd seemed a bit disgruntled over the fact Luc was sending the two men to Maine to join them.

"That's what I really can't discuss yet. Pack Dynamics is a lot more than just a detective agency. They're into some pretty sensitive stuff and we can't risk our conversation being tapped. The point is, Luc feels you might need some extra protection in a few days and he wants to make sure you and Jake are safe. A lot depends on my father's current mission. Just trust me. And Jake. You can trust Jake." She paused, but before Shannon could ask another question, Tia grilled her again. "Well? What do you think of Jake? Is he not the most interesting man you've been with in a long time?"

"Like forever?" Shannon snorted. "You knew exactly what would happen if we met, didn't you?"

This time Tia sounded wistful. "I guess I hoped. Shannon, I'm not sure what Jake's told you, but I've met the most amazing man. I actually knew him years ago when I was a kid, but I never dreamed that we . . . well, I never thought I'd love anyone the way I loved you, but what I feel for Luc is so powerful it's frightening. I want you to find what I've got. I'm hoping you'll find it with Jake."

Shannon was the one to laugh this time. Would she find the same love with Jacob Trent that Tia had with her man? Only time would tell. "I hardly know him. The sex is amazing, and we have this really strange connection. I can't explain it, but there are a lot of barriers between us as well. Maybe in time . . . we'll see . . ."

"I have to go, sweetie. Luc's calling me. He wants to go for a run."

"A run? You?" This time Shannon's laughter felt perfectly natural. "Sheesh. Jake's out running right now, too. In the dark, if you can believe it! I'm going back to my glass of wine and a book. I sure hope this amazing desire to exercise isn't catching."

Tia laughed. "You might be surprised. Take care. Be safe."

"You too."

Shannon stared at the cell phone after she hung up. Tia sounded so happy, more content than Shannon could recall. Rubbing at the increasing irritation along her arms, Shannon turned off the light, grabbed the afghan and her glass of wine and went out on the front porch.

The sky had reached that deep purple-to-black shade signaling the advent of nightfall. Jake hadn't taken a flashlight. Shannon hoped he knew his way well enough to make it home in the dark.

The more she thought about Jake out there in the woods, the more she worried. Finally, Shannon went back into the house, grabbed a kerosene lantern, lit the wick and brought the lantern outside. Like a lighthouse on the shore, it might help to guide Jake home through the dark.

Shannon sipped her wine and watched the stars come out, one by one. She might have dozed, but suddenly she was wide awake and alert, aware of a sense that someone else was near.

"Jake? Is that you?"

She heard a low whine, out in the meadow. Shannon stood up and stared into the darkness. It was brighter than she expected, but still hard to see anything at all, even with the low glow of the lantern behind her. Shannon grabbed the lantern, turned up the flame and held it aloft until a golden light spilled out from the porch.

There, just beyond the bottom step, sitting calmly as if he owned the place, was her wolf.

Shannon walked to the top step and adjusted the wick

on the lantern so she wouldn't hit him in the eyes with the glare. His tongue lolled to one side, there was a mischievous glint in his amber eyes and what almost felt like a flirtatious tilt to his broad wolven head.

Though Jake had warned her against getting too close to a wild animal, Shannon stepped down to the bottom step, so that she was only about six feet away from the wolf. She set the lantern on the step beside her.

The wolf stood up. Its bushy tail wagged slowly back and forth, the ears pointed forward as well. There was no sense of fear, no threat in the animal at all. Mesmerized, Shannon sat on the bottom step. She wished she had something to tempt the animal, then realized the wolf had taken a step closer to her.

As she watched, he took another, then another. Shannon held her breath as the silver-tipped wolf closed the narrow gap between them.

She wanted to hold out her hand. Thought better of it. Couldn't help herself. She reached out and let the animal sniff the back of her hand, as if she were approaching a large yet unfamiliar dog. The wolf's tongue swept across her skin, raising chills along her arms.

There it was again, that strange sensation of skin crawling, bones aching, that she'd noticed most of the day. The wolf licked her hand again and Shannon forgot all about her aches and pains. Slowly she turned her hand and cupped the animal's face in her palm. He leaned into it, his amber eyes focused intently on Shannon's face.

Almost as if he wanted to talk to her. She thought of the strange link she shared with Jake, the emotional and mental communion of spirit during sexual climax. Almost without thinking of how it happened, Shannon opened her mind to the wolf. Gave him permission to come into her thoughts.

Suddenly he was there, a gentle yet very masculine presence in her mind. Vaguely familiar, yet alien all the same.

Shocked, Shannon somehow slammed tight the barriers that protected her, closed her mind off to communion with the wolf.

She wasn't ready. Not for something *this* weird!

The dreams she'd been having flooded her mind, intense, vivid dreams of racing through the forest, of lifting her nose to the sky and crying out in a long howling song, only it was a wolf's nose between her eyes, wolven paws at the end of furred legs.

Blinking, suddenly chilled, Shannon scooted back on the step, putting distance between herself and the animal. She shivered, rubbed her arms, then her legs. This was definitely weird.

The wolf stared at her for a long, almost solemn moment. Then he dipped his head, raised it and looked at her again, his pink tongue once more hanging out between sharp canines. Shannon didn't know whether to laugh or cry. She wasn't about to open her mind to him. For some reason, it scared the crap out of her, the thought of letting this animal have the same access to her thoughts she'd allowed Jake.

Only during sex, at the point of climax.

Yet she'd felt the wolf in her mind now, sitting here on the front porch.

The wolf sniffed the air, turned his head and sniffed Shannon. He lowered his nose from her breasts to her belly, then stuck his snout close to her crotch. She held perfectly still while he drew in a deep breath, then raised his head and stared at her, almost expectantly.

The moment felt surreal, as if she were dreaming while awake. Her body tingled with sudden, unexplainable arousal. Shannon rubbed her arms, more aware than ever of the strange irritation. She wished Jake were here, not only to ease the ache of need, but to share what could only be called magic.

The wolf was magic. Everything about him. Magical and mysterious.

The wolf leaned forward, ran his tongue along Shannon's wrist, took another long look at her face, then abruptly turned and raced back into the forest.

Shannon released the breath she hadn't realized she'd been holding. The night seemed terribly empty now that the beautiful animal was gone. Had she really felt him in her mind?

Impossible. But what of the dreams? The vivid dreams of racing through the trees, of being a wolf?

Chanku? What made her think of those stories Tia used to tell? Bedtime stories Tia had learned from her mother before Camille was killed.

Stories about wolves who changed into humans.

Hadn't she picked the same word out of Jake's mind? She tried to remember, but the memory wasn't clear enough.

Shannon sat there for a long time, staring into the woods, wondering about the wolf, recalling Tia's stories. Was it real, or just a very graphic vision, another of Shannon's dreams? She ran her fingers along her wrist. Her skin was damp from the wolf's saliva. Rubbing her fingers together, Shannon stared once more in the direction the animal had disappeared. Had it really tried to communicate with her? Maybe she should have let it.

More importantly, though . . . where in the hell was Jake, and when was he coming back?

The thick humus covering the forest floor scattered beneath the wolf's paws as it raced along the narrow path. Eyes narrowed, tail stretched out behind, ears laid back against his broad skull, he ran as if the fiends of hell chased him.

Maybe they did. They were certainly spinning their disturbing spells in his brain. Maybe he deserved whatever evil befell him. Maybe his unforgivable act against his leader's bitch condemned him always to run alone.

Maybe he was just a loser. Not the alpha male he'd imagined himself. Maybe he didn't deserve a female of his own. Someone who loved only him.

What if Shannon couldn't love him? Wouldn't love him?

Just now, she'd shut him out, locked down the barriers of her mind, closed herself to the wolf, to that part of Jake that ruled his mind, his body, his heart. He was Chanku. So was she! No mere human would have the power to close her mind to the power of the beast.

She'd only had the pills for two days. Even Tia, whose parents were both Chanku, had taken a week before she made the change. Had she been ready earlier? How long did it take? Jake had needed almost two weeks of supplement before he'd understood the new way his body worked.

Luc hadn't told him what was going on. Couldn't, because if he'd guessed wrong, if Jake hadn't been Chanku, Luc would have had to kill him.

Luc would have done whatever it took to keep their secret safe. Jake remembered the weird dreams he'd had, the strange sensation of his bones practically crawling beneath his skin. He'd been light headed, dizzy, his senses suddenly so acute he'd thought he was losing his mind.

The strangest of all had been the sex. His already powerful sex drive had gone off the charts. Though never all that attracted to men before, he'd still experimented with same-sex relationships since puberty, more to ease his need than anything else. Yet after a week of the nutrients, believing they were nothing more than vitamins, he'd spent a night with Luc that still rated as one of his best all-time sexual experiences ever.

Since then, he'd rarely gone without some form of sexual gratification for more than a day, even if he had to deal with his needs by himself. His body demanded release, a need Jake accepted as part of who and what he had become.

Jake's mad dash through the woods slowed to a trot, to a walk, to a complete stop beneath a thick stand of birch shining almost silver in the moonlight.

Shannon obviously had a sex drive far beyond what most women experienced. She had no qualms about sleeping with either men or women or combinations of both. Could that be one of the signs of the latent Chanku genes? That constant drive for physical release, for sex?

Merely thinking of Shannon, of her heated response, her warm body and delicious scent made him hard. Jake turned his head and stared back along the trail he'd just run. It was time to return. Time to make love to her again. To wait patiently for the supplement to complete the changes in her body that would make her Chanku.

He had to believe. Had to get over the paranoia, the fear that Shannon wouldn't want him. Needed to figure out how he was going to explain to her that he'd made a decision that would change her life, made it without asking her, without consulting her in any way.

He'd started her on a supplement she'd need every day for the rest of her life. None of them knew what might happen should the nutrients be taken out of their diet. Would they regress? Lose forever the abilities that made them more than human? Would that special part of the brain just shrivel up and go away?

None of them knew. None of the pack was willing to take a chance. Jake remembered, on the few occasions when he'd forgotten to take the supplement, his body had cried out for whatever was missing. He'd been driven to find the nutrients he craved.

Nutrients only available growing on the wild Himalayan steppe . . . or in the little brown capsules Ulrich Mason supplied. Ulrich had actually gone a couple of months, but he'd been Chanku much longer than any of them. Eventually, the cravings had brought Ulrich back to the supplement.

Now Jake was forcing Shannon to the same future. Even though he was making it possible for her to have a life filled with experiences beyond anything she might have dreamed, he'd done it without her permission. Without giving her a choice.

But wasn't that exactly what Lucien Stone had done to Jake? Had Jake ever regretted the huge change in his world? He held up one broad paw, the ebony nails covered with mud and tufts of torn grass and realized that if he were told he had to give up the part of him that was Chanku, he would rather choose death.

He turned and trotted back along the trail, back to Shannon. After only two days with the supplement, she was showing subtle signs of the physical changes in her body. She must be Chanku, or nothing at all would have happened. When Jake saw her rubbing the tops of her wrists and forearms, he knew exactly what she felt.

He'd tell her. Soon, in a day or two. The Chanku gene was dominant in females. Maybe they changed faster because of that factor. Maybe women were less resistant to changes in their bodies. There were so many variables, and no one to ask.

No one but Tia. Would she talk to him? Jake still needed to apologize. The wound on his throat had almost healed. It was time to work on the wounds that ran deeper, the betrayal of one friend over another. He would call Tia, find out how long it had taken her before the wolf emerged. Find out the best way to approach Shannon.

After he explained what an ass he'd been, and asked Tia for forgiveness.

The phone rang beside the bed. Luc raised his head in time to see Tia take the call. When he realized it was for her, Luc lay back down. Tinker threw one muscular arm over Luc's hip and pressed close, disturbed only momentarily out of a sound sleep.

Tia grabbed the handset and walked out of the bedroom, talking quietly. Luc thought about following her, then changed his mind when Tinker's lips found the back of his neck.

Obviously, you're not sleeping as soundly as I thought.

Never sleep too soundly for this. Even Tinker's mind talking sounded tired, but he continued his slow assault on Luc's libido.

Exhausted from the trip back to San Francisco, the three of them had fallen asleep together in the big bed without more than a warm hug. From the pressure of Tinker's cock pressing solidly against his ass and the increasing pressure of his lips, it was time for more than hugs and kisses.

Tia would let him know if she needed anything. Right now, Luc realized he needed Tinker as much as the big guy wanted Luc. Rolling over, Luc wrapped his arms around Tinker's broad shoulders and thrust his hips forward. Their cocks met, hard, erect, trapped between their muscular bellies, heat rubbing against heat.

It wasn't enough. It was never enough. Tinker groaned, then slowly pulled away and, kissing and licking his way down Luc's belly, turned his body around to take Luc's cock between his lips.

Luc reached for Tinker's cock, ran his fingers over the silky skin then sucked and licked the broad head, spending an inordinate amount of time working his tongue around the sensitive underside. Sighing, his body straining under Tinker's touch, Luc took Tink's testicles in his mouth, one at a time, then rolled each globe with his tongue.

Tinker copied each move, his mouth hot and wet, his tongue a velvet brush backed by strength. Whatever sensual move Luc made, Tinker increased on Luc. He drew Luc's balls between his lips, tonguing and licking, then wrapped his meaty fist around Luc's cock to add slow, steady pulls.

Luc did the same for Tinker, sliding his fingers over Tinker's dark skin, wrapping his fist around his lover's thick cock. The two men found a rhythm, deliberately paced to build tension, to raise sensation to a peak. Behind the skilled touch of long familiarity and a deep, abiding love, not only for one another but for Tia, as well, was the quiet tension that always accompanied sex between the two of them.

A contest of wills, a battle for control. When Tia was with them, the macho posturing and testosterone battles remained largely under control, but her calming factor was currently talking on the phone in the other room.

Luc's mouth curved in a smile around Tinker's rock-hard penis. It was a game they played, a challenge between alphas. Who would come first? Which one of them could force the other to shoot his load? Ah, crap . . . Tinker's tongue found the sensitive skin just behind his balls. Luc shuddered and pressed his finger deep inside Tinker's ass.

He felt Tink's body shudder and knew the big guy hovered on the edge. Luc pressed his finger deeper, ignoring as best he could the pressure of Tinker's finger against *his* ass.

Impossible. No way in hell could he ignore the exquisite blend of pleasure and pain as Tinker's finger dove deep. Nor could he avoid thrusting his hips forward when Tinker increased the pressure on Luc's cock, sucking harder.

Close. So damned close and Tinker was in his head, multiplying sensation so that Luc felt what Tinker experienced. They hovered there, backing off just enough to prolong the sensation, holding one another on the very precipice of orgasm.

Tia walked back into the room. She flipped on the low light near the bed, and burst out laughing. "I can't leave you two alone for a minute, can I?" Totally ignoring the fact both men were obviously ready to come, she held the phone out to Luc. "It's Jake. He wants to talk to you. Should I tell him your mouth is full?"

Jake? Luc pulled his head back and stared at Tia. Tinker's cock bobbed against the man's belly, but Tink held on to Luc and it was hard to concentrate on what Tia had just said. Tinker's mouth on his cock felt so good, Luc didn't want him to stop, but he frowned at Tia. She'd been gone a long time. What the hell had Jake wanted to say to her now?

He did a quick little journey into her thoughts and came up against a barrier that stopped him cold.

Even more interesting.

"I'll take it." He grabbed the phone out of Tia's hand just as Tinker ran his tongue all the way around Luc's sac. Luc bit back a groan. "What do you want?" He hadn't really meant to sound so aggressive, but damn. Tinker was really working him over!

"Sorry to interrupt. I know it's late."

Jake, you have no idea . . .

"I wanted to apologize. To thank you. I think Shannon is Chanku. She's sleeping, now, but there are too many signs to ignore. I needed to talk to Tia, to find out what it's like for a woman to make the shift. I needed to tell her I was sorry. I am, Luc. I hope you'll forgive me."

Shit. Luc signaled to Tinker to back off, if only for a moment. "You know you're forgiven. What makes you think you're not? Do you think I'd have sent you to protect a potential mate if I was still pissed? Fuck, man . . . you worry about everything. You screwed up. You apologized. It's over. Did Tia give you the information you needed?"

At Jake's affirmative answer, Luc nodded. "Okay. You've got until Friday to make this work. I'd give you more time, but I'm worried about them finding you. Ulrich's taken care of part of the problem, but the guy's associates may not have gotten the message that the hunt is off. I wish I could tell you more, but without a secure line, I can't risk it. AJ and Mik will fill you in."

"Thanks, Luc. I just wish I had more time alone with her."

Luc's sigh carried across the line. "I know. I wish I could give it to you. Tia says women make the change faster then men. She thinks she was ready within about three or four days, a couple days before she actually tried to shift."

"Did it go okay the first time?"

"Like clockwork. Remember though, when you mate, you bond. Whatever is in your head is suddenly going to be in hers. If you have a secret, any secret, it's hers. My big mistake was the fact I wasn't honest with Tia, didn't let her know about my role in her mom's death. I was afraid of what she'd think when she learned the truth, so I backed off. That's why she was unmated when you were with her. Why you even had the opportunity. That never should have happened. Don't let it happen with Mik and AJ."

"I have no idea what you're talking about, about her mother."

"I know. Again, Mik and AJ will fill you in. Be careful. We know of at least six agents who might be searching for you. With their boss out of the way, there's no one to call them off. Don't let them get Shannon."

Luc handed the phone back to Tia and watched while she placed it on the table beside the bed. Tinker sucked Luc's cock back between his lips. Luc glanced up and caught the twinkle in Tia's eye. She dropped her robe to the floor, then crawled across Luc's chest to take Tinker's penis between her lips. With just a minor adjustment, Luc found Tia's pussy with his mouth.

Holding her buttocks steady with his palms, he slowly worked his tongue deep inside for a taste, then settled down to suckle gently on her clitoris while his fingers searched the cleft between her cheeks.

Sighing, Luc centered his thoughts on the woman he loved, the man loving him.

Jake was a big boy. Eventually he'd figure everything out.

Jake set the phone back in the cradle and stared into the dark. Someone might still be after Shannon and he felt as if a noose were tightening around them. She'd had her first supplement on Sunday and already, after only two pills, she showed signs of something happening. Tia had told Jake many of the changes were subtle, internal things only a woman would understand.

Shannon's menses would alter from the typical heavy flow of blood to a mere staining once a month, accompanied by pheromones that were certain to drive Jake wild. *Check one* . . . he'd already experienced her pheromones.

She'd develop an inherent knowledge of how to release an egg for fertilization, something Tia's cousin, Keisha was supposedly considering. A knowledge of self so complete as to change a woman's perception of not only herself, but her need for an alpha mate.

Would Shannon find Jake *alpha* enough to suit her? Only time would tell. Sighing, Jake quietly joined Shannon in the big bed, but he lay awake beside her well into the night.

Chapter 7

The dream was clearer tonight. Shannon knew she dreamed, experienced the dream state as if she were just outside the wolf, running beside her then floating above, watching the animal search.

Nose to the ground, the wolf raced back and forth across the meadow, her thick coat shining blue black beneath the moon.

What did she look for? Why did the sense of something out of place feel so much more intense tonight? Hovering mere inches above the beast, Shannon tried to communicate with the gorgeous animal, opening her thoughts as she'd opened them to Jake.

There was no warning, no sense of movement, nothing to indicate change. Shannon blinked. When her eyes opened, she *was* the wolf.

Unlike her earlier dreams, she'd experienced the wolf as a metaphor, not reality. She'd sensed it was but a part of her mind, the dissatisfied, unfulfilled part of Shannon Murphy, forever searching for some nameless essence, remaining forever beyond her reach.

Now, though, Shannon's nose twitched at the sudden onslaught of scents, her ears perked this way and that with the sound of mice scampering in the grass, of crickets and cicadas and wind in the trees. Her left front foot hurt, enough that she stopped, sat back on her haunches and lifted the foot to inspect the source of the pain.

A large thistle poked out between her toes. Without thinking, Shannon leaned forward and, with a careful nip of her teeth, pulled the thorn out. It stuck to her tongue for a moment, so she licked her furry shoulder and the thistle fell free.

Then she lifted her paw again and licked the injury, tasting blood. After a couple of extra licks for good measure, the small wound closed and she once more put pressure on her paw.

It hurt, but not nearly so bad as when the thorn was still lodged in her foot. This time when Shannon raced along the trail, it was with a sure knowledge she would find what she searched for. Just ahead. She sensed her goal, sensed it growing closer, felt her blood coursing in her veins, the air rushing in and out of her lungs.

Alive. For the first time, Shannon Murphy knew what it felt like to be truly alive. Joyously alive, her heart pounding as much from emotion as the run, she lifted her nose to sniff the evening breeze. The air smelled lush, alive with a million new scents.

There, amid the rich potpourri of humus and rotting wood, the tangy crush of wild herbs and the pungent stink of an angry skunk, Shannon recognized something familiar. She practically skidded to a halt and yipped sharply.

Her wolf stepped out of the shadows. Thick coat glinting silver beneath the waning moon, he waited at the edge of the forest. Shannon's womb clenched. Unfamiliar and bestial, she still understood its workings with a knowledge her human self had been denied. Understood how to release an egg for breeding, how to help the fetus endure the shift from human to beast and back again.

Understood that all those parts of her that had been diseased and damaged were once again whole. In this body, as this creature, she was fertile and complete.

Beneath all the layers of knowledge, Shannon understood the world of Chanku. A world changing, only now, from fairy tale to reality.

Shannon's reality. Why now? How? The answers were close. So very, very close. She almost . . . Oh! There.

Ah. Such a simple little thing.

Shannon tossed the covers back, crying out. The flickering light from a single small candle on the dresser cast her tortured expression in deep shadows. Jake had watched her long enough, tangled in the throes of what must have been a frightening nightmare, yet he'd been unwilling to wake her from her dreams.

Now he brushed her tangled hair back from her face, leaned close and whispered kisses across her cheek to her lips. Shannon's eyes flew open. Obviously disoriented, she stared at Jake as if he were a stranger. Then awareness slowly settled her rapid breathing. She blinked and shook her head.

"So real. Such an amazing dream. It felt so real."

Jake kissed her full on the mouth. Tasted her lips, nipped at the lower one. "What did you dream?"

Shannon scooted into a sitting position, shoved her pillows behind her, and leaned back on the headboard. "I'm not really sure. It was all tied up in some old fairy tales Tia used to tell. Stories about people who were really wolves. In my dream, I was a wolf. I was looking for something but I didn't know what. Then the wolf I saw here at the house was in my dream. Just before I woke up, I had the strangest feeling he was the one I was searching for. Weird. Really, truly weird."

This was more than he'd hoped for. So much more. Jake took a deep breath to steady his racing heart. "You think so? Do you often have dreams that seem real?" He stroked her hair, comforting her. Still sleepy eyed, she called to him with a power that grew stronger each hour of the night, each minute of the day.

Shannon turned and looked at him for the longest time. Jake felt as if she were judging him, reading something in the way he watched her, the questions he asked.

"I rarely dream. In fact, until I started taking those big vitamins you've given me, I've never dreamed like this before. What's in them? What am I taking?"

Crap. This he didn't need. Jake faked a calm he didn't feel. "I told you. They're herbs, extracts from plants. Nothing dangerous. I can't imagine them giving you nightmares."

Shannon shook her head. "I never said they were nightmares. Merely vivid dreams. Have you ever taken illegal drugs?"

Jake shook his head at the non sequitur. "No. I smoked some pot in high school, but that was it. It didn't do much for me."

Shannon shrugged her shoulders. The blanket dropped away, revealing the upper swell of her right breast, the rosy shadow surrounding her nipple. Jake curled his fingers into tight fists to keep from touching her.

"I have. I'm not even sure what the stuff was. I was out with Tia one night and we'd met a couple of guys. They ended up coming home with us. We took something they mixed in our drinks, and I remember dreams like nothing I'd ever experienced before." She narrowed her gaze and pinned Jake with her green eyes. "It was also the most amazing sex I'd ever had with a total stranger. Until you. Jake, are you giving me some kind of drug for sex? Is that what those pills are?"

He laughed. Damn, the way a woman's mind worked. "You think I'd have to give you drugs for good sex? Give me a break." He leaned close, so close that his lips hovered directly over Shannon's. Close enough to rub his nose against hers, which he did.

"I've never resorted to drugs to make a woman come. It takes skill to bring a woman to climax. Not drugs. At least not the way I work." He licked her upper lip with the very tip of his tongue.

Shannon parted for him. Jake stroked his tongue along the soft flesh inside her lower lip, then nipped the sensitive skin between his teeth. He touched her tongue with his, suckled the tip between his lips.

She moaned, then pulled away. "What if I were to stop taking your pills. Would that bother you?"

Jake fought the ripe surge of panic. "Only because I'd worry about you. I want you healthy." He kissed her mouth, then pulled back. "I want you strong. Ready for me."

She practically purred. "Oh, I'm definitely ready. And, very strong." Slowly, Shannon rolled close to Jake. The covers made a soft barrier between them, teasing him with her partially hidden nudity. She rubbed her breasts over his chest, ran her hands along his arms, raised them up over his head.

Kissing and nipping at his lips, his chin, the line of his jaw, she kept a tight grip on his forearms, pressing them solidly against the iron headboard. She crawled higher on his chest, rubbing Jake's lips with her taut nipple. He felt his cock surge beneath the blankets, trapped under the cotton sheets and down comforter.

She held his wrist now with one hand. He felt her other slip under the pillow and wondered what the hell she was up to. Then she rubbed her crotch over his belly and her scent rose, ripe and intoxicating, filling his nostrils, going straight to his cock and aching balls.

Short-circuiting his brain.

Groaning, Jake realized her little bondage games were officially over. It was time to take control—now. Except, he couldn't. Tugging at his wrists, he looked up and groaned. "How the hell did you manage that?"

She giggled and sat back, her knees clamped to either side of his chest, her scent surrounding him. "When I found the necktie in the closet, I couldn't think of a better use for it. I just didn't imagine it would happen so soon."

Jake twisted his arms. She hadn't had enough time to tie it properly, had she?

He couldn't break free. Obviously, she had.

"I was always good with knots."

"I see that. Okay . . ." He dragged the word out. "Now that I'm tied to the headboard, what do you plan to do with me?"

Shannon raised off his body and pulled the blankets away. His cock popped up like a jack-in-the-box. "Anything I want."

He almost shot his load with the promise in her voice. "How'd we go from talking about your dreams to me tied to the bed? Inquiring minds want to know."

"It felt like a natural progression to the conversation. I think it has something to do with control . . . that, and your amazing ego."

Jake glanced down at his cock. It was standing proud, the foreskin forced back behind the broad, plum-shaped crown. "It is amazing, isn't it?"

"Yeah. Right." Shannon lifted her body away from his, scooted over Jake and climbed off the bed.

"Where are you going?"

"Out."

"What do you mean, out? Out where?" This wasn't going at all the way he'd expected. Jake yanked at the headboard, harder this time. The iron creaked but didn't give. All he did was tighten the knots holding his wrists.

"Don't worry. I'll be back. Soon."

Jake twisted around in the bed just in time to see Shannon's naked butt as she went out the door. She closed it behind her. Left him alone with a single candle. A tiny stub that flickered brightly, then went out. Left him tied to the bed, his cock bouncing against his belly, his balls aching for release.

Jake tugged once more at the necktie binding him to the headboard. He glanced at the closed bedroom door.

Then he shifted.

Shannon leaned over and rubbed her foot. It hurt, almost as if she'd stepped on something sharp. When she looked, though, there was no sign of injury. She picked the bottle of pills up off the kitchen table, opened the lid and sniffed. They smelled like dry grass. She palmed a few and stared at them. They had to be the answer. Something in the pills Jake was giving her must be causing everything weird that was happening. The dreams, the way her skin tingled so strangely. Hell, even her bones ached in an odd, expectant manner. As if the ache was a necessary part of . . . what?

She didn't know. Not for sure, but, damn it all, she was going to find out.

Shannon glanced toward the closed bedroom door. She lit a kerosene lantern and carried it, along with the bottle of pills, toward the bedroom. She heard a loud thump and what sounded like an angry growl, and grinned. Jake was going to be really pissed, but at least she figured she'd get the answers she wanted.

Shannon shoved the door open with her hip and, holding the lantern aloft, walked into the room. Jake lay on the bed, the blankets twisted beneath him, his hands still firmly bound. He glared at her. She practically felt the waves of frustration boiling off his naked body.

He was no longer aroused. Shannon set the lantern on the dresser next to the remnants of the small candle, turned around and grinned. It was much more fun talking to him when his cock was straining against his belly. She held on to the bottle of pills and sat on the edge of the bed, the curve of her buttock against Jake's hip.

He didn't say a word, but then he didn't need to. His expression spoke volumes. Shannon was fully aware he wasn't enjoying any of this. Jake was a man who needed control.

Demanded it.

Right now, he didn't have it. He was not a happy man.

Shannon needed control as well. Right now, she had it. She rolled the bottle of pills between her hands. Then, without warning, she leaned over, dragged her hair across Jake's groin, drew his flaccid penis between her lips and sucked hard.

Jake's hips came off the mattress.

"Shit! A little warning would be nice."

Sliding her lips up and down his rapidly enlarging cock, Shannon merely hummed her answer.

Jake groaned in response.

She worked steadily, slipping him in and out of her mouth, working the smooth flesh over the crown with her tongue, dipping lower to lick his sac and nibble at the wrinkled skin holding his balls. She listened to the rate of his breathing, sensed when he was about to come. Took him to the edge and held him there, then sat back and smiled.

"Now, about those pills." She held the bottle up so he could see it in her hand.

Jake glared at her. "You're just going to leave me like this?" Underscoring his complaint, Jake's cock bobbed against his belly.

"For now. Yep. Are you going to tell me the truth about what you're giving me?"

"I told you. They're vitamins. Just herbs and stuff. There is nothing that will hurt you in those pills."

Shannon stared at him for a long, slow moment. There was an obvious tic in his jaw, his dark eyes seemed to be hiding something and she was absolutely positive he was lying.

She stood up. "Okay. If there's nothing in these pills that can hurt me, then there's nothing all that important that will help, either. They're going in the toilet." She turned her back on Jake and marched toward the small bathroom off the master bedroom.

A low, warning growl coming from the bed stopped her. Shannon felt the skin prickle along her backbone, knew with absolute certainty what she would see tied to the bed. Knew, and welcomed it. There was no need for fear, not even for surprise.

Slowly, Shannon turned. Amazingly, she held on to her composure. She'd definitely tied him well. It appeared the wolf's forelegs were larger around than Jake's wrists, his paws too wide for the tightly knotted silken necktie to slip loose. Bound as the man had been, the wolf twisted its shimmering body and glared at her with every bit of frustration the man had shown.

Of course, the wolf had much sharper teeth.

Smiling, moving ahead without fear, Shannon grabbed a pair of scissors off the dresser and walked back to the bed. She stared down at the wolf, at Jake, for a long moment. He was beautiful. Absolutely beautiful.

And truly pissed. He snarled, curling one side of his lip back to reveal long, daggerlike canines. His ears lay back against his broad skull and his shimmering amber eyes bored into her. Shannon had a powerful urge to stroke the smooth fur between his ears, but shook it off. That might be pushing it.

Later. This definitely wasn't the time to pet him like a large dog.

She took a deep breath, let it out. "I had a feeling that was you in the meadow. Especially when I realized you'd stuffed a bolster pillow into bed beside me."

The wolf merely glared at her.

She carefully snipped away the necktie, freeing first one powerful leg, then the other. The wolf slipped down onto the bed, still staring at her out of angry, amber eyes.

"I'm not the least bit afraid of you, you know. You're Jake and you won't hurt me. However, I imagine it's a lot easier to carry on a conversation when you're human. Is it hard to shift back?"

I can talk to you in any manner I choose.

Shannon was still trying to comprehend the clear sound of Jake's voice in her head when the wolf rolled to its belly and rose up on its powerful haunches. By the time it was fully erect, Jake sat on the edge of the bed, rubbing his wrists. He tilted his head and stared at her.

Shannon's poise almost slipped. She'd proved her theory. Now what?

"You play for keeps, don't you?" Jake's slow drawl didn't sound angry. Anything but. In fact, if she weren't mistaken, he was fighting a grin.

Shannon wrapped her arms around her waist. She felt terribly naked, standing here in the soft glow of the lantern with a man who had just switched from human to wolf then back to human again.

Impossible.

"It's my life we're talking about." She held up the bottle. "What do these have to do with . . ." Shannon waved her hand helplessly, "that."

Jake patted the bed next to him. Shivering, Shannon sat beside him. Warmth radiated from his body. He put his arm around her and hugged her close against his side.

"It's a long and convoluted tale. We might as well get comfortable." He scooted back into bed, held the covers up for Shannon and she crawled in beside him. It was warm and cozy next to Jake, leaning back against the plump pillows with the soft down comforter pulled up to their chests.

"Fifteen years ago I was a paramedic with a serious

drinking problem, facing sanctions at work. I always felt as if I was looking for something I'd never find. I didn't know where to look, didn't know what I was looking for, and figured I might find it at the bottom of a bottle. Then I met Lucien Stone."

"The man Tia's with?"

"The same. I was hiking up in the Sierras, working my way through a flask of whisky, wondering if life was worth the effort. I saw a wolf. It was absolutely beautiful and I'd always been fascinated by the beasts. I found myself staring at it, mesmerized, while it seemed to study me. I'm not sure how it happened, but I suddenly realized the wolf was in my head. Only he wasn't thinking like a wolf. I don't know how long I stood there on the trail, staring at the animal while it wandered around in my mind, but the next thing I knew it was almost dark and the wolf was gone.

"I remember shaking my head, figuring I'd had an alcohol-related blackout. I started the long walk back to camp. Before I'd gone very far, I came across a man on the trail. He introduced himself as Lucien Stone, said he was camping in the area, but he'd gone farther from his campsite than he'd planned. He asked if I had a flashlight. I did, so we shared the light going back to the campground.

"We hit it off really well, camped together for the next week. He started sharing the pills with me from the first night, said they'd help me get over my drinking." Jake turned and stared solemnly at Shannon. "I've never gotten drunk since."

He settled back, even closer to Shannon than he'd been. "After about a week, I noticed some strange physical changes, a sense that my bones were trying to crawl out of my skin. My senses seemed more acute, and my libido was making me nuts. I thought it was a response to going without any booze, but then, one night I had the most amazing sex in my life, with Luc. I'm not gay, though I'd never been all that particular about who I screwed, but I was drawn to him in such a powerful manner that it seemed spiritual as well as sexual. We linked mentally at the time of orgasm—more than once."

Jake squeezed Shannon close and kissed the top of her head. "The next day, he told me about the Chanku. I guess he'd read enough signs in me to know I was one of them. He described a race of humans that evolved on the steppes of the Tibetan Himalayas. They had the ability to shift into animal form . . . into wolves."

Jake looked directly into Shannon's eyes. She felt the gentle probing of his mind, clearer now than it had been since their first sexual encounter. She struggled against his intrusion at first, then relaxed her barriers. Control of her mind was coming more easily now.

"As time went on and the Chanku emigrated from the area, they lost the ability to shift. There's a part of the brain that controls shifting, but it needs certain nutrients to function. What those ancient people didn't know was that the chemicals they required were in some of the grasses growing in Tibet. The organ that made them unique remained, but it became inactive. Without the nutrients it couldn't help them shift. Soon, their past became legend."

Shannon swallowed back the questions bursting in her mind. Jake's hand swept over her hair and he kissed the top of her head. "The genes for the Chanku are dominant in the female. A woman of the Chanku race will always give birth to children with the capability to shift, but without the nutrients they will never be anything other than normal—at least almost normal—human beings. Men can't pass the gene on, but they can be Chanku, the offspring of Chanku mothers. However, they must mate with a Chanku female to have children with the ability to shift."

"But my mother wasn't . . ."

Jake nodded. "She must have carried the gene. Was she a happy woman?"

Shannon shook her head. "No. Never. She took one lover after another, even when I was a child. She and my father divorced when I was a baby. Mom died of cancer when I was still very small, so my father took custody, but he really wanted no part of a daughter. I spent most of my time with Tia Mason."

"Your mother was searching. Just as I was. Just as you are. Searching for that part of her that was missing. The part that was Chanku. Much of what drives us is sexual, an almost addictive need for sex, whether or not we've had the nutrients. Once we become Chanku, we exist in a polyamorous society. Our packmates all have sex with one another. The only restriction is against indiscriminate sex in lupine form. That's reserved for our mate. I've heard it's an amazing thing, when true mates tie for the first time. There's a total link, a bond that can't be broken. A bond that lasts for a lifetime."

Shannon's skin felt cold and hot at the same time. Her own voice sounded foreign when she quietly asked her next question. "The pills?"

"Are a condensed form of the nutrient, made from the same grasses our ancestors ate." Jake hugged her tightly, as if proud of her easy acceptance of everything he was saying. As if he wasn't taking her world and tilting it further and further, until Shannon wondered if she'd ever feel right again.

"I couldn't tell you what was going on because there was still a chance you weren't Chanku, but the evidence, even after just two days, is overwhelming. You are Chanku. You're not ready to attempt a shift yet, but if you continue taking the nutrients you should be able to do it before the week is over."

Shannon realized she still had her fist wrapped tightly around the jar. Now she held it up and stared at it, fully aware her hand was shaking. "All those stories Tia's mom used to tell her?"

Jake nodded enthusiastically. "I don't know how heroic the Chanku are, but the essence of the tales is true. We are humans who can become wolves. We make the shift without pain or effort. It's like taking a deep breath and suddenly we're on four legs with senses so far superior to our human abilities it's almost overwhelming."

Overwhelming described the feelings coursing through Shannon. Suspecting and discovering Jake was a wolf was one thing. Learning he was turning her into a creature just like him without warning her, without her having any choice in the matter, was terrifying. Slowly, fighting the desire to start screaming and just not stop, Shannon turned and stared at him.

"So. Let me get this straight. You were just going to do this to me and not say anything? Turn me into a fucking werewolf and then say, oh, by the way, Shannon . . . you know those little pills you've been taking? Don't you think I might have wanted some choice in the matter?"

Jake shook his head, smiling as if everything made perfect sense. "Don't you see? I couldn't say anything. If it turned out you weren't really Chanku, we'd have had to end our relationship. I can't mate with someone who's, well . . ."

"Human?" She felt her skin grow cold. "You mean I was okay to fuck, but for the happily ever after I need to have four legs and a tail?"

"Shannon, it's not like that."

"Yes, Jake. It is. Of course, I'm supposed to mate with you once the change is complete, right?"

Now he definitely looked unhappy. "Shannon, I've only known you a couple days, but you have to admit, we've got something special going. Yes, I want you for my mate. What man wouldn't? You're beautiful, you're smart, you're . . ."

Shannon held up her hand, halting his litany. Then she crawled out of bed taking one of the pillows with her. She tossed the bottle of pills on the bed beside Jake. "I'm assuming Tia is Chanku as well?"

Jake nodded. She thought he looked a little shell-shocked. Good. It served him right.

"And her father?"

"Yes. All the members of Pack Dynamics are Chanku. We've met others as well. A group in Montana. They're the ones who helped rescue Ulrich."

"How nice for all of you. By the way, I'll be sleeping in another room tonight." Shannon turned away and left Jake staring, openmouthed. She walked from the bedroom with as much dignity as she could muster. It wasn't easy, with the only lantern on the dresser and the living room as dark as a tomb, but it was worth a stubbed toe for a night when she could think about all the changes in her life, and whether or not she was ready for them.

Just to be on the safe side, Shannon grabbed the handful of pills she'd left on the kitchen table and shoved them into the small drawer on the end table near the couch.

It never hurt to be prepared.

Chapter 8

Jake stared at the door and fought the urge to howl. What really pissed him off was the fact Shannon was absolutely right. He'd taken steps that totally changed her life without consulting her. There had to be a better way than lying, but for the life of him he couldn't figure out how he could have done it better, short of telling her the truth.

Something he couldn't do until he knew. *Damn*. Talk about your original catch-22. He had to convince her that everything he'd done was for the good, but how?

Jake waited a few minutes, wondering if Shannon would relent. The silence in the room was absolute, broken only by his panting breaths.

He needed to clear his head, to get out of the confines of four walls and a ceiling. He needed to run. This time, though, there was no need to hide his Chanku form. This time Jake merely shifted, leapt down off the bed, sauntered over to the door . . . and realized Shannon had closed it tight.

Shit. He stared at his big wolven paws, the long ebony claws so good for digging and racing through the woods, but totally useless when it came to doorknobs. Shifting quickly to human form, Jake opened the door, then, as a matter of pride more than necessity, regained his wolf form.

Shannon watched him from her seat on the couch. She sat in the corner of the overstuffed sofa, knees drawn up to her chin, the heavy afghan wrapped around her body. She'd lit a few candles in the room and the light flickered and wavered with the gentle flow of air currents. Jake walked slowly across the floor. His sharp nails clicked on the hard wood, muted when he walked over throw rugs. He looked at the door, then back at Shannon.

Her lips twitched until she sucked them between her teeth and bit down to keep from smiling. "So, you want outside, eh? At least you're housebroken." She got up with the afghan wrapped around her body and sauntered over to the door.

Jake caught back a whimper before it escaped. He wanted her more now then he had earlier when she'd straddled his body and bathed him in her rich scent. He wanted her with more than the usual driving force of Chanku.

His cock twitched, and he knew he had to leave now. With a last look over his shoulder, Jake leapt off the front porch and raced out into the night. The dark forest called, the clean scent of the night air, the sounds of tiny creatures scattering out of his way.

He was wolf. Chanku. Sometimes answers lay in the depths of the forest. When the body hunted, the mind allowed the beast to rule and the cares of humanity dropped away. His claws tore at the mossy trail as he ran through the night. Wind caught at his thick fur and his tail streamed out behind him. Still, the sense remained, that no matter how far, how fast the wolf ran, his heart would stay forever with the auburn haired woman he might have lost.

Shannon tightened the afghan around her body and stared at one of the tiny candles flickering on the mantle. She'd started a fire in the big fireplace, more to give her something to do than for the heat it gave off, but the room still had a chill to it.

Jake had been gone now for hours. Sleep was out of the question. She'd paced, angry at first, then curiosity had finally won out. How in the hell did a person shift from human to wolf and back again? Jake made it look so simple. In fact, it happened so quickly, Shannon hadn't been able to follow what his body actually did during the change.

One second he was Jake, the next a beautiful wolf with silver-tipped fur. Shannon rubbed at her arms, more aware now of the strange, itchy sensation of skin crawling over muscle, of muscle twitching as if small currents passed through her.

She couldn't deny it any longer. For better or for worse, Jake had started a process Shannon would finish. The dreams convinced her. In her dreams she ran free, the strength and power of the wolf as much a part of her as the eyes in her face and the hair on her head.

I am Chanku.

Shannon had realized over the course of the last couple of hours that her dreams of wolves started before her first pill. She'd blamed Jake unfairly, for that much, at least. She'd dreamed of wolves the first night, when Jake had rescued her from the kidnappers.

Was it Jake's proximity that made her dream? Had that part of her mind, the wolven part, recognized a fellow Chanku? She'd never dreamed of wolves while living with Tia, but then Tia hadn't taken any of the supplements at that point, either.

Shannon tried to imagine the act of shifting, looked for that knowledge within herself and realized there was merely a fuzzy concept in her mind. Jake had said she'd need to take the supplements for at least three or four days, if not longer, before she could shift.

She threw off the afghan and paced the length of the big

room and back. She envied Jake right now, envied him the freedom of running through the forest with the night wind in his face, the sounds of falling water and tiny creatures scurrying, the whoosh of wings as owls sped overhead or bats darted between the trees.

Suddenly she stopped. How did she know those sounds? Shannon rubbed her hands over her face, aware of a gut-deep knowledge of the forest at night no city girl from Boston should have. How had her mind even recognized the myriad scents, sounds and sensations a wolf would experience while racing through the woods at night?

Was it some kind of racial memory? An instinctive knowledge? Shannon plopped back down on the sofa and threw the afghan over her lap. She concentrated once more on the flickering candle and let her thoughts follow the tiny flame.

Opening her mind to possibilities, to the meaning behind her dreams, to that newly evolving part of Shannon Murphy that was something fairy tales were made of.

As her heart rate steadied and her body relaxed, Shannon slipped quietly into that new part of herself. She explored her own thoughts, her body, her tingling arms and legs and the reflexes that somehow felt faster, sharper. In her most recent dream, she had sensed her internal organs, the workings of her reproductive system. She'd *known* her organs were whole and healthy, had understood the simple method of releasing an egg for fertilization.

Shannon's damaged reproductive organs were no longer an issue. Once she took enough of the supplement, she'd not be able to get pregnant in human form even if they'd been healthy. Only as Chanku would she be able to breed. Mating with another Chanku, as wolf, and only then if she chose to release an egg for fertilization.

She *knew* this. Knew it as if she'd been taught her own biology from birth. Shannon stared, transfixed, at the candle. Saw the deep woods, the darkness not nearly so dark as her human eyes would lead her to believe.

She sensed Jake, knew he ran to control his anger and overwhelming sadness at having deceived her. Sensed the battles ahead of them as her alpha male realized the pack was under the charge of the alpha female.

Shannon smiled, seeing a lot of male adjustment in her future. Even more in Jake's. She thought of the five pills in the drawer, pills Jake didn't know she had. Though his intentions had been good, his methods were wrong. She should have been told what the true purpose of the supplement was.

There was no question she would continue to take them. No question she would fully embrace her Chanku heritage. And, if she were truly honest with herself, there was no question at all in Shannon's choice of mate.

Jake had met needs Shannon hadn't realized existed. He'd come into her life so suddenly she'd not had time to adjust to the change, to the fact her heart was fully engaged with a total stranger.

Stranger than she'd ever imagined.

Shannon sent her thoughts out into the night, realized she had greatly increased her ability to use her mind for communication after only two days on the supplement. She found Jake near a small pond, saw through his eyes when he stalked a rabbit near the water's edge.

Tasted fresh blood when he pounced, grabbing the small creature between sharp teeth and ending its life in a heartbeat. She felt no sense of disgust, no need to back away when Jake devoured the rabbit, leaving little beside the pond to show a life had ended here.

Just as Shannon's was now beginning. A rebirth.

Slowly, carefully, Shannon pulled away from Jake's thoughts with a sense of triumph. He'd not been aware of her presence!

Exhausted, she got up and extinguished each of the candles she'd placed around the room. With only the glow from the fire to guide her, she crawled back on the comfortable sofa and wrapped the afghan around herself.

Shannon could have chosen the extra bedroom, but this room seemed right for her. It was the center of the house. Her center. Jake's.

She was only half awake when Jake let himself inside the cabin, moving quietly on bare human feet. Shannon thought of joining him in the bed, of putting their argument behind them, then thought better of it. Jake needed to know how his actions had hurt her, needed to understand that, just as she wouldn't take control from Jake, he had no right to take it from Shannon.

So, crawling through his brain when he doesn't know you're there is acceptable?

The errant thought might have kept her awake, but Shannon was too sleepy to even consider arguing with her conscience.

Jake paused by the sofa and stared down at Shannon. She lay on her side, the colorful afghan pulled up over her shoulders, her thick mass of auburn hair spread out over the arm of the chair like a dark copper halo.

Halo my ass. There was nothing the least bit angelic about Shannon Murphy. Full of the devil and twice as hot . . .

Sighing, Jake headed into the master bedroom and the big, lonely bed waiting for him. He should insist she join him, but what would that accomplish? He knew he could make her want him. Making her love him was another story altogether.

The jar of pills sat on the dresser, a reminder of everything he'd screwed up. If she didn't take the pills, she would never become Chanku. Was Shannon hardheaded enough to deny herself her true heritage, just to prove a point?

Frustration washed over Jake in heated waves as he turned the spigots on in the shower. The cascade of hot water soothed his nerves, but not his libido. He washed himself, removed the scent of wolf and sweat, then lingered on his cock.

With soapy hands, he pleasured himself, wrapping his fist around his hard girth and stroking, slowly at first, working the foreskin back over the dark crown, rubbing the full length in a steadily increasing rhythm.

Jake imagined Shannon's small hands encircling him, imagined her lips covering the crown. She'd done something no other woman had done to him the other night when she slipped the tip of her tongue under his foreskin, teasing the ultra sensitive spot just behind the head of his glans.

He shuddered, remembering the silken feel of her tongue, the tight clasp of her hands.

Her skin was so soft, her breasts full and firm, her pussy grabbed his cock like a satin fist and drew him in, deeper, deeper still until he felt the hard, rounded end of her womb, met the small cleft of her cervix and heard the soft moans she made when he touched her there, so deep inside.

He felt her fingers stroking his balls as she rolled each nut within his sac, then cupped the weight in her palm. Her mouth came down on him, taking his whole cock between her lips and down her throat, swallowing convulsively, tightening around his engorged flesh until the pleasure was too great, the sensations too powerful.

Grunting, one fist flying up and down his slick shaft, his other hand holding his ball sac in a parody of Shannon's soft touch, Jake ejaculated all over the tile wall of the shower.

Chest rising and falling with each breath, he stared at the thick globs of semen flowing down the shower wall. It mixed with the water, swirling into oblivion down the drain. Jake shook off a sense of self-disgust, rinsed the wall, finished his shower and slowly, methodically dried himself.

His cock lay shriveled between his legs, the foreskin completely covering the once proud crown. It wasn't the first time he'd beaten off in the shower.

It certainly wouldn't be the last.

For the life of him, though, Jake couldn't explain the emptiness he felt, the sense of loss that Shannon's sweet touch had all been fantasy. The knowledge that while he stood alone in the shower with his dick in his hand, she lay asleep on the couch in the other room.

It didn't get much more pathetic than this. Once again, Jacob Trent managed to screw up the one thing he had hoped to do right. Somehow, he had to find a way to fix things before it was too late.

Shannon had the coffee going by the time Jake crawled out of bed. He looked hungover and grumpy as hell, but she handed him a cup of coffee with a smile and went back to preparing breakfast. Jake nodded, took his coffee and sat down at the kitchen table. He stared at the cup for a long time before finally raising it to his lips for a sip.

"It's good."

Shannon turned with the spatula in one hand. "Well, don't sound so surprised. I can cook, you know."

Jake actually smiled at this. "Well, actually I don't know. So far I've done all the cooking."

She threw a potholder at him, but he ducked. At least he was still smiling. Shannon realized she had a stupid grin on her face as well. "Potatoes are warming in the oven with the bacon. How do you want your eggs?"

"Any way you fix them." Jake took another swallow of

his coffee and his expression was one of pure bliss. "You have no idea how it feels to walk out into the kitchen to find a beautiful woman fixing me breakfast. I could get used to this."

Shannon laughed. "Well, I wouldn't get too comfortable with the image. Breakfast is about all I know how to cook." Still, the warm look he gave her made her feel good, sort of tingly all over.

Maybe it's the pill you took earlier . . .

There was that. She'd taken the pill first thing this morning. Now she watched while Jake pulled the bottle out of his shirt pocket and emptied two capsules into his hand. He held one out to her.

She felt like a liar shaking her head. The look on his face almost made her confess, but something held her back. Was it pride? Or pure contrariness, as her mother might have said.

Shannon turned back to the stove and added some chopped onion to the butter in the pan. She'd been thinking of her mother a lot since last night, wondering what the woman who gave her life had really been like. A five-year-old's memories couldn't be reliable.

Still, she did remember hugs and kisses, and cereal at the table when she woke up. There'd been cartoons on Saturday mornings, wrapped close with her mom in an old blanket on the sagging couch in their front room. It wasn't until she was older that Shannon realized she'd grown up in such a seedy apartment in the Tenderloin. As a little girl, it had been home.

Then her mom was gone and her father moved Shannon to his home in the Marina district, which happened to be close to her friend Tia's house. Shannon recalled very little of her father, other than the fact he'd been cold and uncaring, unwilling to spend time with a frightened, needy child. Scared and alone, Shannon had latched on to Tia as her anchor. They'd been friends since they were barely more than toddlers. Shannon knew Tia's mother knew her mother, but not how well or in what context.

Not long after, Tia's mother had been murdered and the two girls had truly bonded.

Friends, then, when they'd reached puberty and their bodies were suffused with unexpected hormones, lovers. They were inseparable as teens, even going away to a private school together. Though she'd never been certain, Shannon suspected Tia's father had paid her expensive tuition at Briarwood.

Was it out of love, or just to find a place to park the two of them? Shannon added the eggs to the softened onion in the pan, stirring carefully, remembering a life that somehow seemed to belong to another woman, another time.

Tia had found Luc. Shannon wished she knew the details. Had it been as simple as meeting the right guy and falling in love? She glanced at Jake, realized he watched her like a wolf staring down its prey.

How could she let him know he was the right guy, just not quite yet? She needed time. Time to adjust, to learn this new body, this new way of thinking. Already she felt the pill from this morning working its miracles in her bloodstream. Her arms tingled, her senses felt more acute. She felt as if she didn't go out and run for miles she might explode.

That alone was the clincher. Shannon hated exercise.

She scooped a large helping of eggs onto a plate, added most of the fried potatoes and half a dozen strips of bacon. She set it in front of Jake, then prepared a smaller plate for herself.

Shannon stared at the small serving of eggs for a moment, then added what was left in the pan, piled the rest of the bacon on her plate and added the remainder of the fried potatoes. There was enough to feed two of her, but when she sat down across from Jake, Shannon knew she'd eat the entire serving.

Her legs twitched. She felt the need to run, to get out of the house and race through the woods. She might not be ready to shift, but suddenly Shannon knew she had to run in the forest.

Jake raised his head. "This is delicious. Thank you."

"You're welcome." Shannon took a bite of potatoes and smiled. They were really good!

"I'm going to be gone for a couple hours. Will you be okay here by yourself?"

Shannon's head snapped up. "Where are you going?"

"I want to go to town without you, check and see if anyone has been looking for us. If you're with me, people will notice. By myself, I just won't stand out as much."

Shannon found that hard to believe. He was gorgeous. His body alone was enough to attract attention, but that over-long hair hanging in sun-ripened waves around his face, those gorgeous eyes . . . who was the man kidding?

Maybe he just needed to get away. She could certainly understand that. Shannon nodded. "Fine. I'll be here. You might want to pick up some fresh eggs and maybe some fruit. A newspaper would be nice."

"Do you need . . . uh . . ." He looked away, obviously uncomfortable.

"What?"

"You know. Feminine products. You said you'd started your period."

Shannon shook her head. "No. It only lasted a day. False alarm, I guess."

Jake nodded, took another bite. He smiled at her and some of the tension eased. His huge plate of food disappeared before Shannon had eaten half of hers. Jake stood up and carried his plate to the kitchen, rinsed it off and left it in the sink. "I can help you clean up when I get back."

Shannon waved him off. "No problem. It'll give me something to do." She watched him walk back to the bedroom, finished her meal, rinsed her plate. Jake came out a few minutes later, dressed all in black leather with his helmet in one hand. He stood in front of her a minute, his stance uncertain.

Shannon reached up on tiptoe and kissed him. It was a brief touch, just a meeting of lips that could have been so much more, but she pulled away quickly. She saw Jake's shoulders rise and fall with his deep sigh, then he turned and left.

She watched him straddle the big motorcycle, heard the low, yet powerful hum of the engine, watched him ride away. Multicolored leaves swirled in the air behind him.

Shannon felt bereft. As if her only friend in the world had abandoned her. Turning away from the window, she started the water in the sink to do the breakfast dishes.

Jake stopped at the one gas station in town and filled the tank on the bike, then slowly headed toward the general store. He loved the sound of the motor on the bike, a silken purr that made him want to aim for the road out of town and never look back.

Except that would mean leaving Shannon, and that was something he'd never do. Jake pulled into the parking lot. Even though it was still early, there were half a dozen cars in the spaces and a couple of old guys sitting on the bench by the front door.

Jake nodded as he entered the store. Shannon wanted fruit, so he checked the produce section, surprised to find a fairly good selection. He filled a basket with bananas and apples, some late-season grapes and a melon that had probably come from somewhere in South America and would probably cost as much as a plane ticket to Chile.

It didn't matter. Shannon didn't ask for much. He'd figured that out at the very beginning. She accepted, she dealt with the situation, she moved on.

Would she move on from him once the effect of the two pills she'd taken had worn off? Jake shivered, terrified of losing her. Standing in the produce section in a funky little country store, worrying that the woman he wanted for a lifetime might leave. Might choose her independence over the genetic heritage that made her something special, something better than human.

He picked up a loaf of bread, a dozen eggs, a couple of nice-looking steaks. There were deer in the forest and a big freezer in the back of the house.

Jake had no business buying meat, but Shannon would like this. He was certain.

He took his basket to the counter and set the items down for the grocer to ring him up. The man stared at him a moment, gave him a long, slow look that made Jake come to attention.

"You the fellow that came into town with that sexy redhead?"

Jake nodded slowly. "Yeah. She's my wife."

Well, maybe one of these days . . .

"There were a couple guys here this morning, asking about a big man on a new Beemer and a tall, sexy redhead with green eyes. You two fit the description."

Jake took a deep breath as he handed the man his credit card. "Did you tell them where to find us?"

The grocer smiled. "I sent 'em that way."

Jake looked in the direction the man pointed. Due east. His cabin was north. He nodded, smiled. Looked up and caught the grocer's eye and winked. "Thank you. I appreciate it."

"Your money's good here. They complained about the prices."

Jake bit back a grin. "That'll get you bad information every time. Personally, I think your prices are just fine."

He signed the tag, gathered up the bags the man handed him and started to leave. Then he turned back to the grocer. "For what it's worth, they're Feds. They want her on a bogus charge and I'm trying to protect her. I appreciate your help." Jake scribbled his cell phone number on the back of his receipt and handed it to the grocer. "I'd appreciate hearing from you if they come back."

The man's smile spread from ear to ear. "I just knew it. No one wears a suit that expensive around here. I didn't trust 'em. Not one bit." He pocketed the number and straightened his shoulders. "You can count on me."

Jake held out his hand. The older man took his in a firm grip. When he left the store, Jake whistled all the way out to the parking lot.

Shannon finished the dishes and wiped down the counters. There really wasn't much to do and Jake probably wouldn't be home for at least an hour or more. She buzzed with energy, as if her body needed to move and move fast, and realized she'd been pacing back and forth in the front room, like a lion in a cage.

Or a wolf.

Adrenaline coursed through her veins and she chalked it up to the changes in her body, the changes Jake had warned her about.

It's really happening. She stared down at her arms, imagined them turning into powerful wolven legs and paws. Felt the skin ripple beneath her gaze. The time was growing closer. Now that she understood the reason for the pills, all the sensations began to make sense.

It explained Jake's nervous energy, the fact he rarely sat still for any length of time. Shannon grinned, giving in to the inevitable. Tia's need to run with Luc even made sense. Finally she went into the bedroom and found Jake's travel bag. She pulled out a pair of jogging shorts, a T-shirt and some socks. They'd be big on her, but better than running naked through the woods.

Shannon might not know how to shift, but the need to run was overpowering. She pulled on the shorts and tied the string at the waist to hold them up, slipped into the shirt, tugged the socks on and laced up her shoes. She thought of leaving a note for Jake, but he'd only been gone about half an hour and she didn't expect him back for quite a while yet. It was obvious he needed his space.

Just as she needed hers. Checking to make sure the fire was banked and the dishes done, Shannon slipped out the back door and jogged along the narrow path to the forest. Jake had gone in from the front, but the trail here looked just as well traveled.

Putting her city-girl fears behind her, Shannon took off at a slow run along the well-trod path. One foot in front of the other, lungs expanding, nostrils flaring. She'd never felt so strong, so in control of her own destiny. In just a matter of days, if all went according to plan, she would run this distance on four legs.

Unbelievable. Impossible.

She couldn't wait.

Chapter 9

Jake thought of going straight back to the cabin, but he wasn't sure if he was ready to face Shannon yet. His cock had been hard ever since he'd left this morning, which made the bike's comfortable seat anything but. He wanted her with an all-consuming, gut-wrenching need, but right now he figured the last thing Shannon wanted from him was sex. Not as pissed off as she'd been.

She hadn't acted all that angry this morning, but her distance had been palpable . . . and painful as hell. He needed time to think, time to figure out how to right all the wrongs he'd done.

This was as good a place as any. The sky was so damned blue and the air almost balmy on this mid-September day. The more he thought about it, the more he recalled how Shannon hadn't minded him leaving, in fact, she probably could use the time alone . . . and the bad guys *were* safely headed in the wrong direction.

Jake pulled the bike off on a side road near his property, tucked it in behind some bushes and stripped off his clothes. Things always seemed clearer to his Chanku mind than to the human side. Of course, the wolf didn't carry nearly as much baggage as the human did.

Shifting, Jake put his nose to the ground and took off at

a steady lope, heading across the brushy meadow toward the forest bordering his property.

He rarely ran during daylight hours, but the sun felt warm against his back and the grasses carried a richer scent than the meadow at night. He smelled warm sap and the aromatic resin of the pines. Even the fallen leaves had a unique smell that reminded him of clean earth and summers long ago.

Jake let his thoughts wander. Unerringly, they found their way back to Shannon. Would she ever forgive him? How in the hell was he going to make her understand his reasoning, his need to bring her over to the Chanku life? Uppermost in his mind was worry. None of them had ever started, then stopped the supplement before the change was complete. How the hell was he going to get her to take the damned pills?

Another thought surfaced, one that brought him to a complete stop. How was he going to get her to mate with him before AJ and Mik arrived if she wouldn't take the pills? The last thing Jake wanted or needed was to find himself in a situation like Luc's, with an available, unmated Chanku bitch surrounded by a bunch of horny males.

Would serve you right, bastard. Payback's a bitch.

It was almost humorous when he thought of it that way. Shaking his head at the vagaries of fate, Jake once again raced through the forest.

Shannon couldn't believe how far and fast she'd run, but it was time to turn back before she ended up lost in the woods. She'd already lost the trail more than once, but her sense of direction seemed stronger, her awareness of her surroundings more acute.

Now, instead of anger with Jake, Shannon felt indebted. She might have gone through life as her mother had, always searching for an identity just out of reach.

Sweat soaked the T-shirt and it clung to her skin. Even the shorts were damp with perspiration. She stopped at a small spring to drink when she realized how much fluid she'd lost. Kneeling down, palms planted in the soft mud at the edge of the woodland pool, Shannon saw she'd knelt as an animal would, leaning forward to lap the water with her tongue rather than bringing it to her mouth with her hand.

The realization stunned her. She sat back, hard, her butt flattening a patch of ferns. The muscles in her arms and legs twitched and she felt a strange crawling sensation along her spine.

Sitting perfectly still, Shannon tried to separate each of the new sensations but they were all-encompassing. Every part of her felt primed for . . . *something*. She tried looking inside herself, much as she had in her dreams when she'd discovered her healthy reproductive system in the body of the wolf, but she wasn't quite sure what to look for.

Maybe one more pill, one more day of change. Shoving herself to her feet, Shannon headed back to the cabin. Tia had gone through this, knowing what to expect. At least, knowing more than Shannon did. She'd call Tia.

Either that, or she could swallow her pride, admit to Jake she was still taking the supplement and ask him how she'd know when she was ready to attempt the shift.

Nah. She'd call Tia. Jake needed a little more time hanging out to dry . . . at least until she got so horny she had to give in. Just thinking about him now brought her nipples to attention and made her aware of the heat between her legs. Damn . . . the man had power over her whether she wanted to admit it or not.

Grinning at her own fickle nature and refreshed from her short break, Shannon headed back down the narrow path to the cabin.

*   *   *

Shannon sensed the presence of others long before she got near enough to see the black sedan hidden off to the side of the long driveway. She worked her way quietly through the thick undergrowth until she was close enough to make certain the car was empty, but it was still way too familiar.

She might not recall her brief time spent in the trunk, but Shannon certainly remembered her time with Jake.

Jake! He could be coming home any time now, and there was no way he'd see the sedan until he was practically on top of the car.

Panic set her heart to pounding. She crouched down behind the thick trunk of a maple tree. *Jake. What the hell do I do now?*

Don't move. I hear you. What's wrong? Where are you?

The mind talking he'd told her about! She hadn't even thought of it. At least her Chanku nature had evolved far enough to understand him. To communicate from a distance. Sighing in relief, Shannon collapsed back against the rough tree trunk.

In the woods beside the driveway, on the north side. The black car is hidden just across from me. There's no one in it. I have no idea where they are or how many, but it looks like those men have found us.

I'm coming. Don't move.

Shannon held perfectly still for what seemed hours, but could only have been about ten minutes or so. She heard a low whine, looked up and saw the wolf watching her from just a few feet away.

Without any hesitation, she held our her arms. The wolf ran to her. Placed his broad head against her chest in what could only be a hug.

Wait here. I'm going to find out where they are.

"Be careful, Jake." There was a quiver in her voice Shannon couldn't hide. Jake stared at her for a long moment, the expression in his amber eyes unreadable. Then he turned and melted away into the thick forest.

Shannon hugged herself, suddenly chilled in her sweaty clothing. Again she waited, but this time at least, Jake kept up a running dialogue with her.

There's one guy under the front deck, just behind the stairs. Hope he doesn't mind spiders . . .

A minute later, he filled her mind again. *Talk about hiding in plain sight. There's a big sucker standing by the back door. I guess he figures we'll come in through the front on the bike.*

Shannon fought a powerful urge to poke her head out around the tree trunk and look at the house, but she managed to hold her position. Jake's voice sounded in her mind once more.

There's one, possibly two men, hiding inside the house, damn it. Hold tight, I'll be right back.

Shannon remained huddled behind the thick tree trunk. Jake slipped through the thick underbrush almost soundlessly, but he saw her head snap up and her eyes turn in his direction when he was still a good twenty yards away.

She was standing up and waiting with her arms open wide when he reached her. Without conscious thought, Jake shifted and practically flowed into her embrace. He felt her body trembling when he held her, felt her heart thudding against his chest, the pressure of her breasts with each breath she took.

She certainly didn't feel all that pissed off.

No, she felt damned hot and sexy plastered close to his naked body, if just a little bit afraid.

Jake kissed the top of her head and tried to ignore the heated rise of his cock. She'd left him horny as hell last night. Horny, and miserable, and filled with regret. Now his only regret was the fact they'd have to deal with the bastards hiding around the cabin before they could get into that making up process he'd heard so much about.

Jake held Shannon away from him, just far enough so that he could see her face, close enough that his cock still rode against her belly, a hot brand between them. Her green eyes sparkled with tears, shimmering like precious jewels.

Shannon was worth more than emeralds. She was more precious than anything else in his life. Jake would protect her, somehow. He swept his palm over her sleek hair, fought the hard desire that made him want to pull her close, to devour her mouth, breathe in her scent.

He took a deep breath, calmed himself. "We have two choices. We can go back to the bike and get out of here. It's parked back at the edge of the property, hidden from view. Or . . ."

"We fight?" Shannon smiled at him, her straight, white teeth flashing in a shaky grin that told Jake exactly where she stood.

"*I* fight. There's no *we* about it. We have no weapons and you can't shift, but I can. I doubt they're prepared for a wolf."

Shannon shook her head. "Didn't you say the wolf got me away from them in the first place? Are these the same guys?"

Jake shook his head. "I dunno. The ones outside aren't the same ones from the motel. I have no idea who's inside, or even how many."

Shannon frowned. "It's the same car we ditched, isn't it?"

"No. Different year. Same make. They look similar. Government issue . . . very little creativity there. When you choose your car, it's this black sedan or that one." He risked a glance around the side of the tree. The only man visible shifted his position beneath the front porch.

"There's a guy at the back door. He didn't look all that alert, probably because he figures we'll come up the driveway. I'm going to take him out first. Next I'll get the one under the steps, but I should have the first man's weapons by then . . ." He grinned at Shannon, imagining the chaos he was going to cause. "I doubt he'll be expecting a naked man armed with his partner's gun."

Shannon slowly rotated her hips against his cock. Jake bit back a groan. "That isn't helping me any, Shannon."

She leaned close and kissed him, her lips a soft benediction against his mouth. "Hmmm . . . just giving you a reason to be very careful."

Jake reluctantly put her away from him. "You've made your point. Now keep an eye on the one under the deck. Let me know if he moves." He turned away, but looked back over his shoulder. Shannon stood straight and tall in the shadow of the ancient maple, her hands clasped in front of her, her lips caught between her teeth.

As much as his cock ached, Jake suddenly realized his heart ached even more. Dear God, but he loved her. Somehow he had to make her realize it was more than Chanku, more than the act of sex, more than anything he'd thought himself capable of feeling.

Jake winked and shifted. With a flip of his tail and one last, backwards glance, he put his nose to the ground and followed the edge of the woods as silently as a wraith.

Do you see any movement from the guy under the porch?

No, unless you count him shifting around like he sees bugs he doesn't like.

Spiders. Big ones. I sure wouldn't go under there.

Jake heard Shannon's soft laughter in his mind. He studied the big guy waiting by the back door. The man was huge, built like a linebacker with shoulders twice the size of Jake's. He held a large semiautomatic weapon in his right hand, but the barrel was pointed at the deck and his stance looked relaxed.

In fact, he looked bored out of his skull. All of a sudden, some movement must have caught his attention, because he turned and stared out across the meadow. He seemed to be watching something at the edge of the woods, but Jake couldn't see what it was from his position in the tall grass.

A musky scent teased his nostrils. Jake raised his head barely enough to see over the grass and spotted the full rack of a large buck. The deer nibbled at one of the shrubs growing along the meadow's edge, upwind from both the wolf and the man on the deck.

It was an extremely welcome diversion. Jake lowered himself to his belly as the man stepped away from the back door and leaned out over the railing. He brought the gun up to his shoulder and sighted. Jake imagined the buck in the crosshairs, wondered if the guy was stupid enough to shoot.

A soft, whispered ka-pow! reached his ears.

The dumb schmuck.

"Ka-pow! Ka-pow!"

The deer continued browsing, reaching above his head to nibble at the tender leaves. Jake quietly followed a line of tall grass to the edge of the deck, out of sight of either of his targets, and shifted back to human.

He'd never mastered the art of walking across a wooden deck without the telltale *click, click, click* from his nails. Moving swiftly on bare feet, avoiding windows in case someone inside might see, he got into position behind the first target, shifted back to wolven form and attacked.

Other than a soft grunt and the thump of the man's gun hitting the grass below the deck railing, Jake's kill was silent and swift. Only someone standing very close would hear the snap of vertebrae, the gurgle of air leaving the dead man's lungs. Clamping his jaws tightly around the limp throat, Jake lowered the man's body to the deck, then leapt silently to the ground below. He crouched over the gun, a modified semiautomatic loaded with armor-piercing shells.

These guys were playing for keeps. If he wanted Shannon safe, Jake knew he'd better be damned careful. He reached for Shannon.

One down. What's going on in front?

If I didn't know better, I'd guess he was jacking off! He's leaning against the piling under the right side of the steps and it looks like his hand's in his pants.

These guys aren't necessarily the brightest bulbs in the batch. Let me know if he changes position.

What if he comes?

Spare me the details.

Her laughter caressed his mind, took away the stink of death, the danger of his next kill. Jake shifted back to human, grabbed the deadly weapon and slowly worked his away round the far side of the cabin.

Shannon wasn't kidding. The guy really was jacking off. He had his dick wrapped in his fist and was doing a slow, thorough job on himself when Jake got close enough to draw a bead on him.

There was something abhorrent about shooting a guy in the back before he came. Jake settled himself against a piling beneath the deck, checked for spiders, and fixed the guy in his crosshairs.

He heard a creak in the floor just over his head around the same time the one he was watching began to groan.

The front door squeaked on its hinges. A strange voice whispered loudly, "What's going on out there?"

The guy jerking off didn't slow his strokes and he was obviously too close to shooting his load to talk. Jake heard the one above him say something to someone else in the house. That answered one of his questions. There were at least two of them inside.

Jake set the gun down and moved forward, quickly, silently on bare feet. He wrapped his forearm around the man's neck just as he reached climax. A twist and a snap and the man slumped in Jake's grasp ... dying with a groan of satisfaction on his lips and his ejaculate all over the piling in front of him.

Jake carefully placed the man's body against the wall and moved to a spot beside the steps, partially hidden beneath the deck. He glanced toward the forest but saw no sign of Shannon.

He breathed a sigh of relief.

Jake? Are you okay?

Yeah. Two down, two to go. Stay hidden.

Be careful. I don't want you hurt.

I don't want me hurt, either, Shannon? I love you.

The minute the thought left his mind, Jake wished he could pull it back. Damn, she'd think he just said that to, to ... what?

He heard a sound behind him, a whisper of movement. Twisting, Jake flung his body to one side, barely escaping the bullet that whizzed by his ear. Tucking and rolling, he fought the instinct to become Chanku. The wolf was no match against two assailants.

Another shot, but this one was close. Dirt spattered beside him. He ducked behind the front steps and reached for the weapon a dead man didn't need.

Footsteps pounded on the stairs above him. A shadow skirted away, hidden beneath the deck. Jake's fingers closed around the gun lying beside the body.

"Hold it. Drop the gun!"

Too late. The man on the stairs had Jake in his sights. The suit under the house held his weapon pointed directly at Jake's heart. Slowly he released his grip on the butt of the dead man's gun.

Shannon. Stay hidden. They've got me. I'll need to get loose later. Don't let them find you.

He waited for her reply. There was no answer.

Holding his hands away from his naked body, Jake slowly crawled out from under his house.

They could have been cloned, the two of them, so much alike Jake had trouble telling them apart. It was as much the attitude and the suits as their appearance. They showed no emotion, no reaction to finding a naked man under the house. There wasn't even a sense of sadness over their two associates lying dead outside.

The one from the steps grabbed Jake by the shoulder and slammed him up against the side of the house, twisting his right arm high between his shoulder blades. The other man came crawling out from under the deck, brushing cobwebs and dust off his dark suit. Neither one said a word.

Jake felt the cold steel of handcuffs around his wrists. He grunted when the one holding him twisted his arm and shoved him into a chair on the deck.

He felt a cold fury, that these men would desecrate the sanctity of this beautiful place. The one spot where he'd felt safe with Shannon.

Where the hell was she?

Jake kept his head down, his chin almost touching his chest. He waited, wondering what they would say, what their plan was.

Finally, the one who'd caught him jerked his head toward the house. "Call the boss. Let him know we got one. The bitch should show up before long. I hear they don't like to be separated."

Jake bit his lip. No way would he implicate Shannon. He heard the second man walk into his house. Jake felt the anger build, to think they'd made themselves at home here. This was his land, his home.

His woman. *Shannon, where are you? Don't come near. They've got me handcuffed and they're waiting for you.*

Good, because I'm coming.

No!

Jake had no time to act. The man guarding him had even less. The wolf leapt over the railing, jaws spread wide, ears flat to her head. There was no hesitation, no fear in her attack. She caught him by the back of the neck, swung her wolven body to the right and snapped his spine.

He didn't have time to make more than a gurgling cry, cut off almost before it escaped.

His body dropped, hard, trapping the she-wolf with its weight. She scrabbled, her sharp claws raking against the wooden deck, pulling herself free.

Jake didn't hesitate. He shifted, thankful the cuffs were loose enough to pull his paws free, and followed Shannon into the house. Questions—and answers—would come later.

The suit inside whirled around the moment the wolves entered the room. He didn't even hesitate. He set the phone back in its cradle and carefully laid his weapon on the floor. Then he stood up and held his hands over his head.

Jake snarled. His hackles rose, his ears went flat against his skull and he crouched, preparing to spring. The bitch moved her body just as fast, blocking his attack. She snarled at the man as well, then turned and stared directly into Jake's eyes.

No way in hell could he look away. Not when she was there, totally Chanku, his alpha bitch giving him a silent, yet powerful command.

Don't kill. She took a deep breath and nudged Jake with her shoulder. There was a loud roaring in his ears when she sat back on her haunches and turned her attention back to the man standing before them, hands over his head, eyes wary.

Can't you tell? He's one of us.

Heart pounding, Jake turned to look closely at the agent. Tall, handsome by anyone's standards, he studied Jake with open fascination through brilliant amber eyes. Jake watched the man's throat constrict as he swallowed, smelled his fear, sensed his overwhelming curiosity.

Could it be? Jake glanced at the she-wolf who shouldn't be, then back at the man who had tried to kill him, and shook his wolven head in a very human gesture.

The agent seemed to relax. He reached behind him, felt for the edge of a kitchen chair, and sat down. Hard. "I hope you don't mind, but it's that or fall on my ass."

He talked to them as if he knew. Jake snarled, the growl low in his throat. The agent held up his hand.

"I know. You don't exist. For what it's worth, I don't agree with Bosworth's plan. The whole idea of a breeding farm disgusts me." He held up the phone. "I just called him. His wife answered. Bosworth is dead. He had a stroke yesterday morning . . . on his front porch of all places."

Jake and Shannon sat perfectly still. Jake sensed Shannon's excitement, the newness of her shift, the thrill she felt in her wolven body, but her thoughts were blocked, and her eyes on the man in front of them.

Bosworth was dead. Ulrich had flown to DC Sunday night. There had to be a connection. This man, however, was a complication. Killing him would have been much easier, but not if he really were Chanku. Jake stood up and moved closer.

The man held perfectly still. Jake sniffed his ankles, his hands, moved around behind him and watched him from the back. There was a sense of familiarity, of brotherhood. How the hell had Shannon recognized it?

How did you know?

When he was stalking you, I heard his thoughts. He was fascinated, reminded of dreams he's had all his life.

Dreams of wolves, dreams of running through the forest, of hunting in a pack. He requested this assignment after hearing rumors of our existence, but he's not part of the regular team.

How did you change?

Shannon turned and stared at Jake for a long moment. *The same way you do. I am Chanku.*

He wanted to be angry. Wanted to tell her she was presumptuous and a pain in the ass. He couldn't. She'd saved his life. He loved her. Seeing her now, her dark coat gleaming with reddish fire, her green eyes boring into him, Jake knew there was nothing he would not do for this woman, this she-wolf. Already she'd stood beside him in battle. She'd killed for him. There was no doubt in Jake's mind . . . this woman was his.

Shannon wished her heart would stop racing, wished she could concentrate on the prisoner waiting patiently in the kitchen chair while she and Jake worked out their differences, but the whole incident had taken on the feel of a very graphic yet surrealistic dream.

Jake had been in trouble. She'd felt helpless. Then the thoughts of the agent stalking him had intruded on her mind and she'd known she had to intervene. The frustration had exploded inside, Shannon's basic instincts had overruled everything her conscious mind said was impossible. Without plan or hesitation, her body had shifted. From one heartbeat to another Shannon's entire sense of self had undergone a permanent change.

She glanced at Jake, sensed his momentary indecision, then the point where he realized there was a step he needed to take, one from which he couldn't retreat.

He shifted. Right in front of the enemy, Jake was suddenly a six-foot five-inch naked male.

Rather than fly into a panic, a slow smile spread across the agent's face. He held out his hand, shook Jake's. "I'm

Quinn. Baylor Quinn. Bay to my friends. You must be Jacob Trent."

There was no matching smile from Jake, only a guarded, wary acceptance. "Yeah. I'm Jake. Well, Bay . . . maybe you can tell me. What the fuck is going on here?"

PART THREE

Detour

Chapter 10

"I heard rumors about Bosworth's plan. People on the hill figured he was nuts but I've always had this weird fascination with wolves. I've dreamed about turning into a wolf for years, so it didn't seem all that far fetched to me, the concept of shapeshifters. I volunteered for the duty. This was my first assignment."

Shannon handed a cup of coffee to Baylor and another to Jake before pouring one for herself. Bay's black suit coat was draped over the back of his chair, his tie tucked into the pocket. He'd rolled up his shirt sleeves when he helped Jake load the bodies of the three agents in their car. Now he looked totally at ease in perfectly fitted black slacks.

Jake had pulled on a pair of jeans. With his chest muscles gleaming in the late morning sunlight, his tousled, sun-streaked hair falling over his forehead and his amber eyes narrowed suspiciously as he watched Baylor, Shannon thought he looked feral, primitive, like the powerful beast she knew him to be.

She'd shifted in the bedroom, unwilling to show herself naked in front of a stranger. Now, dressed in her comfortable sweats, she sat in the sun-drenched kitchen with two breathtakingly gorgeous men. It was difficult to believe that only a short time ago, she'd shifted and become a wolf.

That she'd killed a man.

The deaths hadn't even fazed the men, but then, it appeared Jake had been right when he said that killing was the nature of the beast. It had to be. How else could Shannon have so easily taken a life? Jake was Chanku. So was Baylor Quinn—or he would be, after he received the supplement.

Shannon was absolutely certain of his heritage. She sensed a kindred spirit, heard the unspoken questions roiling in his mind. Admired his patience. Like a wary predator, he waited for the answers he knew would be forthcoming.

Would Jake share the supplement with another man, a potential rival? Already, there was obvious posturing going on, a sense that, while Jake was pleased to have found another of their breed, he wasn't all that thrilled with the fact Baylor was another male, and quite obviously alpha.

Did Jake see Bay as a threat for her affection? Shannon hadn't even though of that aspect of the situation until now. She'd been more concerned about what to do with the three bodies out in the car than the fact Baylor Quinn might be a potential mate.

"What, exactly, was Bosworth's plan?" Shannon sipped at her coffee and studied Bay over the rim of her cup. He was definitely handsome. Almost as tall as Jake, every bit as broad shouldered, he wore his dark hair cropped close to his skull. Bay glanced at Jake, then answered Shannon.

"A breeding farm. He figured out the females carry the gene for shifting. He wanted to capture as many as he could and harvest their eggs. I heard there's actually a facility set up somewhere in California, but I've never seen it. He planned on hiring surrogate mothers, using carefully selected men as sperm donors and essentially breeding his own militia. What he intended to do with them, I have no idea."

"That's disgusting." Shannon slowly set her coffee down. "It sounds like something out of the Third Reich. How could you possibly want to be a part of—"

Baylor held up his hand. "I didn't know of his plans until this trip, which I already said, by the way, was my first assignment with the group. Joe, the guy Jake took out under the steps, was another substitute . . . what a jerk." Baylor shook his head and turned toward Jake. "We were filling in for the two guys you roughed up when you rescued Shannon. Believe me, the only reason I'm here is that I'd heard Bosworth had something going on with shapeshifters. The minute I heard about it, I had to get involved."

Shannon turned to Jake. *His mind is open. He's telling the truth.*

I know. Jake's eyes flashed. *You're awfully good at this for someone who decided not to take her medicine.*

Shannon grinned at Jake, then turned back to the agent. "I imagine you have a lot of questions."

Baylor took a deep breath and nodded. "You have no idea. For the longest time, I've thought I was losing my mind. I don't even know where to begin."

Jake glanced at Shannon, then stood up. "I think we need to begin with disposing of the car and its contents before someone comes looking for them. Even with Bosworth out of the picture, we don't know if there's anyone else on our trail. Four government agents don't just disappear. Do they have families?"

Baylor turned to Jake. "Only unmarried guys were considered for the assignment. Those three were all loners. I don't think anyone besides Bosworth and his original four agents had any information at all about you guys. Two of the originals died here. Like I said, the third was a substitute and probably knew less than me. With any luck, it ends here, unless, of course, the other two, the ones who kidnapped Shannon, saw you shift."

Jake shook his head. "They saw a wolf come out of the

shadows, but neither man saw me shift. They were unconscious when I shifted back." He stood up. "C'mon, Quinn. If you're with us?"

Baylor nodded and rose to his feet.

Shannon followed the two of them to the door. "What do you plan to do?"

"There's an abandoned granite quarry about ten miles from here. It's flooded, but the water is so polluted no one goes out there. These fellas are going to have a little accident and go over the edge. They've all died of broken necks, something consistent with a crash. No bullet wounds. We'll have to hope they aren't found, but even if they are, there's nothing to tie them to this location. We checked the bodies and the vehicle. No maps, notes . . . nothing to incriminate us. Quinn, put your gloves on. You take the car and follow me." Jake leaned over and kissed Shannon.

She wrapped her arms around his neck and held him close. *I don't want you to leave. There's so much we have to talk about.*

I know, baby. I'll be back in about an hour. Lock the doors, just in case. Call Luc. His number's on my cell phone. Tell him what's happened. Oh, yeah . . . one other thing. Jake slowly disentangled her arms from around his neck, then stared into Shannon's eyes with ferocious intensity. *You might ask him to send an extra jar of the supplement with Mik and AJ.*

Shannon clicked the phone off and wished she could do the same with her brain. She felt as if her thoughts were tangled as a skein of yarn in a basket full of kittens. She could definitely see what Tia found attractive about Lucien Stone, though. Calm and levelheaded, he'd listened patiently through her entire story. When she'd told him of her shift and the kill she'd made, he'd complimented her on her quick thinking that had saved Jake. He'd reassured her she'd done what she had to do, what her nature demanded. It didn't totally remove her guilt over taking a life, but did help Shannon accept what she'd done.

Tia had gotten on the phone for just a few moments, long enough to tell Shannon how happy she was to finally know why the two of them had been so close for so long.

They were one and the same. Not just Murphy and Mason, the M&M girls—Shannon had laughed at the reminder of the silly nickname they'd given themselves—but two powerful alpha bitches within a pack of even stronger men.

She still found it hard to believe. Putting the phone aside, Shannon stood up and walked into the bedroom. Facing the large mirror on the closet door, she saw the same woman who had looked back at her last night.

Only she wasn't the same. She would never be the same again. Watching her reflection, Shannon stripped off her sweats. Then, her eyes focused on the woman in the mirror, she shifted.

Baylor helped Jake wipe down the interior of the sedan. They placed the three bodies inside with seatbelts tightly fastened. Wearing his leather motorcycle gloves, Jake reached through the open window, turned the ignition on, put the gearshift in drive and stepped away from the vehicle.

Parked as it was, high on the sloping edge of the abandoned quarry, the car rolled forward easily. It tipped slowly off the precipice, flipped over and landed in the dark water upside down. Within a few seconds, the only sign of its existence was the pattern of bubbles rising to the surface.

Jake turned to study Baylor for a moment. Bay stared solemnly at the water until the bubbles ceased, then glanced up at Jake. "They weren't evil men, but they saw nothing wrong with imprisoning any shapeshifters they could capture. They saw you—us—as less than human."

Jake nodded. He wanted to say, "Not less than human.

More than human." God, he hoped Shannon knew what she was talking about! Jake was almost positive, but the risk was so great. If it turned out Baylor Quinn wasn't Chanku, that he and Shannon had been wrong, the man would have to die. He knew too much.

That would be hard. Real hard to live with. So far, Jake liked what he was beginning to know of Bay.

Still, Jake didn't know enough. There were, however, always ways to learn more. He tilted his head and studied Baylor out of the corner of his eye. "Are you bisexual?"

"What? Why would you ask that?" Baylor took a step back and stared at Jake.

"Just answer the question."

"I'm not gay."

"I didn't ask if you were gay. I asked if you were bisexual. Have you had sex with men before? With more than one person at a time, man or woman or both? Is the need for sex as much compulsion as desire?" Jake closed the distance between them and wrapped his fingers around Baylor's forearm. "These are not frivolous or intrusive questions. Your answer will actually tell me something very important about you."

Bay nodded, but his skin flushed a deep red. He looked away, out over the still waters of the quarry. "Yeah. All of the above."

Jake laughed. He remembered the morning after his first night with Luc, how embarrassed he'd felt over some of the things the two of them had done. How Luc had put him at ease. "It's okay, Quinn. So have I. So has Shannon. It's the nature of the beast. You shouldn't feel any shame for staying true to your nature."

"Sometimes the need can be so strong . . ." Baylor's words tapered off on a sigh.

"I know." Jake wrapped an arm around Bay's neck and pulled him into an embrace. At the same time, he ran his other hand over Bay's zipper. He cupped Bay's sizable package in the palm of his hand, felt the solid length of Bay's cock grow beneath the heat from his fingers.

Baylor groaned and thrust his hips forward, inviting Jake's touch. Jake rubbed Bay's growing erection through his slacks, traced Bay's heat and length as the man's cock stretched down the left leg of his slacks. Jake stroked slowly up and down, then ran his fingers over the softer sac behind Baylor's cock. He made one last pass along Bay's solid shaft, then stepped back and took a long, steadying breath.

Jake's hand tingled from the contact. His own cock throbbed within the confines of his tight jeans, pressing solidly against the metal zipper. It took him a minute to control his breath, and his voice sounded unnaturally husky when he spoke.

"The rules are different in our world, Quinn. Shannon's mine, but if she invites you to share our bed, or even hers alone, you'll be welcome and I'll not interfere. I won't necessarily like it one bit, but the decision will be entirely up to her."

Bay let out a long, deep, shuddering breath, and nodded. His gaze never left Jake's. His pupils were dark pits circled by amber fire.

Jake stuck his hands in his back pockets and rocked back on his heels. He gazed out over the still waters of the quarry and thought of the car they'd just dumped, the men's lives ended. "Will you be missed when someone realizes these guys aren't coming back?"

Baylor shook his head and rolled his shoulders, as if putting himself past the brief incident with Jake. "I was a last-minute replacement, handled by Bosworth himself. I'd been working on getting an assignment to his office once I heard about his plans. It so happened he needed an extra body the first day I showed up to work."

Jake thought about Bay's words. "If you heard of Bosworth's plans, others might have as well."

Bay nodded. "I've thought of that. It's hard to say. Most people thought the man had a screw loose. They didn't pay much attention to him."

"You're kidding?" Jake shook his head. "He was the damned Secretary of Homeland Security."

"Go figure." Bay's laugh lacked humor.

Jake studied him for a long moment. There was no sense of subterfuge. Baylor Quinn looked him square in the eye, his mind open and honest. In spite of himself, Jake realized he liked the guy. A lot. Not only liked him, wanted him. His cock, engorged from the brief episode of touching Bay, twitched, and his balls drew up tight between his legs. Immediately he thought of Shannon.

Jake imagined Shannon kneeling in front of Quinn, slowly unzipping his slacks, lifting the big man's cock out of his pants and testing the weight of his balls in the palm of her hand. Then she'd lean forward, maybe lick the smooth crown, caress his testicles, then work his full length down her throat while Jake slipped into her wet and ready sex from behind. She'd be ready for him. Shannon was always ready, her vulva wet and swollen with desire, the lubricating juices intoxicating, an aphrodisiac all on their own.

Jake's breath caught in his throat as the visual took shape in his mind. He licked his lips, then blinked, suddenly aware his jeans were much too tight and Baylor was looking at him strangely. Jake abruptly turned away from the man and the dark quarry and walked back down the road to the spot where he'd parked the motorcycle. Baylor followed quietly behind him.

They took it slow going back to the house, following narrow country roads that twisted and curved through deep forest and sere meadows. The afternoon had cooled until a bare hint of winter chilled the air. Jake wore his leather coat but Bay merely had his white dress shirt and slacks. Not ideal clothing for riding a motorcycle through Maine in the fall.

Still, Jake was intensely aware of the man so close behind him, of the heat from Bay's body, the taut line of his thighs touching Jake's. Aware and aroused.

Shannon waited on the porch, her feet propped up on the deck railing, a glass of wine in her hand. She stood up to greet them as the men wheeled into the parking spot just beneath the end of the deck.

"Everything okay?" Shannon leaned over the railing. The tops of her full breasts spilled out over her cotton tank, her taut nipples poked against the light fabric. Jake's mouth went dry and the rush of need shooting through him was stronger than anything he'd felt. He glanced back at Bay and realized the man's eyes were practically glued to the cleavage Shannon exposed.

Jake tamped down the instant surge of jealousy, the sense of ownership. He felt hackles rising along his spine, impossible as a human, but all too much a part of the wolf.

Still, the thought of Baylor Quinn getting turned on by the woman he loved made Jake even hotter. It truly was the nature of the beast, but he'd had so little contact with a Chanku female, he had no idea what it would be like, feeling both jealousy and desire, possession and intrigue over the idea of sharing her with another man.

Jake nodded at Shannon. "Everything went fine. We need to check this location carefully, make sure there's nothing that will tie us to any of them." Jake turned and stared at Baylor for a moment. "Of course, I have no idea how to explain you."

Bay laughed and slowly dragged his gaze away from Shannon. "I wasn't with them. Not officially, anyway. Neither was the other temp. This whole operation, from what I can figure out, was totally Bosworth's idea. On paper, anyone who worked for him was listed as personal protection. Bosworth was totally paranoid. It may raise eyebrows that four men disappeared at the same time as the Homeland Security Secretary, but all of us will be considered expendable casualties."

He looked away, out toward the forest, and when he spoke again, Baylor's voice had a rough edge to it. "It's nothing new. That's all I've ever been. Expendable." He rolled his shoulders, as if shaking off a bad memory.

"What's your family like?"

Bay laughed, but the sound held little humor. "One word? Dysfunctional. I can't really think of a better term. My father's in prison for murdering our mother when he caught her screwing the postman. The postman didn't survive Daddy's little temper tantrum, either. My sisters are both totally messed up. One of them lives under a bridge in Tampa, last I heard. The other one got pregnant and married at seventeen, then she miscarried. She's divorced now, living somewhere down in New Mexico. I lost contact with them after the trial about ten years ago."

Jake turned and stared at Shannon. Did she know enough about Chanku to understand the implications of what Baylor just said?

From the smile on her face, she must. Two sisters. Women who carried the Chanku genes. Women they might be able to find, with Baylor's help.

Dysfunctional or not, they would already be Shannon's sisters of the heart.

Jake grilled steaks for dinner, then went outside to tinker with his motorcycle. Baylor helped Shannon clean up the kitchen. He was a comfortable man to work with, quiet and unassuming, yet with a solid strength Shannon admired. He'd taken his first pill with dinner, swallowing it down without hesitation.

Now he appeared thoughtful, somewhat introspective.

Did he have any idea how his life would change?

They'd all been quiet at dinner. Each of them had gone through a life-altering experience today. Small talk had been all any of them seemed capable of. Now Shannon took comfort in the simple, familiar chore of doing the dishes.

"Here, Bay. Can you reach?" Shannon handed him the last dried platter. Baylor slipped it onto the top shelf with ease.

Jake had given him a pair of old sweatpants to wear. The evening had grown cooler, so he'd slipped his white T-shirt on, but his feet were still bare.

Shannon found herself glancing down at his feet, attracted by their long, narrow shape, the dark dusting of hair across the tops. In a very few days, that same foot would become a paw. Could he possibly understand?

Jake walked into the kitchen, went straight to the sink and began scrubbing grease off his hands. "Bay, will you be okay here by yourself? Shannon, are you up for a run?"

Shannon nodded as Baylor carefully folded the damp towel and hung it over the edge of the kitchen counter.

He studied both of them out of his strangely familiar amber eyes. "You're shifting? You'll run tonight?"

"Yep." Jake dried his hands, then cupped his palms over Shannon's shoulders. Their solid warmth eased the nervousness that had been slowly building in her since they'd finished dinner. She leaned back and kissed his chin, rubbing her lips over the dark shadow of a day's growth of beard.

"It will be my first time. I'd never shifted before today. I've only run through the forest in my dreams." She giggled. "Uh, and while you guys were gone today."

Jake laughed. "I wondered if you'd gone out on your own."

Baylor rubbed his palm over his short-cropped hair. "I've run in my dreams as well. Dreams so clear I can smell the forest, hear the sounds of live things moving through the night. I can't believe that in just a few more days . . ." He blinked, seemed to catch hold of his emotions and grinned at Jake. "Yeah, to answer your question, I'll be fine. Jealous as hell that I can't join you, yet. But, I'll be fine."

Shannon stretched up on her toes and kissed Baylor on the mouth. Surprised at first, he slowly raised his hands, rested them lightly on her shoulders and kissed her back with enthusiasm. His tongue easily found the seam between her lips, parted them and entered the damp interior of Shannon's mouth. She touched his tongue with hers, memorized his scent and taste in one arousing kiss, then slowly ended it.

Jake had explained the polyamorous relationships among Chanku, but until her shift today, Shannon hadn't truly understood. So much had finally come together in her mind, so many confusing feelings she'd had about relationships finally made sense. Shannon felt Jake stiffen behind her, but she had to do this. Had to remind Jake of who and what they were.

What Baylor Quinn was, as well. One of them. A brother of the heart. Soon to be a lover.

Chanku.

Baylor stepped back. He looked shaken, as if surprised at the depth of his response to Shannon's kiss, at the lack of response from Jake. Shannon watched as he quickly gathered himself, raised his head and looked directly at Jake. There was no sense of challenge. Merely curiosity and, if she wasn't mistaken, desire.

For Jake as well as herself.

When Shannon turned around, Jake was slowly unbuttoning his shirt. Watching him bare his chest as he peeled the soft flannel over his shoulders made her womb throb and her pussy clench in anticipation. Shannon slipped from between the two men and sat down on the couch.

She removed her shoes, almost preternaturally aware of Baylor's eyes watching her, of his hands clenched at his sides.

The tension in the room was a living thing, connecting each of them in a lush wave of desire, arousal so intense, so powerful, it made Shannon pause, take a deep breath, regroup.

She swallowed, found control and quickly tugged her sweatshirt over her head, then shoved her pants down over her hips and stepped out of them before she had time to think of her audience.

She hadn't worn a bra or panties. She'd never been particularly modest, but standing here naked in front of Jacob Trent and Baylor Quinn, the room practically snapping with the combined need of both men, made her nipples pucker into tight little beads even as a dark red flush spread across her chest.

Feeling terribly self-conscious, Shannon stood very still, posing without intending to. Her nipples ached, they were so tightly beaded. Her pussy throbbed and she was aware of a thick stream of moisture about to trickle along her inner thigh.

Both men stared, lips parted, eyes narrowed and nostrils flared, focusing only on Shannon. She wondered if they were even aware of one another, so intently did they watch her. Shaking herself, she took a deep breath and hoped she could remember how to shift.

She saw herself as wolf, imagined the process of changing from human to Chanku, blinked and immediately felt her world change. She found herself looking up at Baylor and Jake. Both of them grinning, standing there staring at her now as if she'd just done something absolutely marvelous.

Well, hadn't she? Shannon lifted one big paw and studied her nails. They were long and curved and black as obsidian. Probably just as sharp, too.

She turned and glanced along her side, from the stiff hair partially raised along her shoulder, to the softer fur blending into her hip and belly. Black in the lantern light, but when she moved, the fur glowed with red highlights.

Shannon decided she really loved the color, the texture, the fine pelt that covered this wolven body. Still a redhead, even on four legs.

She was so wound up, so excited by her shift, she wanted to laugh. There was no mechanism for laughter in this furry body, so Shannon leapt into the air and yipped, three sharp barks that made both Jake and Baylor burst into laughter.

It would have to do. She turned toward the door, glanced back over her shoulder. Waved her tail in invitation. Jake turned almost helplessly toward Baylor, then in three long strides reached the front door. He yanked it open.

"We'll be back in a couple hours. Stay alert. There are still two agents out there."

Baylor nodded. Shannon thought he looked sad, as if he'd been told to stay back while everyone else had fun. Which, of course, was exactly what was happening.

Jake stripped off the rest of his clothes and shifted. He turned at once toward Shannon, his eyes bright, glimmering like a banked fire in the low light. Then he turned and raced out the front door, crossed the deck in a single bound, leapt over the railing on the deck to land lightly on the ground below. Shannon followed without hesitation.

Jake took off at a steady lope, heading directly toward the dark forest. Shannon followed, tail high, legs stretching out in long strides to keep up with her mate. With Jake.

They were not yet a bonded pair. She thought of him as her mate. Already that link was formed in her mind, but was she ready for a permanent bond? If they mated tonight as Jake expected, if he took her beneath the starry sky with the deep forest all around, took her as a wolf mates his bitch, she would be his forever.

Not yet. This body was too new, this life too changed, her emotions too highly charged. She was no longer Shannon Murphy of Boston, no longer the woman who searched night after night for something or someone to bring meaning to her life.

She'd found that meaning. Found the life she was meant to live. Yes, it would eventually include Jake. Now, beyond her wildest dreams, it could also include children.

But not yet. Not tonight. Tonight she intended to run, to hunt, to learn what this perfect four-legged body could do. If she made love to Jake in the forest, it would be as a woman, lying with her man in the tall grass.

The bitch would wait to take her mate. Tonight she was free. The dreams, so vivid, so much a part of her existence, were nothing compared to the reality of racing through the cool forest, the soft thud of her paws hitting the hard-packed trail, splashing through small streams.

The scents had a perfume all their own. The combination of crushed grass, damp earth, small creatures and rotting leaves acted like an aphrodisiac, exciting her senses, thrilling her mind and heart. Skidding to a stop, Shannon breathed deeply of the clean forest air, so filled with joy, with the excitement of discovery, she couldn't contain herself.

She threw her head back and howled. Her cry echoed in the darkness that was no longer truly dark when viewed through wolven eyes. Small creatures scattered, the flap of wings told Shannon she'd startled an owl from its perch. How could she know? What instincts identified each sound and scent?

Chanku. The power inherent in the beast. The knowledge. Shannon's heart pounded with the joy of self-discovery. She howled again, head back, muzzle pointed to the sky, ears laid back along her skull.

Until now, she'd always thought the sound of a wolf howling in the forest was a mournful noise, a lonely sound.

Tonight she knew differently. Tonight Shannon tasted the joy of her new life, the freedom to run as she was meant to, the strength to race the wind, to run beside her chosen one.

Jake's answering howl drew her onward.

Had it only been three days? How could her world have changed so completely in so little time?

She followed his scent, her Chanku instincts overriding her human disbelief. Shannon Murphy was not the outdoors type. She liked her food served on fine china with utensils properly placed to the side. She wanted her trails covered in concrete, her exercise on a nice, clean machine down at the gym.

Now she followed the scent of her lover though the Maine woods, followed Jake with total confidence, as if a visible line glowed through the woods. Racing on four legs, unafraid of the darkness, the strange territory, the sound of other creatures nearby, she followed her Chanku senses down a narrow trail through the darkest hour.

Cutting between the ghostly white trunks of birch trees, leaping over fallen logs and landing with unerring accuracy, Shannon cut through a silent meadow and found Jake on the far side.

He was absolutely beautiful. Standing strong and proud, he waited for her. Waited for Shannon, expecting, she knew, to take her as his mate.

She halted just a few feet from him, alert, aware. Shifted. Watched Jake as he studied her, as his eyes narrowed.

Why? I don't understand. He followed his question with a growl.

"I'm not ready. Three days is not enough time to commit myself to you forever. I need to be sure."

There. She'd done it. Finally told him how she felt.

Jake snarled again. Louder this time. His ears laid back against his broad skull and he bared his teeth. *Is it Baylor? Do you think he would make a better mate?*

Shannon laughed aloud. "No, Jake. It's not about Baylor. It's not about you. It's all about me. Selfish as this may sound, I need more time to make a decision that will affect me for a lifetime. You made the decision to change my life when you gave me the supplement without telling me what it really was. From now on, I want control of what I do with that life."

Jake shifted. He stepped close and drew Shannon into his arms. She wrapped her arms around his waist and rested her forehead against his chest. His cock brushed her belly, a hot brand against her flesh.

"You're right. I'm sorry for taking the decision away from you. Will you ever forgive me?"

Shannon felt Jake's lips press against the top of her head.

"I have forgiven you." She raised her chin so that she could look at him. Already Jake was so dear to her, so important that it was hard to remember life before him.

"Because of you, I finally feel complete. You are my one, true mate, in all but the final act. It will happen with you and no other, but not yet. You're going to have to trust me."

She felt his chest expand as he took a deep breath, let it out. His arms tightened around her waist, his cock swelled even larger against her belly. When Jake leaned over to kiss her, Shannon was already raising her head, parting her lips to meet his.

Chapter 11

Trust. It all came down to trust. In that one word, Jake realized how right Shannon was to wait. He didn't know her well enough to trust her. He believed he could trust her, wanted to, but didn't really know. Didn't know much at all about Shannon Murphy, other than the fact he wanted her.

She was beautiful . . . brave, strong and fearless. She had killed for him. Risked her own life to save his. Still, he had no idea what made her laugh. Didn't know what colors she liked, what music she listened to.

He knew what turned her on, but not what kept her spirit alight. There'd been no courtship, no time spent talking far into the night, discovering one another.

Unfortunately, Jake now understood all too well what Lucien Stone had felt when Tia invited the entire pack to her bed before she and Luc mated.

Would he have the strength to stand back and give Shannon that freedom? Another thought intruded. An unwelcome thought. Hell, it wasn't his place to *give* Shannon anything. He would have to learn to accept her decisions.

It wasn't going to be easy.

Jake leaned down and caught Shannon's mouth with

his, intending gentleness. He realized immediately that wasn't what she wanted.

She raised up on her toes and caught the sides of his head in her palms, holding him still as her mouth opened to receive his thrusting tongue. Jake groaned. Her mouth was hot and sweet, her tongue sliding along his, teasing the roof of his mouth. Her fingers slipped through his hair and one long leg wrapped around his waist.

Her pussy pressed tightly against his belly, hot and wet and tantalizing him with her rich scent. He grabbed her taut buttock with one hand, pressing her even closer, helping her ride against the length of his erection.

Shannon whimpered against his mouth. He felt her body shudder and realized she'd climaxed merely from the combination of their kiss and the friction of their bodies. Slowly Jake lowered her to the thick grass, wishing with all his heart he could take her in their wolven form.

Not tonight. Nor would he pressure Shannon for what she wasn't ready to give. Trust. He would have to trust her.

She lay in the grass, legs spread wide, one arm flung loosely over her eyes. Jake knelt between her thighs and rubbed his hands along her legs, just to the juncture where her pussy swelled beneath his touch. Even in the faint glow of the waning moon, he was able to see the glistening moisture between her legs. Her scent was intoxicating, drawing him closer.

He lifted her, his palms gripping her firm cheeks, lifted her high enough to feast comfortably on her slick folds. He swept his tongue into her slit, avoiding contact with her clitoris, teasing and nipping at the swollen lips, dipping his tongue deep inside to lick and stroke the sensitive walls of her vagina.

Shannon bucked against his mouth. Her hands tangled in his long hair and held him close. He stroked his tongue from her perineum to her clit, over and over until she cried out with each gentle slide. When he puckered his lips around the hard nub of her clit and worked it with his tongue, she bowed her back, curled against his mouth and screamed.

He felt her climax with his lips, tasted the gush of fluid, arched his back as her heels dug into his shoulders. Unwilling to quit, Jake continued licking and sucking, bringing her to another peak.

He slipped his finger between her cheeks and found the tightly puckered opening of her anus, already slick with her fluids. He gently rubbed, teasing the taut muscle, then pressed and gained entrance as Shannon whimpered and cried. Her legs had gone limp, her body still shuddered but he brought her to life once more. Licking softly now, working his tongue over her labia and clitoris in time with the in-and-out thrust of first one finger, then two, he slowly eased Shannon once more into orgasm.

Slipping his fingers free of her tight warmth, Jake moved forward on his knees, grabbed his aching cock in one hand and directed it toward Shannon's spasming sex. Her hot pussy clenched him like a satin fist, holding him tightly as he slipped deep inside. Her muscles tightened even more as he slowly withdrew.

Wrapping Shannon's legs around his waist, Jake found his own rhythm, going deep, reaching all the way to the hard mouth of her womb, then slowly withdrawing to the point where he almost left her warmth.

Almost, but not quite.

Over and over again, driving deep and hard, burying himself until his balls rested against her firm ass, until his entire cock was clenched within her silken vise. Shannon whimpered with each thrust, lifted her hips to meet him, stroked his back, his hair, finally dropped her hands to her own breasts and plucked at the engorged nipples.

The sight of her touching herself, the vision of her fingers pinching and twisting her puckered nipples, almost took Jake over the edge.

"I love you. Shannon. Hear me out. Believe me. I love you!" He buried himself deep, felt the tight grasp of her vaginal walls holding him, milking his seed, squeezing the entire length of his cock in her wet heat.

His climax came hard and fast, almost painful in its intensity. Jake arched his back, felt the hot coil of semen all the way from his balls to the end of his cock. Shannon grunted with his final thrust, spreading her legs even wider to take all of him.

Wrapping her arms around his back, holding him close as he pumped his seed deep inside her waiting body, Shannon climaxed once more. Her scream this time was a harsh cry of exhaustion as much as completion. Jake lowered himself to lie atop her for a moment, savoring the warmth of her body, the soft swell of her breasts against his chest.

Then, well aware of his weight, he rolled to one side. His cock slipped free and she whimpered in denial, a soft sound as if she'd been abandoned. Jake leaned over and kissed her, a soft and gentle connection.

He tasted salt. Reached up and touched her cheeks with his fingertips and realized she was crying. His heart suddenly stuttered. "Sweetheart? Are you okay? Did I hurt you?"

She shook her head, as if words were beyond her. *No. My God, Jake. No. That was amazing. Beautiful. Overwhelming. I do love you. I love you very much. Do you understand, though, why I have to wait?*

I understand. I love you. I can be patient. He kissed away her tears. *That doesn't mean I have to like it.*

Shannon smiled, kissed him back, nodded. "Thank you." She ran her finger along his cheek. "Should we go back? I'm really tired."

"Okay." Jake thought of Baylor. Wondered if Shannon wanted to sleep with their new packmate tonight.

She must have been in his thoughts. Shannon shook her head. "No. Not tonight. Tonight I want to sleep beside you. Just sleep, and only you. I really am exhausted. Is that okay?"

"Definitely okay. Let's go home."

He stood up and held his hand out to Shannon. She grabbed his fingers. Her hand felt warm, the palm smooth and callus free. Jake pulled her to her feet.

This time her shift was slower, as if her fatigue affected her speed. Jake watched the metamorphosis from human to wolf and was amazed at the beauty inherent in Shannon's change. She absolutely flowed from one form to the other, as lovely a wolf as she was a woman.

Jake shifted quickly and nudged her shoulder. Shannon turned and nipped him lightly on the flank, her eyes bright with a teasing glimmer, and the two of them headed back along the trail, trotting now, a more moderate pace than earlier.

His heart felt light. Lighter than it had felt in ages. Trotting along beside his woman, Jake realized he knew more about Shannon tonight than he had just hours ago. She loved with a purity and determination that rocked his world. She might not be ready to mate, but she was already his one true mate in every other way.

He fell into line behind her, watched the sway of her brushy tail, the steady glide of her powerful legs, and realized how much his own life had changed in three short days.

Baylor waited for them on the front porch. Shannon spotted him first, sitting back in one of the big wooden chairs, a beer can dangling from his fingers. He looked lonely out there in the dark. She bounded up the steps and shifted, not even thinking of her nudity until she caught the interested gleam in his eyes.

She laughed as Jake shifted and stood beside her. "Not tonight, big boy. I'm headed to bed to sleep."

Bay flashed her a sheepish smile, then turned to Jake and shrugged his shoulders. "A guy can dream, can't he?"

Jake chuckled. "Shannon's pretty tired. It's been a long day." He kissed her cheek, his soft breath feathering across her face, then she felt his body expand as he took a deep breath. "On the other hand, I'm too wound up to sleep. Got another beer?"

Shannon sensed the spark of interest that flew from Baylor to Jake and back again. Jake's cock already stood at half mast, something Bay had to have noticed. Or not . . . he was obviously entranced by the sight of her dark nipples, tightly puckered in the chill air. Maybe he hadn't noticed Jake's interest at all.

Shannon covered her mouth with her hand and coughed, but only to hide a smile. "I'll get a beer and a warm blanket for you. Then I'm going to take a shower and get some sleep."

She headed into the kitchen and grabbed a can of beer, then tugged the heavy afghan off the couch and took it to Jake as well. He leaned over the deck railing next to Baylor, obviously unconcerned with his nudity.

Bay wore the soft sweats, but they did nothing to disguise the lean lines of his body, the strong, muscular back and broad shoulders. Shannon swallowed, already regretting her decision not to have sex with the agent tonight. From the tension she sensed between the two men, she might not have Jake in her bed, either.

Shannon handed the beer to Jake and draped the blanket over his shoulders. "I don't want you to get chilled." She leaned close and kissed him on the shoulder, running her tongue over the smooth skin, tasting just a hint of salt from their run. He turned his head and caught her mouth with his for a long, searing kiss that left her breathless, her heart racing and her pussy slick. Shannon laughed and stepped back. She waved her hand in front of her face. "Whew. My mistake. As hot as you are, chilling isn't an issue."

Moving away from Jake, Shannon turned to Baylor and kissed him lightly on the mouth. He leaned closer, his hand came up to hold her, but she stepped back out of his reach. "Good night. Both of you. I'll see you in the morning."

Jake watched Shannon walk into the house, mesmerized by the sleek line of her hips as they swayed with each step, the long indentation along her spine, the soft curve of her buttocks. He glanced to his left and, in spite of the quick flash of jealousy, chuckled. Bay had the same shell-shocked expression on his face that probably marked Jake's.

"She's something, isn't she?"

"Shit." Baylor just shook his head. "I feel like I've tumbled down Alice's rabbit hole. It's not often a drop-dead gorgeous woman kisses me, much less a naked one, in front of her man. I don't get it."

Jake took a deep breath and released it slowly, letting out some of the tension still racing through his system. "A few more days of the supplement and it'll all start to make sense. Something seems to change in our wiring. We truly are pack animals. Shannon and I aren't mated, though she's promised herself to me. Even so, she'll want you in our bed once you become Chanku. Maybe even before." Jake shrugged his shoulders, wishing there were a better explanation. "It's the way of the pack, for better or worse."

"That overwhelming sex drive, right?" Bay chuckled, but he'd turned to look at Jake rather than the direction Shannon had taken. His nostrils flared and his pupils dilated. In fact, Bay studied Jake with more than mere curiosity.

His body language screamed arousal and desire with every tight move he made.

Jake realized he liked this man more every minute they spent together, something that truly surprised him. The idea of sharing his woman with other males without a fight wasn't easy to accept, but exploring his feelings for Baylor? Now, that was different.

Baylor certainly didn't try to hide his feelings . . . or his interest. Jake turned and propped his elbows on the wooden rail. "Yeah. That overwhelming sex drive. Except what you've always thought of as a strong sex drive is nothing compared to the way you'll feel once your body finishes the change from human to Chanku. Our senses are more acute, our needs greater, the desire to satisfy them sometimes bypasses our common sense. I think that's part of the reason we tend to settle in groups. There's always a companion available."

Silence stretched between them, punctuated only by the quiet night sounds of the forest. Finally Bay's soft words, slightly hesitant, little more than a whisper, drifted over Jake. "I'm available."

Jake turned around and leaned his hip against the railing. He looked Baylor over in the dim light and once more realized how much he liked what he saw. "I was hoping you felt that way. C'mon. Your room is at the opposite end of the house. We won't disturb Shannon."

Bay followed him through the dark main room. Shannon had left a single candle burning. It flickered, casting more shadows than light. Jake picked it up and carried it with him to the bedroom.

Bay closed the door when they entered the room. He leaned back against it and watched Jake, eyes narrowed, his stance tense, expectant. Was he having second thoughts?

Jake didn't think so. He set the candle on the one long dresser in the room, shrugged out of the afghan hanging capelike over his shoulders and leaned back against the tall bedpost.

Jake folded his arms across his chest and watched the man across the room. It was Bay's turn to make the next move. Right now, he stood motionless, watching Jake. Bay's eyes glittered, their amber light shining almost green in the candlelight. Chanku green, like the eyes of a wolf. The familiarity of their color gave Jake hope.

In one, smooth motion, Bay reached down and grabbed the hem of his T-shirt, then slowly dragged it up over his muscled chest. Jake felt his mouth go dry as the perfect six-pack abs were exposed, the flat brown nipples nestled in a thick mat of dark hair, the long column of Bay's throat.

Jake's cock rose against his belly. Absentmindedly, he reached down and wrapped his fist around the base, then stroked his hot length, rolling the foreskin back and forth over the broad head. Bay held his shirt against his chest. It was obvious he saw nothing but Jake's slowly moving fist. After a long moment, Bay dropped the shirt, then slowly peeled his sweats down over his slim hips and stepped out of them.

Jake's hand stilled and his mouth went dry. Damn, the man was hung like a moose. Uncut like Jake, Bay's cock jutted straight out of a dark nest of hair, as if too heavy to rise against his belly. The crown was broad, almost black in the dim light, the foreskin stretched back behind the curve. A drop of liquid glistened beneath the dark eye at the end.

While Jake watched, his left hand slowly stroking his own cock, Bay reached down and wrapped his fist around himself. Slowly he squeezed along the length until he reached the crown, then he smeared the drop of pre-cum around the smooth head.

The two of them stood there, separated by the six foot distance between the bed and the door, each man slowly stroking himself, their gazes locked on one another.

Jake took the first step, pushing himself away from the bedpost. He moved slowly across the few steps to stand directly in front of Baylor. He reached out, covered Bay's hand with his own, followed him stroke for stroke along the length of Bay's cock.

Bay groaned and reached for Jake. He raked his fingernails lightly along the underside of Jake's erect penis, rolled his palm over the thick fluid already leaking from the end and smeared the moisture along Jake's full length. Bay stepped even closer until he could press the length of his cock alongside Jake's. He gripped both in his hands, one hand wrapped around the base of his own cock, the other holding the crown of Jake's, holding the two of them tightly together.

Jake copied Bay's moves, smearing the lubricating moisture from the crown of Bay's cock, then holding himself against Bay's erection, sliding his slick cock against the other man's, both of them tightly gripped in each other's hands. Pre-cum leaked from both, adding more moisture to the palms of their hands, the length of their cocks.

The sensation was exquisite. Jake rhythmically thrust his hips forward, more aware of the feeling of Bay's hands wrapped around him than of his own. The heat from Bay's cock was a fiery brand along his, but it wasn't enough. Not nearly enough. Jake jerked his head toward the bed. Bay nodded and released his grip on Jake.

The two of them crawled across the bed, obviously with the same thought in mind. Turning head to toe, Jake grabbed Bay's huge cock in his hands just as Bay found Jake's. Jake licked the moisture at the tip, tasting him. He bit back a moan and sucked at the small opening, wanting more of the salty, almost sour taste of Bay's, then quickly encircled the hot crown with his mouth.

Bay groaned. The sound vibrated over and around Jake's cock and he felt himself slipping deeper into the agent's hot mouth. Felt the scrape of teeth, the rough surface of Bay's tongue, the tight suction of his cheeks . . . the hard ridges across the roof of his mouth.

Groaning, Jake worked his lips around the broad head of Baylor's cock, savoring the musky, salty flavor, taking Baylor deep. Jake relaxed the muscles in his throat just as Baylor took him every bit as far down his throat.

They quickly found a rhythm, sucking hard, scraping tender flesh with their teeth, cupping testicles with strong hands, raking the sensitive flesh behind one another's balls with their fingernails.

Jake circled Bay's tight sphincter with his fingertip, stroking gently at first, teasing the puckered muscle, then pressing hard, attempting to force entrance without lubrication.

Pain, sharp, fiery pain lanced through Jake as Bay did the same to him. One thick finger roughly probed and pushed at his sensitive ass, but the pain was offset by the exquisite heat from mouth and tongue, the tight suction holding his cock.

There was none of the gentleness Jake felt when making love with Shannon, yet the sensations were arousing to the extreme, an encounter between two sexual alpha males, a carnal battle for dominance that neither man could really win, yet both could enjoy.

Jake achieved entrance first, slipping deep inside Bay's heat, first one finger, then two, stretching the tight muscle, reaching for the smooth, round gland that could take Bay over the edge.

Jake searched for Bay's thoughts but found only a jumble of sensation, a mixture of pain and pleasure without words. The man was definitely turned on! Bay's finger pressed harder against his ass. Jake grunted at the sharp pain of forced entry, then pushed back against Bay's finger, helping to ease the way. He gasped around the hard cock in his mouth when Bay added a second finger, stretching him, bringing Jake even closer to climax.

Jake did the same, pumping in and out of Baylor's ass with three fingers as he suckled the man's cock, matching the inward stroke with each deep swallow. He found Bay's prostate, massaged it, rolled the small gland beneath his fingertips.

Jake knew Bay's climax was close, felt the tension in the other man's body. He tried again to read his thoughts, but Bay's mind was closed to him. Jake reached between Bay's thighs with his free hand to cup his testicles once more, squeezing them lightly just as he applied more pressure to Baylor's ass.

Jake's timing was perfect, each movement coinciding with Bay's—as Bay's fingers went deeper inside Jake, as his hand wrapped around Jake's balls and gently squeezed, as his mouth clamped down hard on Jake's cock.

There was no warning, no time to react. Jake climaxed, shooting his seed into Bay's mouth, clamping his lips around Bay's cock to swallow the thick stream of ejaculate when Baylor climaxed at the same time.

Jake's body convulsed, stiffened. Stuffed full, surrounded, his balls drawn up tight between his legs, every muscle in his body clenched in spasm.

Jake held Bay's cock in his mouth long after his orgasm ended. Licking and sucking, bringing him down slowly. Enjoying the same courtesy from Bay, the same sweet tenderness so totally absent during coitus.

He shivered, an aftermath of pain and pleasure, of the deep, emotional connection he suddenly felt with a man who was still a stranger . . . a man who might also be a brother of his heart.

It certainly hadn't been lovemaking, not by anyone's standards. No, they'd shared the rawest form of sex. Basic man-to-man pleasure, each of them trying their best to make the other come first. Damn, why was it always a contest?

Jake rolled over to his back and laughed. Within moments, Baylor had joined him, turning around so that they were both oriented in the same direction.

"Damn. Is it always like that?" Bay propped himself up on one elbow and grinned at Jake.

"Nope. Usually it's even better. Before long, you'll be able to read my thoughts, experience what I'm feeling. Then there's another thing to consider. Imagine Shannon between us."

Bay flopped over on his back. "I'd rather not. I think it would kill me."

Bay's comment hung in the air between them. Jake glanced at the man beside him and felt a tight fist squeeze his heart. Damn he hoped Shannon was right. There was still no convincing sense of Baylor as Chanku, nothing beyond the sense of closeness Jake felt to the man, the sexual desire.

The glittering amber eyes.

Baylor's dreams were another clue, but there was still no proof. If it turned out Shannon had been wrong, that Bay lacked the Chanku genes, Bay wouldn't have to worry about the sex killing him.

No. Then it would be Jake's problem.

Shannon lay in Jake's lonely bed, her fingers slowly stroking between her legs in the aftermath of orgasm, and wondered if Jake realized his mind read like an open book. She'd been there, inside his head, part of some of the most intense sex she'd ever experienced.

Damn. No wonder men enjoyed fucking each other. The raw beauty of sensation, the lancing pain when they penetrated one another, the sweet suction of hot mouths on warm cocks. Too much. Way too much.

Shannon grinned into the darkness and wondered if Jake and Baylor would mind very much if she joined them. In spite of her orgasm, she wanted more. Wanted penetration by something more substantial than her own fingers. Wanted two lean, hot, muscular bodies pressed against hers.

She'd had group sex before, but never with two men she desired as much as she wanted Jake and Baylor. She stared into the darkness for a few seconds, than sat up.

"Screw it. I'm not going to get any sleep at this rate." Slipping out of bed, Shannon walked quietly into the main room. The guest room was on the far side of the house, but the low rumble of male voices told her the men were still awake.

Shannon moved silently, praying the floorboards wouldn't creak and give her away. The darkness was absolute but her Chanku senses helped Shannon find her way even in her human form.

Each day the beast within became more powerful, more well defined. Jake had told her the time would come when Shannon was truly Chanku at all times, merely a wolf existing in human form, not just a woman able to shift to wolf. Already Shannon felt the changes, the subtle differences in all of her perceptions and senses.

In fact . . .

She paused, aware suddenly, of something *wrong*. A sense of intrusion, of *other*.

Quiet laughter came from the men's bedroom, but the feeling of unease persisted. Shannon sent a light, searching thought toward Jake.

He was in her mind immediately. *What's wrong? Where are you?*

In the main room. I was coming to surprise you and Baylor, but something isn't right.

Did you hear someone?

No. *Just a sense, a feeling . . .*

I'm coming. Go into the kitchen. Put the counter between you and the front of the house.

Shannon turned to her right, toward the kitchen. A hand clamped over her mouth. Dragged her against a powerful body.

Jake!

Shannon twisted her hips, swinging her elbow back into a taut belly. Her captor grunted, but held on. She heard the roar of an angry wolf, felt whoever held her, twist and stumble.

They went down, hard. Gunshot splintered the night. Glass shattered above Shannon's head, the acrid scent of kerosene almost overwhelmed her senses. The shriek of toenails searching for purchase on wood, a loud yip and a snarl . . . then the clatter of a gun skittering across the floor.

A man screamed. The sound twisted in upon itself, became a loud, sucking gurgle, the hiss of air through blood.

The one holding Shannon turned her loose. He scrambled to his feet but the wolf caught him before he could reach the door. Again, the harsh scream of a dying man.

The cry ended in the crunch of bone, the gurgling rush of air escaping through a torn windpipe.

Shannon wrapped her arms around her knees and leaned her head forward. She shook so hard she knew she couldn't stand. Fought the nausea that threatened.

"Are you okay?" Baylor knelt beside her, his nude body warm and strong and very comforting.

Shannon nodded. As okay as she could be, considering.

"Come with me." He brushed his hand over her tangled hair, practically lifted her to her feet. She stood on wobbly legs, lungs heaving, heart still pounding.

Baylor wrapped his arms around Shannon's waist.

Offering comfort, moving her away from the unseen remains of the intruders.

The scratch of a match head against stone, a flash of light. Jake lit one of the lanterns on the kitchen table. Shattered glass and spilled fuel marked the spot where a second lantern had been turned to rubble. The bullet appeared to be buried in the wall just over the sink.

Shannon hated to look, but knew she had to. While Jake scrubbed the blood from his face at the kitchen sink, she walked with Baylor to inspect the first body, the one who had shot at her.

It was the same agent, the one she had mistaken for Richard that first night. His arm, encased in a fabric cast, lay twisted beneath his body. Heart pounding, Shannon turned to look at the other man. Long scratches marred his wrist. She'd never really gotten a good look at his face. Still, she'd marked him well the first time he grabbed her.

Both men had bandages on their heads and abrasions on their faces from Jake's attack the night they'd tried to kidnap her.

Neither man would ever threaten her again.

Shannon raised her head and looked at Jake. "Will it ever end? Will others just keep coming after us?"

"Bay? What do you think?" Jake dried his hands and face on a kitchen towel, then reached for Shannon.

She drifted into his arms, feeling as if she'd just awakened from a terrible nightmare. The scent of death filled her nostrils and the blood soaking into the wooden floor made this nightmare all too real.

"These are the only two I know of who were part of Bosworth's plan. They won't be telling anyone anything now."

Jake nodded. "Still, we don't know who, if anyone, they might have talked to." He kissed Shannon. "Go back to bed. Bay and I will take care of this."

She nodded, still horribly shaken, and returned to the bedroom. An hour later, Shannon heard a car and Jake's motorcycle pull out of the yard. She was still awake when they returned, just as the sun spilled its light over the eastern hills.

Chapter 12

Shannon got up and made coffee. When she walked into the main room, there was no sign of a struggle, no hint of the deaths that had occurred just a few short hours ago. Jake and Baylor had cleaned away the blood, the spilled kerosene, the broken glass.

The bodies.

Shannon guessed the agents had joined their brethren in the dark waters of the granite quarry. Neither Jake nor Baylor mentioned the men, though they seemed unusually introspective this morning. They'd showered and changed as soon as they returned, but neither man had wanted to sleep. After so many hours awake, they had to be exhausted. Still, Shannon sensed more than mere fatigue.

What did they feel, knowing four men were dead, four men who would never return to their homes? Baylor insisted they were all loners, men without families or lives outside of the private agency Bosworth had built, but Shannon couldn't help but wonder if any of them would be missed, now that Bosworth was dead.

She wrapped an afghan around her shoulders and took a steaming cup of coffee out onto the deck. The sun was barely over the treetops and dew still sparkled on the leaves. Shannon heard the door open and close behind her, lifted her chin to receive Jake's quick kiss.

And Bay's. Following close behind Jake, he leaned down and kissed Shannon as if they'd known each other much longer than a single day. He stood beside her, one hand resting on her shoulder, almost possessively. Shannon glanced in Jake's direction, noticed he was as aware of Bay's lingering touch as she was.

Shannon reached up and patted Bay's hand. He chuckled softly.

"All the way back here, I thought of what you said last night. That you were on your way to join us. I want you to know that concept has remained uppermost in my thoughts."

Shannon turned and grinned at him. "I'll be sure and keep that in mind."

Jake continued to watch both of them. Shannon sensed his concentrated stare, his tension. Was he jealous? She wasn't certain. She didn't sense any deep-seated emotion that might warn her off.

Shannon did, however, sense Jake's curiosity. She slid her gaze from Jake to Bay and back again to Jake. Definite curiosity, from both men.

The muscles between her thighs clenched and released and Shannon felt a sudden rush of moisture. Maybe, just maybe, she had the solution to the tension affecting all of them.

She set her coffee cup down on the railing. Turned to smile first at Bay, then at Jake. Her gaze lingered on Jake, on the powerful shoulders, the long, lean line of his torso. The tangle of sun-bleached hair. Soon, she would mate with him as wolf. Give herself and her future over to the one alpha wolf who claimed her heart.

For now, though, the thought of loving two men without commitment was oddly tantalizing. Two absolutely beautiful men. She'd taken her nutrient pill this morning.

So had Bay. His second, only twelve hours after the first, but it was easier to remember in the morning.

As if either of them would forget. Shannon wondered if he felt anything at all, if his body had begun any of the subtle changes that led to a life as a shapeshifter.

She stood up and let the afghan fall to the wooden deck. Her nipples tightened in the cool morning air. Goosebumps covered her arms and legs, raced across her chest and belly. Both Jake and Bay were suddenly alert, their attention focused entirely on Shannon.

Jake's thoughts entered her mind. *Are you sure?*

Of course. Are you?

I don't know. I don't know anything anymore. Jake shook his head and grinned. *It's your call. We might as well find out.*

Bay twisted his gaze from one to the other and back again, obviously wondering what they discussed as Chanku. Shannon reached for his hand. He took hers without hesitation.

"I have just the thing to relax you and help you get some sleep. Both of you. It's been a long night and you both need your rest." Grinning, she tugged lightly on Bay's fingers. He followed her as if he were sleep walking. Jake shook his head and grinned, then moved ahead to open the door. The three of them walked toward the master bedroom, following Shannon's lead.

She began with Bay, slipping his T-shirt over his shoulders, slowly tugging his sweats down over his slim hips. When he was naked, his cock angled out from his body and his breath coming in short, sharp gasps, she gave him a push toward the bed.

Bay stumbled, as if surprised by her move. Shannon laughed and turned to Jake while Bay stretched out on the rumpled sheets. She helped Jake out of his clothes, running her palm along the width of his chest, pausing to tease the taut nipple over his heart. She leaned close and licked him there, felt his gasp as he sucked in a quick breath. Then she pointed him toward the bed and gave him a light shove.

Laughing, Jake tumbled onto the bed and stretched out next to Bay. Shannon stood beside the bed and stared at the two men. They smiled back at her, inviting her with heated looks. Bay, so serious yet unbelievably beautiful. Jake, ruthless and perfect, the bite wound on his neck finally fading away to a pale pink scar.

Someday she wanted the entire story, but not now. Now she wanted to experience both of these men, she wanted to know what her future held.

It felt different, here in the morning light, comparing the bodies of two of the most perfect male specimens she'd ever seen. Shannon couldn't help but think of the night she met Jake, when she'd suffered the attentions of yet another poor lover. Richard and Big Dick were part of a past she had no intention of revisiting. Looking at Bay and Jake, at their perfectly sculpted bodies, their muscular chests dusted with dark hair, the rippling abs and powerful erections standing at attention, she knew she'd never waste another night of her life like that again.

Shannon crawled over Jake's thighs and straddled his right leg and Bay's left, locking the men together in a tight grip between her legs. They both raised up to come close to her. Stretching to meet them, Shannon brushed one breast over Bay's lips, then the other over Jake's. Neither man needed further invitation. They leaned together, each of them drawing a nipple between his lips, each man stroking her sides with a powerful yet warm and gentle hand.

After a moment, she straightened, smiling at the sound when Jake and Bay released their hold on her. Her nipples stood straight out, glistening dark red against her pale skin. She plucked at the sensitive tips, arching her back, then running her palms along her torso.

Shannon tilted her body close and kissed Jake. His lips parted beneath hers, his tongue tangled, gently at first, than more forcefully, with hers. Jake drew her into his kiss, making love to her mouth, focusing so intently on Shannon she found herself falling into his sensual spell.

She was only peripherally aware of Bay shifting around behind her, of his hard chest pressing against her back, his erect cock sliding up and down the crease between her buttocks.

His fingers found her wet and wanting sex. Sharp teeth nipped her shoulder and Shannon arched into the pain. Bay licked the small bite, then nuzzled her neck. "Lube?"

Jake grunted. Without breaking contact, he reached over Shannon's shoulder and passed something to Bay. She felt Bay's fingers stroking the sensitive skin around her ass, felt the cool, slick cream he applied.

His fingers moved slowly, gently against her anus, slipping back and forth in time with Jake's tongue. Somehow she'd changed position again. Now she lay atop Jake with his fully erect cock pressed between her legs. Shannon still felt Bay's slow back-and-forth strokes, but her attention focused on Jake and his mouth, Jake and his hot penis brushing over her clit, slipping between her sensitive lips, teasing the entrance to her sex.

Slowly, almost as if by accident, his cock found her warm, wet center and slid home. She felt the hot length of him, felt the hard crown pressing deep, finding the mouth of her womb and pausing there.

At the same time, Bay's fingers entered more than her consciousness, pressing, teasing, rubbing, then pressing again at her tightly clenched anus. Shannon forced herself to relax, forced acquiescence as first one, two, then three fingers entered her, stretched her . . . readied her.

Jake slipped in and out, gliding on her natural lubricants. Bay added more cream to his fingers until her passage was soft and ready. When he pressed the broad head of his cock against her anus, it was merely a matter of Shannon pushing back against him to allow entry.

Even so, he felt huge. Already filled with Jake, she shifted her hips, took a deep breath and let it out, then did it again. Bay's long fingers grasped her hips and she felt him slide into position between her legs, between Jake's legs.

Jake drove deep with a slow, sure stroke. As he withdrew, she felt Bay push forward.

The broad head of his cock moved beyond the tight muscles, thrusting deep within her. She took quick, sharp breaths against the burning pain, forced herself to relax, to make room for Bay's cock. He moved slowly, finding a rhythm in time with Jake.

In, out, in again.

She felt him shift behind her, adjusting the height of his hips to a better angle. His hands clasped her hips, his huge penis slid forward, deeper.

At first, it was all about the logistics. Making something so big fit into a passage so tight. Timing each movement with Jake's to make it work. Shannon concentrated on her breathing, on relaxing her muscles, on the exquisite fantasy of two gorgeous men filling her body at the same time.

The burning subsided when Bay stilled. She'd never taken a man so large, not this way. Shannon wriggled her hips, pressed back against Baylor's groin, deeply aware of Jake's stillness beneath her as she adjusted to this new intrusion deep inside her body.

Shannon felt pain each time Bay pressed forward, exquisite, burning pain that tripped over into a dark and dangerous pleasure when he withdrew. His body molded her back, hot and insistent, pressing her down on Jake, holding her tightly to the man she loved.

She was aware of the rough texture of coarse hair on Bay's thighs, the soft pressure of his balls touching the lips of her sex. Then Jake arched his hips, filling her. Shannon spiraled deeper into pleasure and desire and overwhelming arousal.

Jake arched his hips and drove deep inside Shannon. He felt Bay's cock slide along his. Separated by the thin tissue between Shannon's pussy and ass, their cocks were sheathed in nothing more than hot, wet, woman. It felt as if he and Baylor made love to one another, with Shannon the sweet filling in the middle.

Shannon's breasts pressed against his chest, her nipples hard as pencil erasers against him. Jake had never experienced pleasure such as this—his cock buried in a hot, wet and swollen pussy, his hands molding and squeezing those two perfect breasts, his thighs pressed down by the powerful thighs of another man.

Grunting with either pleasure or effort, or both, Bay thrust deep. Jake felt the hard ridge of Bay's cock slipping against his own. Shannon whimpered, totally caught in the moment. Jake tried to enter her thoughts and found only sensation, amazing light and color, pleasure and a dark yet seductive pain.

He took all her sensations into himself, experienced what Shannon felt and grunted with each thrust of Bay's hard cock sliding deep inside her body. Shannon arched, catching Jake by surprise with her sudden orgasm.

He felt the tense clenching of her vaginal muscles, drove deep when she screamed, felt Bay's solid erection pressing solidly against his cock, both of them buried deep inside Shannon.

Jake opened his thoughts once more, searched for Shannon . . . and found Baylor. Clear as the spoken word, Bay's pending climax tipped Jake over the edge. He felt the tight passage trapping Bay's cock, the soft rise of Shannon's buttocks against Bay's groin, the hot, wet, living flesh, squeezing, clasping, spasming out of control.

Jake shouted, the sound tearing, unexpected, from deep within his chest. He arched his hips, driving hard. He reached out to hold Shannon and found his hands clasped tightly in Baylor's strong grasp.

Forearms straining, they locked Shannon within their embrace, rocking slowly as the final spasms of their orgasm slowed, stilled . . . stopped on a sigh shared by the three of them.

Bay released Jake's hands. He lay forward across Shannon's back, but he held his weight off of both her and Jake, resting on his elbows.

Shannon's cheek pressed against Jake's chest, her sweat-dampened hair clinging to his chin and shoulder. He felt her lips, the soft tip of her tongue as she licked slowly at his nipple. Jake's cock stayed hard, trapped inside her, held in place by Bay's solid length.

Jake swept his hand over Shannon's hair, lingered on Bay's hard shoulder. Baylor raised his head and smiled at Jake over the soft curve of Shannon's back. His steady gaze lingered for a moment, filled with promise, with a sense of expectation.

Jake sighed beneath the weight of both lovers. His cock stirred within Shannon's heat, and he felt Bay harden against him. Something seemed to fill his throat, a hard lump he barely recognized.

Damn, he wasn't going to cry, was he?

No, not when he'd never felt this happy in his life. Not when he hadn't had this powerful sense of belonging before, a love that surpassed anything he'd ever known. This woman was his. So was the man. Three of them, all Chanku. Together they wielded the strength of the pack.

Together, as soon as Bay completed the change. They'd been inside each other's heads this time, both of them loving Shannon, both of them experiencing her heat and warmth, her giving spirit. Jake had thought of opening to Shannon's thoughts, but he couldn't. Not yet.

Not until they mated. Until Bay changed. Until all the parts came together to complete the whole.

When, he wondered, would Shannon finally be ready for their true joining? What held her back?

He lifted his hips, sliding deeper into her wet heat, sliding the thick length of his cock along Bay's, and he felt Shannon sigh. She raised her head just enough to kiss him, then lay her face back against his chest.

Her body was his . . . theirs. She'd given him this much. Soon, Jake thought, she would give him her heart.

Early Friday evening, Shannon soaked in the big tub, feeling replete and more sated than she could recall. Soft voices filtered into her consciousness. Jake and Bay, sitting out on the front deck, sipping at cold beers and talking about whatever it was men talked about on a cool fall evening.

Dipping her head back to thoroughly wet her hair, Shannon had to bite back a grin. She kept picturing herself as a virgin sacrifice, preparing her body for the altar. Absolutely an hysterical image, considering the last three days she'd spent with Jake and Baylor.

She swept the washcloth along her legs, then brought it slowly up between her thighs. There wasn't a place on her body that didn't ache, but she wouldn't have it any other way.

Grabbing a disposable razor, Shannon began shaving her legs, but her mind was far from simple chores. Since that first time Wednesday morning, she and Jake and Bay had tried just about every sexual position physically possible . . . and they'd laughed uproariously at the ones that proved impossible.

She still wasn't sure which was her favorite, though

lying back while Bay licked and sucked between her legs as Jake took Bay from behind had to be one of the most erotic things she'd ever experienced. Watching Bay's face as Jake slowly lubricated his cock then penetrated Bay had left Shannon dripping her own lubricant down her inner thighs. Even now, her pussy clenched when she recalled the deep thrusts of Baylor's tongue each time Jake drove deeper into Bay's ass . . . dear God but she'd gotten hot. What really took her over the edge was the look of pure ecstasy on Jake's face when he'd come.

She'd turned the tables on Bay, then, slipping around after Jake was through to take Bay's hard cock in her mouth. She'd reveled in the power she felt, the strength, the control over two strong men who loved it when she touched them, who loved each other.

Shannon licked her lips, remembering the taste, the differences in both men, the similarities. Every time they had sex, it felt totally fresh, completely new. That alone made relations with both men extra special. Tonight, though Jake didn't know it yet, Shannon intended to experience something even more unique.

It was time. After talking to Tia this morning, Shannon realized she couldn't put Jake off any longer. There really was no reason. She loved him. He loved her. They both loved Bay, and that was part of the problem, part of the reason it was time to mate with Jake.

She knew Bay's feelings grew stronger each time they made love. His needs more powerful, his drive more all consuming. The nutrients were doing exactly what they were meant to do, but the drive to mate was growing stronger as his Chanku genetics gained strength.

When Tia told her what Jake had done, how he'd tried to rape her as Chanku, to force Tia to mate with him instead of the one she'd chosen, Shannon knew it was time to remove any chance of that happening between her and Bay.

Nor did Shannon want to be the cause of putting Jake

in an untenable position with his friends. Tomorrow Mik and AJ would arrive. Two more Chanku males. Bay couldn't shift yet, but there was no doubt it would happen soon. She'd noticed him rubbing at his arms, the intense look in his eyes whenever she and Jake shifted.

Mik, AJ, maybe Bay as well, all of them alpha wolves, who managed to co-exist only because of the human restraints they put on themselves, each one capable of taking a Chanku bitch, of mating her before she could shift.

Shannon's thoughts wandered and she tried to picture the physical act of sex as a wolf. Tia had explained a lot of what happened, including the fact Chanku definitely mated for life. She said the bonding with Luc, when it happened, was the closest thing to a true religious experience she'd had. Shannon had laughed at Tia's description, but she'd been deeply touched, as well. Hearing about mating from Jake was one thing—having a woman who was as close as a sister explain the facts was something else altogether.

For life. Was she ready? Shannon stood up and reached for a towel. *As ready as I'll ever be.*

She dried herself and grabbed a heavy terry cloth robe hanging from a hook on the door. In just a few short minutes, she planned to ask Jake to join her for a run. As a wolf . . . a beautiful she-wolf with furry legs.

Why she'd worried so much about shaving her legs, she wasn't quite sure.

Laughing, Shannon tucked the belt around her waist and went out to join the men.

Jake watched Shannon with a growing sense of expectation. She'd been unusually quiet today and then disappeared into the bathroom for almost two hours. Definitely a long time spent bathing or whatever women did when they locked themselves away like that. Whatever, it had worked with Shannon.

She was always beautiful. More beautiful than any woman Jake had ever seen, much less made love with, but right now she took his breath. Her damp hair glistened, her wide smile hinted at pleasures he'd experienced, others he'd only dreamed of. Jake tried to imagine how it would feel to lose her, to have another male take her away from him.

The enormity of what he'd tried to do to Tia and Luc struck home like an bolt of lightning. What a fool he'd been! What a total idiot. Jake suddenly realized he was rubbing at the healing scar on his throat. He dropped his hand as if he'd been scalded.

Shannon glanced at the movement and smiled. *Run with me? Now?*

Baylor glanced up. Did he hear the unspoken request? Bay couldn't shift yet, but Jake was sure he was getting close. Their sex had certainly grown more intense over the past few days, as if the Chanku part of him was breaking free.

Jake stood and shrugged out of his jacket. He nodded in Baylor's direction. "Shannon and I are going to run. Will you hold down the fort?"

"Sure. How long will you be gone?"

Jake chanced a quick glance toward Shannon. Her eyes were shining and she licked her lips in blatant invitation. He barely caught her quick nod, but Jake knew exactly what she intended. He turned back to Baylor and bit back a grin. "As long as it takes."

Bay sighed and looked away. If he wasn't so anxious to finally be alone with Shannon, Jake might have felt guilty at leaving their friend and lover behind.

He stripped out of his clothes and shifted as Shannon dropped the robe and joined him. She looked back at Baylor just once, yipped loudly and followed Jake with a long leap off the deck.

The air seemed colder tonight. Jake sniffed the gentle

breeze and wondered if the weather was about to change. Winter came early to the Maine woods. Thin clouds scudded across the sky. He wouldn't be surprised to find a dusting of snow by morning.

Now, though, the brisk air suited his need to run, to race with Shannon by his side. Her reddish coat gleamed in the glow coming from the house and her green eyes sparkled with hidden fire.

Neither one had said anything, but Jake knew tonight was one they would never forget. He nipped at Shannon's shoulder, then sped ahead of her. She bit his flank, hard enough to bruise, and Jake knew he was right.

He twisted to the left, taking a small, narrow path that led to a secluded meadow not far from the house. They'd run this way before, but he'd never approached it with such a powerful sense of destiny, never experienced the certainty of his actions.

Shannon raced on ahead, passing him on the narrow trail as if she were as anxious as Jake to reach their goal. Not just the meadow, not even the act of sex between two beasts.

No, this was, in essence, a marriage. Two adults choosing to become one. She would know everything in his head, know all his doubts, all his needs. As he would know hers. Did Shannon understand the ramifications of their act?

Jake was almost afraid to ask.

Which was, of course, the very reason he had to.

They reached the meadow, a small, grassy glade with a tiny creek running along one side. Shannon stopped at the edge, sniffed the air carefully before stepping out from the protection of the thick underbrush. Jake followed, coming into the meadow from another angle. He followed Shannon to the creek and dipped his muzzle close to hers to drink.

They both raised their heads at the same time. Drops of water glistened in the stiff whiskers beside Shannon's nose.

Her eyes were a clear green, even in the darkness. Somehow they seemed to capture whatever light existed, shining it back on Jake.

He leaned close to her and licked the drops from her muzzle. *I love you. You know I've wanted you since the beginning, but I've discovered, in the past few days, how very much I love you.*

Shannon's eyes closed briefly. She sat back on her haunches. *I wanted to be sure. I am. More certain than I've ever been of anything else. I love you. My life wouldn't be complete without you in it. I want you to know I talked to Tia this morning. I know what this means.*

Jake took a step closer. *No secrets. You'll know everything about me, my weaknesses, my failings, hopefully, my strengths. I'll learn everything about you. I promise to accept your secrets, to love the woman no matter what she carries in her memories.*

And I promise to accept the man. Forever.

Jake shivered, more deeply affected than he would have imagined. As if they'd each written their own vows, he felt he had just experienced a formal wedding ceremony. He leaned his body against Shannon.

She turned and nipped him on the shoulder, stood and turned away. Stared at him over her shoulder, her full tail waving gracefully in front of his nose.

An invitation Jake couldn't refuse. Rising stiffly, he pawed at her back and his long claws left deep marks in her dark pelt. Shannon's scent rose to meet him, rich and inviting, calling him to mate.

She yipped once, twice. Twirled away playfully, as if to escape, her jaws wide, sharp canines glistening in the pale light of the waning moon.

Jake positioned himself behind her, raised his paw and planted it firmly on Shannon's back. Felt his cock begin to stretch, knew it slipped free of the loose foreskin.

Shannon turned her head and stared at him, watching

over her shoulder. Jake searched her thoughts and found them open, inviting him to enter.

Rising up on his hind legs, Jake reached for balance, resting his paws on Shannon's strong shoulders. Need thrummed within him. His heart pounded and the urge to mate, to drive deep inside his bitch, to cover her with his body and make her his own, overwhelmed him. Snarling, he thrust forward, anticipating her heat, her tight sheath surrounding his lengthening cock.

Instead of acquiescence, Shannon snarled a sharp warning, twisted her body and rolled to one side.

Entirely black, mouth open, haunches bunching for the strike, a huge wolf launched itself at Jake. Jake whirled away, scrabbled for purchase in the short grass and narrowly avoided the gaping jaws and sharp teeth aiming for his throat.

Jake feinted, twisted out of the range of the snapping jaws and bit down on the beast's neck. Thick fur kept him from getting a killing grip. The wolf jerked to one side and pulled free.

Shannon was suddenly standing beside Jake, her eyes narrowed, her stance aggressive. With the changing odds, two powerful wolves standing shoulder to shoulder against him, the unknown wolf backed down, snarling, saliva dripping from its jaws.

Shannon lowered her head. Her chest heaved with each deep breath. Then she moved away from Jake and shifted, standing tall and glorious in the dark meadow, hands on her hips and fire in her eyes. Before Jake could shift as well, she turned on the interloper. "Baylor Quinn, you asshole . . . what the fuck do you think you're doing?"

Chapter 13

The wolf snarled, its every move radiating aggression and anger. Shannon stood her ground with Jake beside her. He hadn't shifted. She was certain he waited to see what the wolf would do next.

Are you sure this is Bay? I can't read his thoughts. He feels wild to me.

"Oh, that's Baylor, all right. I can tell by the size of his prick . . . can't you see? It's a lot bigger than his brain right now."

Once more the wolf snarled. Stiff hackles rose along his spine and his muscles bunched, as if he intended to leap. Jake moved closer, partially blocking Shannon's legs.

Don't make it worse. I think he's really close to losing it.

Why would he do this? Why would he ruin what we were doing? Shannon didn't know whether she wanted to kick the damned wolf or cry. He snarled once more, showing ivory canines, but there was a sense of indecision in his stance, the possibility he realized how stupid his actions were.

He really doesn't know what he's doing. He shifted before his body was ready . . . he's more wolf now than human. I hope he remembers how to shift back.

Shannon wrapped her arms around her body, shivering. Now that the first rush of adrenaline was wearing off, she felt the chill night air, the fear, the sad sense of tragedy should they lose their friend and lover.

"Bay? Are you in there?" Shannon lowered herself to the grass and, ignoring his aggressive stance, wrapped her arms around the wolf's wide neck. He snarled once, his teeth a hairbreadth from Shannon's face, then his body went limp and he leaned his full weight against her.

"Oh, Bay. Damn it." Shannon sniffed back the tears that suddenly clogged her throat. "Bay, I wanted to mate with Jake tonight to avoid this very thing. Why'd you have to go and screw it up?"

She swept her hand over his head, between the dark ears lying flat against his skull. "Did Jake ever tell you what happened to him? Did you know he was almost kicked out of his pack for trying to take the leader's mate? It doesn't work. Don't do this, Bay. I love you, but I'm not *in* love with you. Not the way I am with Jake."

She felt the tremor in the wolven body, sensed the sudden shift from wolf to human moments before it occurred. Suddenly, Shannon's arms were holding a grown man, holding Baylor around the neck as he sobbed against her breast.

She glanced at Jake, feeling helpless and uncertain. He shifted and sat close to Shannon, wrapped his arms around both Shannon and Baylor, and held them tight.

Shannon looked at Jake and he shook his head. "I don't know. That wasn't Bay. That much I know. He wasn't acting in character at all."

Shannon nodded. "Let's get him home. We're not far."

Jake nodded and stood up. He grabbed Shannon's hand and she stood as well, bringing Bay with her. Awkward as it was, they stood there in the darkness for a moment, holding on to one another.

Bay shuddered, then stood straight. He looked from

Jake to Shannon and hung his head. "I'm sorry. I don't know what happened. I watched you leave, then suddenly I was here, in the dark, hell bent on attacking Jake, on taking the wolf, not you, Shannon. I felt an overwhelming need to fuck the she-wolf, but there was nothing familiar about it, no sense of who you were . . . of who I am. I don't remember shifting, I don't remember coming here. I'm sorry. Something's gone terribly wrong."

Jake stepped forward and wrapped his arms around Bay. "No. Something went terribly right. I've been so afraid you weren't Chanku, afraid . . ."

"You might have to kill me?"

Jake nodded. "Yeah. I don't know if I could have done it. Bay, I love you. In fact, partially because of you, I've made a decision I haven't even talked over with Shannon, but it's something I have to do."

Jake stepped back and looked from Baylor to Shannon. She saw determination in his eyes and a strength she'd always suspected he held close to his heart.

"I don't want to return to San Francisco, to Pack Dynamics. As much as I admire and respect him, I don't think I could serve under Lucien anymore. I want to start my own pack here, in Maine. Maybe an eastern division of the company? I dunno, but I know it's something I have to do, something I want." He grabbed Shannon's hand, then Bay's. "With you. Both of you. Shannon as my mate, you, Bay, as my second. What do you think?"

Bay stepped back, his eyes shifting from Jake to Shannon and back again. "I tried to kill you. Tried to take your mate. How could you want me beside you? How can you trust me?"

"Should I not trust you?"

Bay shook his head. "I don't know. I'm not sure what happened. I'm not sure it won't happen again."

Shannon touched his arm, felt the tension in him. "Can you shift? Do you know how you turned into a wolf?"

Baylor frowned, stepped back and stared off into the darkness. After a moment, he shook his head. "No. I can't remember how I did it before. It just happened. I saw you leave together and it's like something inside me snapped. I don't remember."

"That's because you weren't ready." Jake squeezed Bay's shoulder. "You need the supplement for a few more days. The shift was probably a result of hormones and adrenaline when Shannon and I left. Sometimes the beast takes over if we're not strong enough to grab control and hold it tight. Give it time."

Bay nodded. "I'll go back now. I'm sorry. I . . ."

Shannon reached up and kissed him. "Don't apologize. The beast took over before you had the controls you need. You'll be fine." She pressed her palm to his cheek, letting him know all was forgiven. "Can you find your way back?"

"Yeah. That much I can do." Baylor turned away then, following the narrow trail back to the house. Barefoot and naked, it wouldn't be an easy trip.

"Bay?" Jake's call stopped him. "Let us come with you. We can show you the way."

Jake shifted before Bay could answer, then went to stand just ahead of him. Shannon shifted as well. Together, they led Bay through the dark. He rested a hand on the shoulders of each of them, all the way back to the house.

Still acting unsettled and nervous, Bay chose his own room once they returned to the house. Shannon closed the door behind her and shrugged her shoulders when Jake glanced her way. "I hate to leave him alone. He feels horrible."

Jake grinned and held out his hand. Shannon folded her fingers within his stronger grasp. "He should feel horrible. He almost killed me!"

Shannon raised up on her toes and kissed Jake. "Not a

chance. You're too tough for him. I'll put my marker on you any day."

Jake draped his arms over Shannon's shoulders and stared deep into her eyes. "Would you? Do you trust me that much?"

She nodded. "Always. The more I get to know you, the more I find to respect. You were good with Bay tonight. A lot of men wouldn't have been able to forgive."

Jake shook his head slowly. "I realized almost from the first that I love him. It's my fault he changed here, all alone for his very first time. I should have been with him. Hell, you were forced to make the first shift on your own . . . killed a man your first time out as a wolf. Now Bay . . . I'm screwing up lives right and left here, aren't I?"

"No, you're not. Bay will be fine." Shannon realized she was staring at Jake's chest, at the flat nipple mere inches from her mouth. "I, on the other hand, was interrupted in the midst of something quite important." She leaned close and raked her teeth over the hard point. Jake sucked in his breath. When she twirled her tongue around the sensitive tip, he groaned.

"Something we really should find the time to conclude."

Jake cupped her face in his warm palms, tilted her chin to meet her lips in a deep, wet kiss. "Are you sure?"

Shannon nipped at his lower lip, drawing it between her teeth, then licking the sensitive inner flesh. She felt Jake's tongue exploring her teeth, the roof of her mouth—which suddenly seemed much too sensitive for his touch.

She broke the kiss and leaned her head against his chest. "I want you. I need to feel you inside me. Now."

Breathing hard and fast, Jake slipped out of his sweat pants. Shannon did the same, but when she tossed her clothing aside, she headed for the front door instead of their bedroom.

Jake covered her hand just as she grabbed the door

knob. His eyes asked the same questions he'd asked earlier. Shannon put him out of his misery with a simple finger to his lips.

"Yes. I understand this is forever. Whether we mate or not, I'm yours. Get over it. You worry too much about the small stuff."

He laughed then, kissing her finger in the process. "Mating for life is small stuff?"

Shannon grabbed his hand and tugged him out into the chill night air. "In the overall scheme of things, yes. It's definitely small stuff." She turned around and cupped the side of his face with her palm. "Ya know why? Because it's going to happen no matter how much you worry, no matter how afraid of failing you might be. You saved my life and got me as a prize. Get used to it."

Shannon shifted, leapt over the deck railing and ran, not waiting at all for Jake. She knew he could catch her, no matter how fast she ran. The chase excited her.

She ran really fast.

When Jake finally caught up to her, she stood in the middle of the same meadow where they'd gone earlier. Where they'd shared what could only be described as vows. Words that had seared themselves into Shannon's heart with their simplicity yet powerful promise.

After so much fear, so much agonizing worry over whether or not they should do this thing, Shannon discovered that sex with a wolf was every bit as wonderful, yet no more special, than when they were human.

She loved Jake, no matter if he walked on two legs or four. She knew he loved her just as much, and that in itself was priceless.

When he nipped at her shoulder, raked his claws along her back, when he finally mounted her and drove deep inside her willing body, Shannon merely braced her four legs to carry Jake's heavy weight and gave her animal-mind control.

She'd forgotten about the bonding, the mental link that truly made them one. Forgotten so completely that she almost fought the sensation of Jake slipping silently into her mind. Suddenly Jake was there, so deep inside he *was* Shannon.

So completely, Shannon became Jake.

Like a light shining across a dark page, Shannon finally understood. Truly understood the doubts that ruled him, the questions he couldn't answer, the sadness and insecurity that often colored every decision Jake made.

With that knowledge came the certainty that Jake saw all her weaknesses as well. Saw, understood, and accepted. Her need to be loved, to take sexual gratification when her emotions were left adrift. Her unwavering desire to be a mother, to have a child she could love as she had never been loved, and her despair when she'd learned her sexual indiscretions had cost her that joy, had cost her the ability to reproduce.

She knew he experienced her unbelievable elation when she'd discovered the healing her Chanku heritage had done to her reproductive organs, and she rejoiced with Jake when she felt his indescribable joy, his happiness that, when the time was right, they would have a child.

All this in a link so complete, so soul-searingly deep, it would never fully come undone. This was what she had committed to when she'd agreed to mate with Jake.

This was the gift he gave her, the gift she could return in kind. A gift of self, a sharing of thoughts and memories so private, so close to the heart that only an individual's one true love could keep them safe.

Still reveling in the sharing, Shannon's awareness shifted to the sounds and smells of the night, to the alpha wolf driving deep inside her. He grunted with effort, she whimpered, as much from some primal fear as the building sense of completion, a climax unlike that of her human counterpoint.

Jake's thrusts came fast and hard, she felt the hard knot slip between her vaginal lips and lock them tightly together. Whining now, caught close against the panting beast she loved, Shannon dropped to the grass and watched him.

Her mate. In mind now, as well as body. A part of her soul. She wanted to weep with the beauty of this moment, this time in her life when she felt truly complete. It was almost finished, this strange yet necessary act that took them beyond their humanity, fully into the world of Chanku.

Jake regained his human form as the last tremors of his climax finally subsided. As if she were an extension of him, Shannon shifted to the woman he loved at almost the same moment.

He felt stunned. Light-headed, and humbled beyond belief. He hadn't realized how profound such a mating would be. Had only expected a fast, hard fuck as wolf, his bitch beneath him, her body clinging to his when they tied.

Not the sharing. He'd heard about it, had been told the link was much more complete than anything they might experience during sex, but nothing like this. Nothing so profound, so intimate. This had stripped him bare and left him lying naked under the spotlights, his every weakness and flaw exposed.

Exposed to Shannon. His cock still throbbed in time with his pulse, buried deep inside Shannon's warm and welcoming pussy. She met him equally, her muscles clenching in rhythmic spasms, her breathing every bit as labored as his. Her back was turned to him, her wild mass of dark red hair tangled over his arms, covering her face.

Her warm buttocks pressed against his belly, one arm was flung out over her head, as if she reached for something unattainable.

"I'm here. I love you. Are you okay?" Jake brushed the tangled hair away from her shoulder and kissed her. Would she reject him? Was it too much information, too much she'd rather not know?

Shannon slowly rolled her torso so that she faced him. She propped herself up on one elbow and stared at him for a long, solemn moment.

Jake's heart stuttered in his chest. She smiled. Tears coursed down her cheeks, but she smiled at him, reached for him.

He grabbed her fingers and turned her face to his. His penis, flaccid now, slipped free of her warmth, but it was more important to see her face, her eyes, her beautiful mouth, than it was to keep the physical connection.

We'll always be connected. From now on. Your thoughts are mine. Mine are yours. I love you.

Jake's breath stopped in his lungs. He felt her words in his heart, as if she were a physical part of him. *I love you. I had no idea. None at all.*

Tia tried to explain. She couldn't. *No one can understand until they experience this kind of bond. It's as if you're another half of me. As if you're part of my heart and soul.*

Not as if. It just is. Jake rose to his feet, reluctantly separating himself from Shannon. With that physical separation came the realization the true connection between them would never be severed. Not so long as both of them still lived.

He held his hand out to Shannon and tugged her lightly to her feet.

When she stood in front of him, her tall, willowy body leaning close to his, Jake kissed her. Then he shifted, knowing Shannon would be there, knowing she could read his every thought, know his every intention.

It was frightening and exhilarating all at the same time.

As they loped slowly back toward the house, back to Baylor and the coming dawn, Jake knew he wouldn't want it any other way.

* * *

Jake slipped into the shower beside Shannon and grabbed the washcloth out of her hand. She leaned forward without comment and let him scrub her back, then she turned and did the same for Jake.

They dried themselves, quietly and quickly. Jake didn't question Shannon at all when she wrapped the towel around her torso and led him toward Baylor's room instead of to their own bed just outside the bathroom door.

Shannon tapped lightly on the door and stuck her head in. As she'd suspected, Bay lay awake, his powerful arms folded behind his head as he stared into the darkness.

He glanced from one to the other and sighed. "Is it done?"

Shannon sat on the edge of the bed. "You make it sound as if we went to an execution. All we did was make love."

"Actually, it was a lot more than that." Jake cupped Shannon's shoulders in his palms and planted a quick kiss on the back of her neck. "It was really pretty amazing. At some point, Bay, you'll find a mate and experience a bonding just like Shannon and I did tonight. There's no way to describe it, but what we did doesn't exclude you. It connects Shannon and me in a way that's unbreakable, but it leaves us both free to love you."

Jake slipped by Shannon and reached his hand out to Bay. "We do, you know. We both love you. It hurts us to see you hurting like this."

Bay turned his head away, but not before the tears glistening at the corners of his eyes made visible tracks through the growth of beard on his face. "I don't feel like myself. I'm a stranger in my own body. I can't explain it."

Shannon lay down next to Bay and put her arms around his waist. He kept his back to her, but she knew he listened. "It's the supplement. We just don't know that much about how the change affects people. We're all different. It took Jake a couple of weeks to get it right."

She turned and winked at Jake. "Of course, he's sort of slow that way."

Bay rolled slowly over and stared at Jake. "Two weeks? I've only been taking it a few days."

"Exactly." Jake sat next to Shannon's hip. "You rushed things, bro. You shouldn't have attempted the shift so soon. Your body's not ready."

"No shit, Sherlock." Bay scooted up and leaned against the headboard. "I've been trying to remember what happened. It's like there's a big black hole in that part of my memories."

"Give yourself a few more days before you try it again. We'll be careful not to do anything that sets off the wolf."

Bay laughed. "What? No sex?"

Shannon punched him in the shoulder. "You've got to be kidding. With this guy around?" She nodded in Jake's direction.

"Me?" Jake slowly reached down and grabbed the edge of the thick towel Shannon had wrapped around herself. With a flick of his wrist, he tugged it free and sent it flying. "Actually, sex was exactly what I had on my mind. It's relaxing. Good for what ails you."

Bay's eyes widened at the sight of Shannon's nude body. She felt her nipples pucker into tight little beads beneath his stare.

Jake laughed. "See. What'd I tell you. Feeling better already, aren't you?"

Shannon slipped over Bay's legs and, without any preliminaries, licked the crown of his suddenly very erect cock, then wrapped her lips around the top. Bay groaned and arched into her mouth.

She took him deeper, positioning herself between Bay's legs, raising her hips in the air in invitation to her mate.

Jake knelt behind Shannon and rubbed her buttocks with his warm palms. She expected the solid pressure of his cock against her pussy, but instead she felt the warm, damp caress of his tongue.

Shannon took Bay deeper into her mouth, suckling hard, her cheeks hollowing with each hard draw. Her fingers gently fondled the sac between his legs, rolling the hard balls between her fingers, stroking the sensitive skin between Bay's thighs.

Bay twisted his fingers in the sheets. Shannon felt the tension in his legs, heard his soft moans of pleasure when she explored his cock more thoroughly with her tongue.

She licked the full length of his erection, tracing the thick vein along the bottom, nipping at the retracted foreskin behind the crown. His sac felt hot and heavy in her palm. She realized there was something amazingly arousing, cupping him this way as she licked and suckled his cock.

As if the taste and feel of Baylor wasn't enough to turn her on, Shannon couldn't ignore Jake behind her, his heat, his touch, his mental caress. His warm palms caressed her thighs, his tongue gently explored between her legs.

He nipped her right buttock, a gentle bite not meant to hurt. Chills raced up Shannon's spine. She felt the rush of cool air on damp flesh as Jake backed away.

She sensed his shift, felt his Chanku spirit and smiled around Bay's cock when her legs and thighs shivered in re action to Jake's coarse wolven coat. A cold nose bumped against her inner thigh, a long tongue snaked deep inside her sex. Shannon shivered again and her entire body clenched at the slick intrusion.

She was aware of Bay's tension the moment Jake shifted, understood his fear the wolf inside him would take over, that he'd shift again without control.

Jake's tongue swirled deep and his mental voice tickled

Shannon's consciousness. *Bay has control. He'll discover he's stronger than he thought, that the wolf doesn't own him.*

Jake punctuated his thoughts with a flick of his tongue over Shannon's clit, then a long slow lick that swept from her mons to her tailbone.

Ahhhhh . . . is that why you shifted?

She felt his laughter in her mind. His tongue drove deep inside, lapping at her sensitive tissues with quick, smooth strokes.

Partially. Mostly it was so I could do this . . .

He nuzzled her legs farther apart, pressed his muzzle between Shannon's thighs and literally fucked her with his tongue. In and out, over and over again with deep, curling strokes while she matched Jake's rhythm with her mouth on Bay's cock.

Bay buried his fingers in Shannon's hair and his hips rose to meet her mouth. She tasted him, tasted the salty drops of fluid, and knew Bay wouldn't last much longer.

Nor would she. Jake's tongue was a thing alive, sweeping deep inside, licking at the spasming walls of her sex. She felt the taut curl of the tip, the rough surface as he stroked tender tissues.

Jake's stiff wolven whiskers abraded her inner thighs, his tongue retreated to sweep her from clit to anus, over and over again. Bay's cock jerked within her mouth. He hovered on the edge of climax. Shannon wrapped her fingers around the base of his cock to control his powerful thrusts, tasted him and sucked harder, deeper.

Bay's hips bucked. Shannon's belly clenched as one last sweep of Jake's long tongue took her over the edge. She arched her back and screamed, mingling her voice with Bay's shout. Hot spurts of semen splattered Shannon's breasts and throat and she felt Bay's body shudder beneath her. Felt the pulsing in his cock perfectly aligned to her own body's response.

Her orgasm seemed to go on forever, fading slowly away under the gentle, yet insistent licking, from Jake. When Shannon rolled to her back, Jake lapped the hot splashes of Bay's ejaculate off her breasts and throat, sprawling across her body like a warm, furry blanket.

He shifted then, becoming once more the man who loved her. Shannon kissed him, then slowly, feeling almost groggy, raised her head to look at Baylor.

One of his thighs was trapped under their combined weight. Shannon started to move away, but Bay stopped her. "Don't go. I like the feeling, the weight of both of you holding me down. I was afraid, after what happened out there, you'd want me to leave."

Jake shook his head. "Never. Another few days and you'll be ready to try a shift under your own terms. We'll do it with you, help you through it. In the meantime, it feels damned good to know you're truly one of us."

Jake raised up on one elbow and looked at Bay for a long, slow moment. Then he shifted his gaze to Shannon. "You are both my family. The first family I've really had in a very long time. Nothing will break that apart. Nothing."

He'd barely gotten the words out when Shannon heard the sound of a car pulling into the yard in front of the house. Startled, she raised up and stared first at Bay, then Jake. It was barely four in the morning.

Not a time when most people came calling.

PART FOUR

Decision

Chapter 14

"Hey, Mik! AJ! I didn't expect you two reprobates until late tonight. It's good to see you." Jake vaulted the porch railing and hugged the first man to climb out of the SUV. The tall newcomer looked either Hispanic or American Indian, Shannon wasn't sure. His hair hung in glossy black waves down his back. High cheekbones and a perfectly chiseled mouth set off brilliant amber eyes.

Eyes that saw way too much, as far as Shannon could tell.

Wrapped in a worn bathrobe, Shannon stood in the doorway with Baylor close behind her. She felt Bay's hand on her shoulder and reached back to rub his cold fingers. This had to be tough for him right now, the addition of strangers, both powerful looking men, when he must still feel so fragile.

"Fragile" certainly described Shannon. She chewed on her bottom lip, watching silently while Jake greeted men who were like brothers to him. Men who were his lovers.

Who might, quite possibly, become Shannon's lovers as well.

The driver of the SUV opened his door and got out. He stretched and arched his back, and Shannon's mouth went dry. Weren't any of these guys average? Tall and lean, his body was the thing fantasies were based upon. So handsome, Shannon would describe him as beautiful, it was hard to believe he was actually an ex-con.

Both of them were, according to Jake, inmates from Folsom Prison, who Ulrich Mason had discovered years ago. Mason had done his homework, realized they were Chanku, gotten their convictions overturned and took them home as the newest members of Pack Dynamics.

Jake hugged the second man just as fiercely as he had the first, then turned around to grin at Shannon. "Other than the fact their timing sucks, as usual, I'm glad they made it in one piece. Especially since Mik let AJ drive most of the way."

The Hispanic punched Jake lightly in the arm and laughed. "It was quite an experience, that's for sure. So, we got you guys out of bed, eh?"

"Of course you did. Haven't you noticed it's still dark out? It's four in the morning, you jerk. C'mon, I'll help you carry your bags in." Jake grinned up at Shannon, obviously glad to see the men in spite of the hour. "Shannon Murphy, Baylor Quinn, this is Miguel Fuentes, otherwise known as Mik."

He nodded in the direction of the driver. "And that's Andrew Jackson Temple, AJ for short." After making the introductions, Jake turned back to AJ. "Why'd you show up so damned early in the morning? Is there trouble?"

"Not really." AJ reached into the back seat and grabbed an army-style duffle bag. "We were told to drive fast. I always follow instructions." He laughed and tossed the heavy bag to Jake as if it were nothing.

"Truth be told, I think Luc was worried about you out here so far from the pack. It was quiet at home, Tia's busy with her class—teaching special-needs kids keeps her running—and there's not much going on. We decided to drive instead of fly."

"Straight through. Very fast. It's a long way from

California." Mik grinned in spite of his deadpan grumble, but Shannon thought both men looked exhausted.

Jake took AJ and Mik to the remaining bedroom next to Bay's while Shannon started breakfast. Bay went in to shower. Jake joined Shannon in the kitchen once he got his packmates settled.

Jake took the cup of coffee Shannon poured for him and leaned his hip against the counter while she peeled potatoes. "I didn't think how much extra work it would be for you." He leaned close and kissed her.

She tasted coffee and toothpaste and Jake. It wasn't easy to end a kiss that could have easily taken her so much further. "It's not extra work, not for people you love. I love you and I love Bay. You really love those two. They love you. It's obvious."

Jake nodded. "Yeah. I'm going to need to explain Bay to them. AJ said Luc hadn't mentioned him. They had no idea he was Chanku."

Shannon turned with her hand planted firmly on one hip and grinned at Jake. "Neither did you. Not for sure until last night. Have you called Luc? Have you told him about Bay? About us?"

"No." Laughing, Jake took a sip of his coffee. "Damn. It's been a full week." He covered Shannon's hand with his. "You're the best part of it. You know that, don't you?"

"So are you." The emotions of the past week slammed into her, like a fist directed at her heart. Shannon felt her throat close up and knew if she didn't get back to work, the rest of the guys would catch her standing in the kitchen with a potato peeler in her hand, sobbing her eyes out. Not a great way to make a first impression.

"I'll set the table." Jake leaned close and kissed her cheek. "I'll call Luc later. It's still the middle of the night in San Francisco."

Shannon snorted and glanced at the clock. "It's still the middle of the night in Maine, too."

* * *

By the time everyone had time to shower and gather in the kitchen, Shannon had produced a feast that thoroughly impressed all four of the men. The table was piled high with plates of scrambled eggs and fried potatoes, sausage and bacon and freshly baked biscuits.

Conversation almost disappeared as everyone piled food on their plates, then returned for seconds and thirds.

Jake couldn't take his eyes off of the woman who was his bonded mate. His woman, with her sparkling eyes and contagious smile. He'd never seen Shannon in a group situation before, never had the chance to see her interact with others besides Bay and himself.

She was amazingly self-confident, teasing and chatting away with men she'd never met, putting Baylor at ease and making Jake so proud of her he thought he'd explode. Her thoughts were open to him, her concern that she make a good impression, her pride in Jake and, most of all, her love.

Jake knew, here in the light of day, he loved Shannon Murphy even more than he'd realized the night before.

Mik took a bite of one of the hot biscuits Shannon placed in front of him, and sighed. "Damn it, man. How'd you get so lucky?" He might have been talking to Jake, but his eyes were on Shannon.

Before Jake could answer, AJ interrupted. "You've already bonded, haven't you?" When Jake nodded, AJ grinned. "Congratulations. Have you told Ulrich and Luc yet?"

Jake glanced at the clock. "It's only a little after three in California. Too early to call."

Mik exchanged a quick glance with AJ. "You mean it just happened last night?" He laughed. "Wow, our timing really sucks, doesn't it?"

Jake gave him a deadpan stare. "Uh, yeah. It sucks."

AJ grinned at Shannon. "I know you're new to all this,

but what we've done is pretty much the equivalent of inviting ourselves along on the honeymoon. I really am sorry. You don't deserve it . . ." AJ pointed at Jake. "But he does."

When the laughter finally died down, Shannon turned to Jake and smiled. *I love you . . . and I really like these guys.*

For the first time all morning long, Jake felt himself relax. Another thought entered his mind, a voice he'd not heard so clearly before.

He glanced up and caught Baylor smiling at him from across the table. *So do I. They're good people.*

It really couldn't get much better than this. *So are you, Bay. So are you.*

Later, after the guys had cleaned up the kitchen and Shannon finally had a chance for her shower, she headed straight for the bedroom. Sleep was merely a fond memory, one she fully intended to refresh. The low sound of men's voices in the other room made her feel safe and protected, and lulled her into sleep. She drifted off, her mind filled with the sounds and scents of the forest and the constant, reassuring promise of Jake's thoughts touching hers.

Jake's warm lips kissing her right breast brought Shannon fully awake.

"It's almost four in the afternoon." He kissed her mouth this time. "You've slept the day away."

Shannon touched the side of his face with her palm. He'd shaved and her fingers glided over smooth, warm skin. "And what have you done all day?"

A dark flush spread over his cheekbones. At the same time, sensual images of arms and legs entwined, of Bay, AJ and Mik all sharing the same bed as Jake, their hands touching, mouths sucking, cocks thrusting . . .

"Oh, my." Shannon scooted up against the headboard,

suddenly wide awake. She swallowed, aware her heart pounded and her breaths were suddenly coming fast and shallow. "You've been busy. Let me see more, okay?"

Jake laughed out loud, but he flooded her mind with memories, sensations, scents. Shannon felt the deep throb of arousal, knew her sex flowered in readiness.

Jake pulled the blankets down over her toes and settled himself between Shannon's legs. Still filling her mind with images of the afternoon's activities, he filled her pussy with his tongue, lapping slowly, holding her at the edge of orgasm.

She almost came with the first touch of his tongue, caught herself, and held on to the sensation. Part of Shannon's mind concentrated on the hot sweep of Jake's tongue, the pressure of his lips around her swollen clit, but her main focus was on the images. The amazing, arousing images of men pleasuring one another in every way imaginable.

The faces excited Shannon most. The dark desire on Bay's handsome features as he mounted AJ, the straining muscles in Mik's throat and chest as he tried to hold back his climax when AJ filled his ass and Bay sucked his cock.

Over and over again, each man finding release, each one of them growing closer, accepting Bay fully into their midst, their bodies straining and thrusting, faces contorting, voices crying out . . . all viewed from Jake's perspective.

Shannon touched his shoulders. Even though she was on the edge of her own orgasm, she scooted away from Jake's mouth. "What about you? Didn't you . . . ?"

Jake sat back on his heels. His lips and chin glistened with her fluids, his eyes sparkled. "A little. It was more important to get them to accept Bay. Besides, I . . ." He shrugged and looked away a moment. "I wanted you there with us. I wanted the guys to know you the same way. I wasn't sure how you'd feel about it . . . adding two more men you've hardly met."

Jake chose that moment to run the callused tip of his finger across Shannon's clit. She screamed, convulsing in a powerful, muscle-clenching orgasm.

One touch. Just that one small touch of his finger . . . and the promise of four sensual men taking her to heights she'd never even fantasized.

Four. All at the same time. It took Shannon a moment to catch her breath. Another moment to reassure herself she wasn't dreaming. Even more effort to force an answer between parted lips.

"Yes. When?"

Jake cocked an eyebrow and grinned. "Now?"

Shannon wrapped the bathrobe around herself and stepped out of the bathroom. The bedroom door was open and she heard men talking in the other room. Taking a deep breath, she walked into the main room of the house.

Jake and Bay sat on the couch. Each man had a cold beer and they were obviously deep in discussion. There was no sign of AJ and Mik.

Shannon wasn't sure if she was disappointed or relieved. She walked across the room, leaned over and kissed Jake, then planted one on Bay as well. He scooted over and made room for her.

She sat in between them and leaned back against Jake. "Where'd everyone go?"

"Mik and AJ decided to go for a run. Bay thinks he's ready to try a shift again, and they wanted to give us time alone."

Bay's lip quirked up in a self-deprecating grin. "They didn't want to watch me make a fool of myself."

Shannon laughed. "I doubt that's it, Bay."

"Actually, they were more concerned of the potential problems with an untried wolf faced with so many other males." Jake brushed Shannon's hair back from her eyes as he spoke. "Your shift might bring out all kinds of alpha traits you're not used to. It will be a lot easier with just the two of us here to help you through it."

"After the supplement this morning, I felt as if something clicked. The image of shifting was suddenly very clear to me. When we were all together . . ." Bay's voice faded off and he blushed.

Shannon laughed. Deadpan, she said, "I know what you were doing when you were all together."

"Yeah, well, I came very close to shifting, but I was able to control it. Yesterday, I wouldn't have been able to."

Jake stood up and slipped his sweatshirt over his head. "C'mon, then. There's no reason to waste any time."

Bay slipped out of his clothing. Shannon dropped her robe and heard Jake's clothing hit the ground behind her. Grinning, she opened the front door. "See. I learned my lesson."

"Good girl." Jake touched Bay's shoulder. "Get in my head, Bay. Sometimes it's easier if you watch someone else shift from the inside."

Bay focused on Jake. Shannon sensed his intense concentration, realized she'd entered Jake's mind as well. It was such a natural thing to do, now. Becoming one with her bonded mate.

Jake shifted. As always, Shannon found the process mesmerizing. She followed him, shifting and sitting beside Jake, both of them waiting for Bay.

Other than a brief look of panic, Bay managed his shift perfectly, morphing from man to animal in less than a heartbeat. Covered in a pelt of glossy black fur, he looked big and powerful and absolutely gorgeous.

Shannon leaned forward and touched noses with him. *Are you okay?*

Oh, yeah. Amazing. This is utterly amazing. I don't remember the shift last night. Nothing but fear and darkness and the sense I was in a stranger's body. This is unreal.

Totally unreal . . . it's fucking amazing! He stood up. Yipped once, and bounded toward the door. Looked back with his mouth open and tail wagging slowly from side to side. *What are you waiting for? Let's go run.*

They met up with AJ and Mik just a few miles away from the house. After a few tense minutes of wolven posturing, walking stiff-legged with ears flat and teeth bared, the four males each peed on a tree or two then charged off along a narrow woodland trail.

For the next two hours, Shannon knew Bay experienced wonders he'd never imagined. She thought of her first run as a wolf, just a few short days ago. Of the sounds and scents her Chanku mind had suddenly been able to read like an open book.

She wondered if Bay noticed the sensual nature of the world around him. If he grew aroused, just as Shannon did, when faced with the abundance of sights and sounds and scents unnoticed by their human side.

Shannon ran beside Jake. She joined her thoughts with his, thrilled to see he thought of her not merely as Shannon, the woman he loved, but as his bitch, his bonded mate for life. She ran with the full knowledge each of the wolves in her pack—for it was her pack and fully under her command—would mate with her tonight. Would take her in their human guise, acknowledging her leadership, her position at the top.

Though she fully intended to be on the bottom at least a few times . . . anticipation drove her on. Love of Jake might keep her grounded, but Shannon knew the wolf that was her soul, the Chanku nature Jake helped her discover, had truly set her free.

There was no moon at all tonight to light their way, but the pack had no trouble finding the trail home. Five wolves, muddy, chilled by a sudden drop in temperature, tongues lolling and tails drooping, slowly trotted through the dark forest to Jake's cabin and climbed the front steps to the deck.

Shannon was the first to shift, shivering and sore from the long miles and the ferocious hunts that had favored the woodland creatures more than the wolves. Baylor was next. Then Mik, AJ and Jake, all of them tired, dirty and cold, yet collectively wound tight with the thrill of the hunt, the adrenaline still coursing through their veins . . . and the deep, all-consuming sensual need that was so much a part of Chanku.

"I'm going to shower." Shannon smiled and winked, catching a quick glance at the four obviously aroused males. She went inside before any of the guys had time to react, but the image of their taut erections had burned itself into her brain. She'd caught Jake's sexy grin, his obvious awareness of her need, but she'd quickly blocked his thoughts.

After the intensity of the run, Shannon needed time alone. She took her time in the shower, forced her mind to go blank while she scrubbed away the sweat and dirt, then rinsed carefully with the hand-held sprayer. Adjusting the controls to a gentle pulse, she turned it on herself for just a few seconds, long enough to raise her already aroused body to another level of awareness.

Her arousal grew with each second that passed, the sense of destiny over what was going to happen in a very short time. Grabbing the robe off a hook by the door, Shannon held it in her hands and stared at the soft cotton. Should she cover herself like a virgin sacrifice?

No. Among the Chanku, the female led. Shannon Murphy had four unbelievably sexy men at her disposal for the rest of the night. Even longer, depending on how long AJ and Mik planned to stay. A bathrobe was the last thing she wanted.

Shoving her wet hair back over her shoulders, Shannon

walked naked into the main room. AJ, Mik, Baylor and Jake sat talking quietly, unaware of her presence.

The men had taken time to fix sandwiches. They sat in a group talking, drinking beer and eating, acting as if nothing more exciting were planned for the night. Shannon might have felt insulted, except for the tangible sexual tension in the room.

She waited, standing in the open doorway from the bedroom, her shoulders back and head held high. Slowly, one by one, each man turned and looked her way. Jake first, then Bay, then Mik and AJ. Conversation died.

Jake stood up. He walked to her very slowly, as if he crossed the room in a dream. He raised his hands and lightly cupped her face. Then he kissed her, taking Shannon's mouth with his own, thrusting his tongue deep inside, suckling at her lips, her tongue, marking her mouth as his.

When he finally broke the kiss, both of them were breathing hard. There was absolute silence in the room, broken only by the sound of air hissing in and out of parted lips.

Are you absolutely certain? No one will be offended if you change your mind.

I love you. I love your packmates. I have never been so aroused, so turned on as I have tonight, just imagining what might happen.

Jake grinned, took Shannon's hand and led her out into the room. "Gentlemen, I believe Baylor's room has the biggest bed." He swept Shannon up in his arms, catching her surprised gasp with another kiss.

Then he carried her down the hall to the room with the biggest bed.

Trembling, Shannon wasn't quite certain what to expect, but Jake set her in the middle of the oversized mattress while he shoved his sweats down over his lean hips. Baylor lighted a few small candles while AJ and Mik stripped off their jeans and crawled onto the bed next to Shannon. Bay undressed as well and settled at the foot, between her feet.

Shannon realized she was trembling, whether from nerves, arousal or anxious anticipation. The room quickly filled with four large, extremely sensual naked men, all intent on sex, all focused on Shannon.

She glanced from face to face, saw nothing but smiles and warmth, but when she lowered her gaze, the size and power of each man's erection was enough to make her shiver all the harder.

Then Bay picked up Shannon's right foot and began to gently massage her instep. "Tonight was amazing," he said, looking at her foot as he spoke. There was a sense of awe in his voice, as if he still couldn't believe what he'd done. "I had no idea what to expect, but it went beyond my wildest fantasies."

Bay's thumb traced a firm path across the top of her foot, this time sending exquisite shivers of pleasure through her body. "Oh, Bay! That feels heavenly." Shannon hadn't known what to expect, either, but it certainly hadn't been this!

Bay's fingers continued to work their magic. There was nothing overtly sexual about his touch, but the shivers she felt seemed to race all the way up her leg directly to her sex.

Mik took her left hand in his and began to rub it with the same intensity as Bay. AJ did the same to her right.

Jake sat beside Baylor and picked up her left foot. His long fingers wrapped around her ankle and the ball of her foot, gently pressing and stretching the sore muscles and tendons.

No one went near her sex, no one touched her breasts or any other part of her body. The tension thrumming throughout Shannon's body melted away as the men gently massaged her hands and feet and talked among themselves, their soft, sexy voices enough to make Shannon's insides melt. She closed her eyes. The self-imposed darkness heightened her senses, made each caress even more intimate.

After a few minutes, Jake said he remembered a jar of scented oil he'd seen in the bathroom. He found it and passed the jar around. The room filled with the seductive scent of vanilla.

Jake's hands moved to her calves. Then Bay's did the same, while AJ and Mik worked on her arms. Shannon groaned aloud as her thighs and torso received the same treatment.

She was almost asleep when someone rolled her gently to her stomach and the massage continued. Strong hands kneaded her back and thighs, worked lovingly over her buttocks, her shoulders. Warm lips followed some of the strokes, a kiss here, another there. She'd lost track of which man massaged what part, and in this half awake state was only aware of sensation, of warmth and pressure and the slow, gentle movement of bodies working close to hers.

Mouths and tongues, fingers and lips, the occasional brush of a swollen cock against her side. She was gently turned again. Warm mouths found each breast, gently suckled her nipples, rubbed the soft underside and stroked her belly. Large hands pulled her thighs apart, lips traced the line from navel to groin, from her knee along her inner thigh.

It all had a dreamlike quality, arousing, seductive, sensation building with each kiss and touch. She felt something warm and satin-smooth brush her lips. Shannon parted her lips and stroked the smooth, hot flesh with her tongue, recognizing the firm head of someone's cock, licking up the salty flavor of pre-cum. Not Jake's. She already knew she'd recognize his flavor anywhere. Not Baylor either. She knew his as well.

AJ or Mik. Did it matter which one? She opened her mouth wider, took him all the way to the back of her throat. Licked his full length when he withdrew, twisted her head and took his sac into her mouth, rolled the hard balls inside with her tongue.

She heard a low, heartfelt groan. Shannon grinned around her mouthful. The scent alone was an aphrodisiac. Clean, musky male with an overlay of vanilla. She licked and nipped, then released him. Warm lips touched hers, a tongue licked the seam of her mouth, invited her to open once again.

The kiss was deep, searingly hot, exciting. She thought about opening her eyes but the fantasy of nameless mouths and hands, of tongues and cocks and pure sensation was much too wonderful to end.

Someone worked between her legs, licking, suckling, finding each sensitive spot that craved attention, and satisfying the need. The rich vanilla scent grew stronger. She wondered if someone had decided to heat the oil, and had her suspicions confirmed when warm drops spilled across her chest.

More oil dripped onto her neatly trimmed thatch of pubic hair. She felt it run down the crease between thigh and sex while some dripped directly over her clit then mingled with her own juices. Her pussy clenched when the warm oil found its way between her swollen labia.

Strong hands raised her knees, pressed them back against her chest. Oil dribbled over her perineum, strong fingers slipped back and forth in the slick crease between her buttocks.

A tongue lapped at her sex and she hoped the oil tasted as good as it smelled. Fingers pressed against her anus as the tongue swirled deeply inside her pussy.

One of the men must have shifted. No human tongue could go so deep, find so many sensitive spots and she realized it was so, recognized the coarse coat of a wolf against the back of her thighs.

Just as the sensation of wolven coat and searching tongue began to make sense, the finger pressing against her butt slipped through her tight sphincter muscle and was quickly joined by a second. Shannon's world narrowed, centered on the burning heat of fingers thrusting in and out of her tight anal passage, of the long tongue licking and stroking deep inside her sex.

Her right hand was lifted, the fingers opened, then carefully wrapped around a swollen cock covered in the sweet oil. The same happened with Shannon's left hand. Awash in sensation now, she gripped each cock tightly, and slowly, steadily stroked all the way out to the crowns of each, then back to the thick nest of coarse hair growing at the base.

Shannon opened her mind to the sensations, the minor differences in each man. She had no idea who she held, what male she pleasured, only that their thoughts began to mingle with hers, mindless images of pleasure multiplied as each man shared, one with the other, then included Shannon in their sensual link.

She drew them closer, closer until she could reach out with her tongue and stroke the satiny head of first one, then the other. The images in her mind grew more intense, more defined, and she knew that AJ was on her right, Mik on her left. She searched deeper with her thoughts, entranced now by her mental ability to define the nature of each man by their touch, almost as if they carried a specific fingerprint linked to their arousal, their own sensuality.

Ah . . . Jake had shifted. His tongue filled her, stroked the sensitive tissues, held her at the edge of climax. Bay was the one who penetrated her darker passage, who stroked in perfect counterpoint to Jake's tongue.

The pressure built, the sense of impending climax as each of them came closer to their peak. In Shannon's mind she saw how Mik took Bay's cock deep down his throat, bringing Baylor ever closer to climax. The images, all of them, linked together, expanded, one upon the other. Brighter, more powerful, until Shannon's mind was bursting with sensation, with the combination of Mik and AJ and Baylor, growing, expanding, climaxing.

Mik stiffened, his cock grew even harder in her grasp. AJ did the same. Shannon heard their groans, felt the warm streams of semen hitting her breasts, her belly, as she stroked each man through his climax.

Bay cried out, his fingers slipped free of her body and she knew he'd come as well, but Shannon resisted, held at the brink of orgasm by Jake's tongue, his unspoken desire that she wait.

Her eyes still closed, her mind open, Shannon heard the raspy breaths of three satiated men, heard her own heart thundering in her chest, felt one last, long sweep of a wolven tongue between her legs.

The wolf crawled up her body, nuzzling her belly with his cold nose, licking the spatters of warm ejaculate from her torso, but when he reached her lips it was Jake, the man she loved, who kissed her. Jake who thrust his cock deep inside, who shared the feeling of her ripe and ready sex clasping his cock, who brought her to climax with one powerful penetration.

His body was hard and rigid in her arms, his heart pounded against her chest. She heard his shout of triumph as he filled her, felt his love, his possession, his need to own her heart and soul.

Shannon smiled when she sensed something else, something unexpected and therefore treasured. Jake's pride. Pride in Shannon as his mate, in his fellow packmates for their easy acceptance of his chosen partner, in Baylor for his successful shift and easy acceptance of the Chanku way.

So tightly linked, Shannon was reminded of Jake's

hidden vulnerability, his need to feel wanted, to be loved. *Both of us, my love. We both share those same needs.*

I love you.

And I love you. Shannon finally opened her eyes. She wasn't quite certain why it had been so important to keep them shut during this first time together with all four men, but deep in her heart was the sense that it had been the right choice.

She glanced to her left, at Mik, propped up on one elbow smiling at her. AJ, to her right, still lay flat on his back, his lungs pumping like a bellows. Bay leaned up against the headboard, but the smile on his face told Shannon this was something he'd never grow tired of.

Jake still sprawled over her body, a welcome weight that probably kept her from floating off the bed. Shannon had a sudden image of a basket of puppies, all of them sprawled and tangled together, and she started to giggle.

It didn't feel appropriate, giggling after the best sexual experience she'd ever had in her life.

The more she tried to bite it back, the harder she laughed. She caught Mik's eye and realized he was biting his lips. Jake raised his head, frowned, then snorted.

In seconds, all of them were laughing, giggling, wiping tears from their eyes. Holding their sides, roaring with laughter and sharing an overwhelming sense of joy.

Chapter 15

Shannon awoke later, dreaming she was on a boat rocking on rough seas. Instead, gazing through sleep-swollen eyes, she saw Jake kneeling beside her with Mik's cock deep inside his mouth. Baylor knelt behind Jake, his face twisted with what could only be described as unimaginable lust. His hips thrust forward then tilted back as he slammed rhythmically in, then pulled out of Jake's ass.

AJ suckled Jake's erection. His cheeks hollowed as he drew Jake's swollen cock deep down his throat. At the same time, his hands were busy with both Baylor and Jake, carefully massaging each man's sac.

Mik pleasured AJ, his head moving slowly up and down over his mate's erection. All four men, their faces contorted with expressions of pain and pleasure and unmitigated lust, appeared to be totally caught up in their own pleasure as well as each of their partners'.

Shannon had never seen anything quite so amazing, nor been aroused so completely by a visual such as this. Her fingers stole down to the waiting heat between her legs and she stroked herself, unintentionally finding the same rhythm as Baylor. The same rhythm each man shared.

Bay's fingers dug into Jake's lean hips. He grunted now

with the force of each thrust, his balls slamming close against Jake's each time he buried his cock deeper, harder.

Each time Bay rammed home, AJ's fingers stroked him and Bay groaned.

Shannon hadn't seen Jake on the bottom before, had only seen him cover Bay, something she'd found so arousing she used the image to fantasize, to bring herself to climax.

This aroused her even more, seeing the man she loved as the recipient of Bay's cock, watching Jake pleasure Mik. The scene was both dark and addictive, from the rigid expressions on each man's face and the slide of powerful muscles beneath smooth skin to the musky scents of each man, the sounds they made, all melding together, building, spiraling higher with each second that passed.

Almost afraid to open her mind, Shannon was seduced by the need to experience, the overwhelming desire to be a part of this while still remaining apart. She linked to Jake, just his mind alone and arched her back with the jolt of profound pleasure she found.

He acknowledged her presence . . . barely. Shannon stayed with him for just a moment, experiencing the burning thrust as Baylor's cock speared deep inside his bowels, the dark pleasure when he withdrew. She tasted the smooth crown of Mik's cock and realized his was the one she'd suckled earlier.

Emboldened now, Shannon tentatively tapped into the group consciousness of all four men. Lust slammed into her. Powerful, all male, carnal to the extreme. Need and desire, the sense of competition so inherent in strong men, and over all, pleasure so wondrous and a love so deep it brought Shannon to tears.

Lights flashed behind her eyes, electricity sparked in her mind and raced to her toes and fingers. She thrust deep inside her clenching sex, pinched one nipple with her free hand, twisting painfully as orgasm claimed her.

Shouts, groans, the combined power of four strong and vital men reaching a simultaneous peak, carried Shannon even higher. When she finally fell, it was with a boneless, mindless drop into pure pleasure.

Her body stilled, though the muscles in her pussy continued their rhythmic contractions. She pulled her slick fingers free with a brief pause to stroke her throbbing clit. A broad hand grabbed hers, moist lips and a wet tongue licked the juices from her fingers. Shannon opened her eyes and grinned at AJ, who sucked at her fingers with a look of pure bliss on his face.

This time, there was no laughter, just a quiet contentment brought on by total satiation. However long it would last didn't matter. The pack would be there to see that no one went unfulfilled.

Bay lay across Jake's back, hugging him close, stroking his chest and belly, then gently cupping Jake's balls in the palm of his hand. Finally he pulled out and headed for the bathroom.

A few minutes later, Jake snuggled close to Shannon and Bay returned to the room, crawled into bed and tucked himself against Shannon's other side. She was aware of AJ and Mik crawling off to their own room, then nothing but the sound of quiet breathing and the steady beat of three hearts . . . three hearts beating as one.

Shannon crawled out of bed around midmorning, took a quick shower and slipped into a clean pair of sweats. Her body ached in spots she'd ignored for years, but each sore muscle was a reminder of something wonderful she'd done with the pack the night before.

Saturday night? One full week since Jake rescued her. Shannon heard a noise behind her, turned around and saw Jake peeking around the corner of the bedroom door.

"Good morning, lazybones. I was just checking on you."

Shannon pushed her hair back out of her eyes and threw her arms around Jake. "Good morning to you, too. Happy anniversary!"

Jake leaned back, still wrapped in Shannon's arms, and cocked one eyebrow. "Anniversary?"

"Hard to believe how much has happened in one week, isn't it? You rescued me just a week ago." She reached up on her toes and kissed him, then backed away before Jake could take the kiss any further. "In fact, it was more than a rescue. You saved my life, Jake. I was in such a terrible downward spiral."

Jake's arms settled around Shannon's waist and he rested his chin on top of her head. "You weren't the only one. And the rescue works both ways. C'mon. The guys have been talking. I want you in on the conversation."

He took Shannon's hand and tugged, pulling her out into the main room.

Shannon felt as if she'd walked into a *Playgirl* photo shoot. Bay was stretched out on the sofa wearing his black slacks and white dress shirt with the sleeves rolled to expose his forearms. The shirt was unbuttoned, allowing a suggestive glimpse of his muscular chest and the dark whorl of hair linking his nipples, trailing down to disappear beneath his waistband.

His feet were bare. In fact none of the men wore shoes. Shannon decided there was something both subtle and sexy about bare feet.

Mik sat near the wood stove with a paperback novel held loosely in one hand. He wore faded blue jeans, but had skipped the shirt. Shannon sighed quietly, grateful for small favors. Unlike Bay, Mik's chest was perfectly smooth, a deep bronze shade defined by spectacular muscles and two perfectly flat nipples. A narrow trail of black hair ran from his navel down his flat stomach and disappeared beneath the unsnapped fastener at the top of his zipper.

Shannon licked her lips and had to swallow back a soft

moan. She remembered following that same happy trail with her tongue. After last night, she'd never be able to look at Mik without getting turned on.

Her gaze slid down to AJ where he sprawled on the floor, his back against Mik's legs. AJ made Shannon think of cowboys and horses and dusty rides, but when he turned and smiled at her, all she could think of was the blissful look on his face when he'd licked her juices off her fingers.

Shannon sighed again, turned to Jake and shook her head ruefully. "All they wanna do is talk? Damn."

Jake grabbed her hand and tugged her to one of the overstuffed leather chairs. He sat down and pulled Shannon into his lap. "Mik called Luc awhile ago. They're trying to figure out what's the best approach for Bay. We need to get him as far away from contact with the missing agents as we can, and somehow get him honorably discharged from the agency. Ulrich is thinking of putting Bay on the Pack Dynamics roster as an employee. In a few months we'll open an eastern branch with me as head, and Bay can transfer back here."

Shannon frowned. "Transfer back? You mean Bay has to leave?"

Baylor straightened up and planted his feet on the ground. "I'm not real crazy about leaving you guys either, but it wouldn't be for long. It makes sense. I'll take over Jake's position in San Francisco while he gets things set up here. From what I know of Lucien Stone and Ulrich Mason, it shouldn't take long for them to figure out how to get me cleared. Plus, it'll give you two some time alone together."

"Such a concept." Jake's dry comment made Shannon smile. They really hadn't had any time alone together. "We won't be alone for long. I need to take Shannon to San Francisco to meet everyone. I imagine Tia's anxious to fill her in on all my bad points."

"Darling, you have no bad points." Shannon smiled sweetly while the other three groaned.

AJ draped his arm over Mik's knee. "Besides, how're you guys gonna go anywhere if Baylor stays? I can't see three adults on that sweet little bike Jake managed to snag on this trip. We really do have to take Bay with us."

"Ah. The bike." Mik laughed. "You should have seen Luc's face when Ulrich told him the pack had just bought you a new BMW. You've certainly redeemed yourself in our eyes!"

"Yeah," said AJ. "Why did you get a motorcycle? It's hardly practical transportation in Maine in the winter. You plan to run it with chains on the tires? I mean, that one's really sweet, but why not a sleek little sports car? If you're planning to stick it to Luc . . ."

Jake laughed and shook his head. "I had no desire to stick it to Luc. In fact, I've got every intention of paying him back. I didn't have enough cash and wasn't about to use a credit card that could be traced."

Mik frowned. "Okay. Now I am curious. Why did you buy it? Why now?"

Jake turned to Shannon and brushed her hair back from her forehead. His eyes sparkled and she felt his smile all the way to her heart.

"To get Shannon in leathers. Why else? It was worth every penny to get her perfect behind in a pair of tight, leather pants." He turned to the guys and held out one hand, imploring.

Shannon giggled. She'd had no idea, but she had to admit, it was sweet . . . and very *Jake*.

Mik nodded solemnly. "You've made your point. I'd have bought the bike, too."

They ran together late that night, one last race through the dark Maine woods before Mik, AJ and Baylor headed west. A light snow was falling by the time they dragged themselves up the steps and into the house.

Jake would have fallen into bed alone with Shannon, but she pulled him into the shower with her, scrubbed his back, kissed him hard and insisted they join Bay.

"I've created a monster, haven't I?" Yawning, Jake let Shannon tug his hand and lead him down the hall. Mik and AJ were in Bay's room already, though the three of them were merely talking.

That didn't last long.

When Jake finally awoke hours later, it was to the smell of bacon frying and freshly brewed coffee.

He was the only one left in the bed.

Jake wandered out and stood in the doorway, watching as Shannon flipped pancakes like a master, a cup of coffee in her left hand, the spatula in her right. AJ and Mik sipped cups of coffee and it looked like they'd already eaten. Baylor was merely waiting for seconds. The perfect domesticity of the scene stole Jake's breath.

He'd come out here filled with resentment, taking the assignment to protect Shannon because he felt he had no other choice. He'd been an outcast. Wondered if he'd ever be accepted back into the pack or if he'd spend the rest of his life alone.

So much had changed in just a few short days.

It's been one hell of a week.

Shannon looked up and smiled. *Didn't I say just about the same thing yesterday?*

Yeah. You did. He leaned over and kissed Shannon. Traced her lips with his tongue, found his way inside. Deepened the kiss until she moaned softly against his mouth.

Then she dropped the spatula.

Jake leaned over and picked it up, rinsed it off and handed it back to Shannon. Her lips, still parted, were moist from his kiss. She blinked and turned back to the stove, just in time to keep the pancakes from burning.

Grinning like a damned Cheshire cat, Jake poured a cup of coffee and sat down at the table. The guys greeted him. Bay only grumbled a little when Shannon put the pancakes meant for Bay on a plate in front of Jake.

He could get used to this real fast.

It hit Jake like a fist to the solar plexus. For the first time in as long as he could remember, he looked forward to tomorrow. They had so much to do. There was that insidious breeding farm that might or might not exist. Bay's two sisters out there, somewhere, probably carrying the Chanku genes.

A mate he wanted to get to know a whole lot better.

Maybe, some day, a family to raise.

Jake realized he was sitting at the table grinning like a damned fool. No one seemed to mind.

Still smiling, Jake dug into his breakfast.

For a sneak peek at more delicious erotic romance, turn the page for an excerpt of KISS OF THE WOLF, by Morgan Hawke, on sale from Aphrodisia in February!

1

November 1876

The Fairwind, *American Line steamship*
En route to Constantza, Romania

Thorn gasped and jerked upright, knocking the pillows off the small brass bed and onto the floor. Her entire body shook. She pressed one palm over her slamming heart. "A dream . . . just a dream." She shoved the long pale brown strands of hair from her damp cheeks. It was long since over and done.

She jerked the white cotton sheets from her naked, sweat-soaked body and slid from the cot to stand. The waxed hardwood deck of the steamship's tiny iron-walled cabin was cool and rocked gently under her feet. She turned to stare out the cabin's porthole. The moon floated among rags of cloud, and the sound of the sea rushed in her ears.

Once upon a time, she had been Kerry Fiddler, an ordinary girl, with an ordinary paper route, who had found an extraordinary white dog. And then the Doctor had found them.

But that was years ago.

She couldn't stop shaking. She moved to the corner and

the small washstand. "It's over and done, over and done, damnit!" She had long since become used to being someone else, some*thing* else, something wilder, something fiercer, something feral. She splashed water on her face.

The moon's light silvered the mirror's glass. Beneath her dark slashing brows, her dark gold eyes caught the light, and the hearts caught fire, glowing like two green-gold coins—wolf eyes.

The night shadows within the ship's small cabin seemed to close in on her. Her sweat-slicked skin chilled in the cool air of the cabin. She shivered and gasped for breath. She couldn't get enough air. She shook her head and forced herself to take deep, slow breaths. It was over, it was done, and she had escaped. It was nothing but a memory.

Thorn turned to look back at the moon floating outside her small window. The damned nightmare came whenever she spent too much time in too small a space. She needed to get out of this tiny iron box. She needed to run.

She took three long steps to the cabin door and jerked it open. The wind from the ocean caressed her naked skin and swept through her waist-length hair. Moonlight tinted the fine straight strands with silver. She lifted her face to the moon and let her wolf rise from her soul in a tide of fur and joy. She dropped to four paws and shook her silvery fur into place. Ears forward and long tail lifted, she trotted down the deck, her black claws clicking on the slick wooden surface.

"A large white dog was seen running loose on the ship last night." Seated behind his elegant golden oak desk, carried onboard for his express use, Agent Hackett, fine, upstanding representative of the United States Secret Service, wrote with a hasty hand. His Parker fountain pen scratched busily across the very fine parchment. "What do you have to say for yourself?" He did not look up.

Thorn Ferrell's hand tightened on the brim of her charcoal-gray leather hat. "I needed some air."

Agent Hackett scowled at his writing while working the top back onto his fountain pen. "So you ran around the deck on four legs? You couldn't do it on two like a normal human?"

Thorn didn't bother to answer him. He wouldn't have liked the reply. Why should she act like something she wasn't?

In complete contrast to her farmboy appearance, he was fashionably dressed in the attire of most governmental associates. His restrained frock coat of midnight green was buttoned over a severely understated waistcoat of black damask, and a floridly knotted cravat of black silk was tied around the high collar of his white shirt. With his blond hair combed back into a ruthless wave, and neat mustache, he was considered handsome by many.

Thorn considered him a self-righteous prig.

Agent Hackett tucked the fountain pen inside his jacket's breast pocket. "This makes four times you've exposed yourself." He gently blew across the damp ink.

Thorn rolled her eyes. "They saw only a dog. . . ."

"That is not the point." Agent Hackett ruthlessly folded the paper and reached for his stick of sealing wax. "If you cannot be trusted to control your baser urges and at least act like a human, I do not see why you should be treated as one." He struck a lucifer match against the side of his desk.

The stench of sulfur burned in her nose. She winced back. The bastard knew damned well she hated the smell of those things.

A smile twitched at the corner of his mouth. "Perhaps your return trip should be done at the end of a leash." Melted wax dripped onto the folded paper. "Or better yet, in a cage."

A leash? A *cage*? Thorn's temper flared white-hot. Did

he honestly think she would allow either to happen? She swallowed to hold back the growl that wanted to boil up from her chest. His attitude clearly begged for a reminder of whom, and what, he was dealing with, but a show of temper would only work against her. She needed something far more subtle.

She dropped her white canvas pack and dark gray, black fleeced, sheepskin coat on the expensive carpet. Casually she stepped slightly to one side, choosing a spot by the corner of his desk very carefully. She adjusted her position to allow the light from the small oil lamp to shine directly into her highly reflective and inhuman eyes. It had taken ages to figure out the exact angle, but the results were always worth the effort. Pleased, she jammed her thumbs into the pockets of her faded dungarees, relaxing into her pose.

"Now then, Courier Ferrell . . ." Agent Hackett looked up from his desk and froze, staring into her gaze. The pupils of his eyes widened, and the acrid scent of his sweat perfumed the air, betraying his instinctive alarm.

Perfect. Thorn smiled. Yes, my dear Agent Hackett, your brain may be dense, but your body knows very well that it's in a small room with a dangerous predator.

Agent Hackett tore his gaze from her eyes and lunged to his feet. Scowling, he yanked opened a desk drawer and pulled out a small brown-paper-wrapped parcel with a white card. He came around the desk to tower head and shoulders over her and offered them. "This is the package. You already know the route. The card has the address you are to deliver it to. It is vital that you arrive as swiftly as possible."

Thorn took the package and card from his hands and then knelt to tuck them into her small canvas pack. She knew the "preferred" route, all right. It hadn't taken much to memorize the map they had provided and to deduce that she would cover the territory a hell of a lot faster if she didn't bother with roads. But Agent Hackett didn't need to know that.

He held out a second card. "When you return to Constantza, I will be at this address." His blue eyes narrowed, and his painstakingly neat mustache twitched. "No delays on the return trip, either, you wanton little beast. I don't want to remain in this godforsaken country any longer than necessary."

Still kneeling, she looked up at him. He was standing so close her lips were but a kiss away from his crotch. Well aware of her suggestive position, she smiled. "Do I really look like a wanton to you?"

Agent Hackett's eyes widened, and the perfume of lust rolled off him. She could smell the evidence of an erection growing under his knee-length midnight-green coat. He jammed the card into her hand and jerked back a step. "You look like a street urchin." His voice dropped to a growl. "However, your reputation for shameless exploits precedes you."

"Dungarees are better suited than skirts for what I do, Agent Hackett." She rose to her feet and dragged on her fleeced coat. "And I'm not ashamed of my exploits." She shouldered her pack and smiled. "I like sex."

He jerked his chin up, refusing to look at her. "Why in God's name did they saddle me with you?"

Thorn snorted. "My guess is you pissed off somebody upstairs."

His cheeks flushed, and his jaw clenched. He pointed at the stateroom door. "Get out of my sight!"

Thorn headed for the door and jammed her hat on her head, chuckling softly. Agent Hackett simply could not accept his physical attraction to her. His morals wouldn't let him. Too bad. He obviously was in dire need of a good fuck.

She stepped out onto the steamship's crowded deck and blinked against the late-afternoon winter brightness. The icy wind from the dark Romanian port city smelled bitterly of coal smoke. The Black Sea, behind her, smelled just as strong, but far cleaner. Damp chill crept down past the collar of her sheepskin coat and up the legs of her faded dungarees. She'd thought to bring her good boots and flannel shirts, but she should have brought a heavy sweater, too.

Among good-natured farewell shouts and horrific blasts from the steamship's horns, she eased in among the ship's debarking third-class passengers and marched toward the narrow roped walkway leading down from the steamship to the dock. Setting her hand on top of her battered hat to keep the wind from blowing it away, she tromped down the gangplank into a maelstrom of humanity.

Keeping her head down, she jogged across the busy docks, dodging drays hauling freight and coaches with passengers. The occasional steam carriage chugged by, disturbing the horses with their whistling pops and loud, grumbling hisses. The train at the far end loosed a long, high whistle that raised the hair on her neck.

She entered the city proper and jogged swiftly through the wasteland of crumbling buildings, garbage heaps, and casual violence. She dodged gazes as she hurried by, just another kid in a battered sheepskin coat and faded dungarees. She snorted. The illusion would have been a lot more effective if she'd been a little more flat-chested and narrow-hipped.

Thorn reached the city's limit just at nightfall. Farmland stretched before her, and, beyond that, clean forest. Strands of her hair escaped her braid and flitted around her cheeks. Snow scented the wind.

The next leg of her journey was the easy part. Run. A lot.

The snowstorm finally ended, and moonlight bathed the snow-covered mountains and forest, creating near-daylight brilliance.

The she-wolf ghosted out from under the snow-heavy,

ground-sweeping conifer, her silvery winter coat blending perfectly with the fresh snow. The chill hadn't been a problem, not with her thick arctic coat, and the long nap under the draping tree had given her a much needed rest. She gave herself a firm shake to settle the white pack strapped to her long slender back and then launched into a gliding lope.

Her long strides and wide paws carried her atop the snow and through the moon-bright forest with blinding haste. Her sensitive nose caught occasional traces of the far smaller, and darker, red-coated European wolves that lived in the small mountain range she was passing through. They weren't too difficult to avoid. They stank from eating human garbage. She smelled them long before they could scent her.

A trace scent of human drifted on the breeze.

She stilled and lifted her nose to sift the wind. What the hell was a human doing all the way out here? Along with wool and sweat, there was something odd about the scent, something subtly wrong. . . . Her tail switched in annoyance. She figured out where the scent was coming from and moved away, deeper into the trees. She preferred avoiding humans as much as possible. She had no interest in their noisy, cramped spaces, their stinking food, and their lies about what they wanted and didn't want.

Her loping pace ate distance, and the moon drifted across the sky, marking the passage of hours. Her long strides carried her out of the forest and higher, into the mountains. The pass she was headed for was impassable for humans in winter but not for a wolf.

She moved swiftly upward over rock and snow. Her muscles burned with the effort. Her time on the ship had held far too much inactivity. She was going to need to rest again. Dawn was only a few hours away, so finding a safe place to sleep through the day was probably a good idea. She could start out again at sunset.

Halfway up the mountain, among the cliff heights, she found a small opening in the rocks. The opening proved to be the mouth of a small tunnel. She squeezed into it and wove her way into the back, where she found a rather roomy cave. There wasn't one speck of light, but her nose told her that a tiny runnel of water slid down one wall and a crack offered a draft for a small fire.

Perfect.

She shivered into her human form. Her breath steamed out and chill bumps washed across her naked skin. It was way too cold to play human, even with a fire. She hastily dragged her pack off her back and pulled out her sheep-skin coat. Throwing it on the rocky floor, she slid back into her wolf form. Warm and comfy in her thick fur, she curled up, nose to tail, on the black fleece lining of the gray coat and promptly drifted into sleep.

Scrabbling among the rocks at the mouth of the cave's tunnel jolted her out of a sound sleep and onto her paws. The fur along her back rose, and she snarled loudly. Whatever was trying to enter needed to get the hell back out or she would kill it and eat it.

Shifting stones betrayed that whatever had entered was moving deeper into the tunnel.

Her tall ears flicked forward, and her tail switched in annoyance. Just how stupid was this creature? Other than a bear, she was the biggest predator on the mountain. Her snarl should have given that away. She snarled again and gave it some serious volume.

It progressed closer.

She jolted, dancing back on her paws, thoroughly alarmed. Whatever it was, it wasn't heeding her warnings. That meant it thought it could take her in a fight. What the hell thought it could take out a wolf? It couldn't be a bear; a bear was too big to fit in the cave. It had to be her size or smaller. Was it insane?

Scent drifted into her section of the cave: wool, leather, dust, earth, old blood, and cold human.

A human? She sifted through the more subtle scents. The human was male, with silk, oil, steel, and gunpowder. A gun. She snarled in pure reaction. A stinking hunter? This high in the mountains in winter? The scent of oiled steel smelled small, like a pistol. What kind of idiot went into a wolf's cave carrying only a pistol?

She crouched, her muscles bunching tight, in preparation for a lunge. If he wanted to kill her, he was in for a nasty shock. It took a hell of a lot more than a mere pistol shot to kill her. Her voice dropped to a deep, rumbling growl. *Last chance to escape death, idiot.*

Light flared in the inky blackness of the cave.

She blinked and flinched back, but her growl remained.

A man, with long straight silver-white hair, swathed in a bulky black wool coat, knelt at the tunnel's exit with one gloved hand held palm up. A tiny ball of light floated above his hand—a ball of light that did not smell like fire.

Her ears flicked forward briefly. Light without heat?

He spoke in a language she didn't know, but there was no mistaking his meaning. "Wolf."

She curled back her lips and flattened her ears to her skull. Stupid human. What else did he think was growling, a bunny rabbit?

His eyes opened wide and reflected the light above his hand with an emerald-green shimmer.

Every hair on her body rose. This might look human, but it wasn't human. Human eyes reflected red, like a rat's, and they did not reflect easily.

The light rose from his palm, floating toward the cave's low ceiling.

Her gaze followed the curious floating light.

The man smiled, showing long upper incisors and shorter lower ones, the teeth of a hunting predator.

Her gaze locked on the creature's bared fangs. A deliberate challenge? Snarling in anger, she dropped to a crouch. *Fine, die*. She lunged, teeth bared to rip out his throat.

He caught her by the fur of her throat and was bowled over backward by the momentum of her charge. He snarled, baring his long teeth in her face.

She snarled right back, writhing in his grasp, snapping for his arms, his face, his throat, anything she could reach.

Twisting with incredible dexterity, he kept her fangs from his skin while holding her with ferocious strength.

She writhed and stretched her neck. Twisting suddenly, she sank long teeth into his forearm, tearing through the wool of his coat to reach flesh and blood. *Got you!*

He threw back his head and shouted in pain.

His blood filled her mouth, thick and hot—and nasty. It burned in her throat like whiskey. She pulled her fangs free but couldn't escape the taste.

His black eyes wide, he stared straight into her eyes and shouted.

A black spike slammed into her mind and sizzled down her spine. She yelped in surprise and pulled back.

His fingers closed tight in her neck fur, holding her gaze locked to his. He spoke. She didn't know his language, but the meaning was crystal clear. "Be still."

Black pressure smothered her anger. Her growls stilled in her throat, and she froze, trembling.

He spoke again, his words an indistinguishable waterfall of liquid syllables, and yet she knew their meaning. "Your bite is deep, but my blood is strong, yes?" He sat up slowly, easing her back and off him while holding eye contact. Gripping her neck fur with one gloved hand, he stroked his other gloved hand down the silver fur of her shoulder. His voice dropped to a low croon. "Yes, wolf, be stilled. Be at ease."

Languid ease infiltrated her mind and spread, making it

hard to think, making it hard to stand upright. Off balance, she rocked on her paws.

"Yes, very good, you are a brave wolf." He stroked her neck and shoulders with both hands. "Rest. Lie down, and sleep."

Pressure increased on her mind. She wanted to rest. She wanted to lie down and sleep, just like he said. She stilled. Like he'd *said*? It was him; he was in her head! She jerked back.

"Wolf?" He caught her by the neck fur. "What disturbs you?" His narrowed gaze pierced into her mind, probing her thoughts with smoky black fingers.

She twisted sharply, fighting to break away, and a frightened whine escaped her throat. *Get out! Get out of my head!*

"What?" His silver brows rose and then dropped. "A wolf should not have such thoughts."

She froze. He could hear her? He was listening to her thoughts?

His gaze focused. "Human intelligence? How is this?" His curiosity drove fingers of darkness deeper into her mind, questions looking for answers.

Panicked, she twisted her head to break eye contact. *No, no, no! My secret!*

"A secret!" He gripped her neck fur and fought to keep eye contact. "Tell me your secret!"

No! She reared up and back, dragging him with her.

"Yes!" He wrestled her to the cave floor and pinned her on her side, holding her down with his greater weight. He caught her long muzzle and forced her gaze to his. "Tell me now!"

A steel spike of power slammed through the center of her skull. She howled in agony—and changed.

Thorn snapped aware, naked and curled up on the icy stone floor. She shivered and opened her eyes.

The silver-haired man poised above her on his palms, framing her naked body with his. His expression was one of complete astonishment. His eyes narrowed, and his long teeth appeared. "Who has done this sorcery?"

She wrapped her arms about herself and trembled with cold and fear. He had forced her to change into her human form. Would he kill her now?